CONTENTS

CHAPTER ONE

Rock Bottom

He had decided to end his life. At least that's what he kept saying to himself. The decision was not yet firm. He was in an exploratory phase. He called it morbid dating. He was not ready for a commitment. After all, it was a matter of life and death. It was a one-way ticket. There was no option of divorce from death. He had been dating for a while, but nothing had clicked. Nothing had come closer to him saying, that's how I want to die. He didn't give up. He was ready for another date. He preferred the weekends. Less traffic on the roads you know.

He set an alarm for six o'clock, but he was awake well before that. It was summer; the sun was already up. He had to leave early; Highway 401 and QEW to Niagara Falls filled up quickly. He checked the traffic news before leaving. It was imperative as summer was construction season in Canada. It was also a season of bumper-to-bumper traffic. Getting stuck in a traffic jam would have been a disaster. It could have pushed him over the edge; an impulsive decision. He had no desire to throw away his life like that. Spontaneity was not his thing. He didn't skip breakfast. He considered it the most important meal of the day. It had to be quick, healthy, and cost-effective. It was always the same: corn flakes sprinkled with baby cereal. Yes, baby cereal. He believed baby cereal had the best and the safest ingredients for discerning adults, and he liked the taste. He filled the gas tank before embarking on his journey. Gas was cheaper on the weekends, and he believed in cheap dates.

Sadeep was a closet agnostic, which meant he prayed with cynicism. Nevertheless, he did pray daily. It was part of a habit, like washing your face or brushing your teeth. It was less of a prayer but more of a wish list from a probable God. The prayer was fast and efficient. It had elements of all religions mixed up; a tailor-made request to God. He wanted to cast the net wide and considered it a wise move. He cursed himself for forgetting to do the prayer before leaving. It was against the norm, but better late than never. He could break someone's heart, but he had a hard time breaking a habit. He recited the prayer while keeping his eyes on the road. It was a sort of distracted driving but not against the law. He had forgotten his sunglasses as well. He was annoyed and knew a migraine was on its way. He had a supply of ibuprofen if migraine came with a vengeance.

The route was familiar. He had been to Niagara Falls dozens of times, but this time it was different. The experience had changed over the years. The highway was wider, but the traffic was even denser. It had become a game of cat and mouse; a curse of modern society. Resources were not enough to meet the ferocious appetite of modern life. It had made people restless and anxious about the future. The speed of goods churned by the corporate world was accelerating, but it was not making people happy. Materialism was no match for the avalanche of melancholy that was drowning the human spirit. Sadeep missed the good old days. He watched vintage videos on YouTube and indulged himself in the nostalgia of the past; Paris in the '20s, New York in the '40s, London in the '50s, Toronto in the '60s. However, it was no time to get lost in the psychodynamic analysis of the past. His priority was to contend with the traffic cops who were laying their traps. He knew their hideouts. He smirked at the sight of a flashing cruiser ticketing a caught speedster. He felt proud that he got the better of the cops. An empty highway was a luxury and a speedster's paradise. Speed did kill but it was better left for another date. He was slapped hard by his superego for contemplating such a reckless act.

He parked his car far away from the Falls. It was a smart move. Parking rates were half and there was a free shuttle. He was tired after a two-hour drive. He needed his black coffee; being in Canada, coffee shop was right there. There was a long lineup, but he had no choice. He grabbed the coffee and went to the outside observation area. The direction of the wind was favorable. The mist was blowing towards the American side. He didn't need an umbrella. He spent his time glaring at the majesty of the Falls. As he stared, the water felt still, and he was moving backward against the Falls. It was an optical illusion, showing the equivalence of rest and relative speed. He wondered about the human fascination for Niagara Falls. It was an acknowledgment of the fragility of human life and a morbid desire to see the face of death but at a safe distance. There had been a long history of daredevils trying to push the limits of human survival. He was also trying to do the same but through his thoughts.

He stared at the birds that were flying over the Falls. They had no fear. They had wings. He wished if he was one of them. He was hypnotized by the Falls. His meditation was frequently interrupted by visitors trying to take the perfect selfie. He obliged, gave them the coveted spot, took family photos. It was a nice thing to do. It was a Canadian thing to do. It was nice to hear a thank you. He had to hurry as hordes of tourists were on their way. He wanted a few moments of solitude amidst the tourist frenzy. He contemplated the fate of the human body against the overwhelming power of the Falls. He wanted to die but not quite. This question had tormented many. Shakespeare had asked this question in Hamlet. It was Sadeep's turn to answer the difficult question of to be or not to be. He wanted to jump, only to be rescued by a savior, an angel, a comic book hero, a good Samaritan, or anyone who had the superpower of empathy. A memory that was ingrained from old VHS tapes, fairy tales, and comics to his grey matter. Where was his savior? Where was his angel? He heard a voice.

"Here I am."

He was startled. He looked around and up and down but couldn't find the source of the voice. Maybe it was a figment of his imagination. Maybe it was a comment not directed at him. He started walking briskly. He wanted to get away from the crowd. He was unsettled by the voice. It felt loud and clear even in the background noise from the Falls and the tourists. Someone was listening to his thoughts; that was the scary part. He decided to head back home. The date had ended on an abrupt note. It was nothing new in the world of dating. He was used to failures in his life and failing to end his life was the best kind of failure he ever had. He planned his life to the last minute. Anything unexpected rattled him. He walked all the way back to the parking lot. He didn't have the courage to take the shuttle and get into close contact with people. He kept looking around to see if someone was following him. There was no one. The passersby said hello to him. He reciprocated but didn't like the gesture. He wanted to be left alone. He did not hear the voice on the way back. It was some kind of a fluke, he thought.

CHAPTER TWO

An Intruder

The journey on the way back was not pleasant. He was stressed and hoped for an interruption-free drive. Alas! It was not the case. He was going against the traffic but even a fender bender was enough to create chaos. He was stuck in a traffic jam for over two hours. He was waiting for the journey to end. The only saving grace was his love for the car. He had a two-door sports car. It had a red matte finish. The original owner had spent five grand on the special paint. He had a bargain on his hand. The car was holding its value as it had a gem of an engine: a naturally aspirated V8. He revved it to eight thousand rpm, creating a mechanical symphony. He enjoyed driving it, even though it meant frequent trips to the gas station. It was a gas guzzler that fed on premium fuel. Gas prices had collapsed in wake of the shale oil revolution. He took full advantage of it. He persevered with the sports car despite its harsh ride. There was a price to pay for self-indulgence. Driving it on twisty roads was amongst the few happy moments he had in his life and was worth the cost. He had a sigh of relief on reaching home. He carefully got out of the low-lying car to avoid twisting his knee, which was already giving him trouble. He took a few slow steps and turned around to admire the car; a sign of a true car fanatic.

"The color of the car doesn't match your personality. You

should have gone for grey or black."

"Who's there?" Sadeep looked around nervously. "Come forward, if you have any guts."

There was no response. He was afraid. He ran to the door; his hands were trembling, and he was desperate to find the keys to the house in his cluttered pocket.

"Come on, come on," Sadeep said.

The alarm was triggered as he entered the house. He deactivated the alarm and looked outside through the glass door. There no one was around. He had a terrible headache. It was a double whammy: tension headache with a migraine. It needed double-dosing; he took fast-dissolving 325 mg acetaminophen and 200 mg ibuprofen gels. He believed in taking the minimum effective dose. His experience had taught him what worked and what didn't. That day, the medications were not effective. He had delayed taking the capsules. He had to contend with the headache taking its own course. But he had a bigger problem on his hand: the voice. He had heard it twice; it couldn't be a coincidence. He had never heard such a voice before. He was not even sure if it was a male or a female voice. He couldn't make out the accent either, but the voice was undoubtedly in English. The voice was loud and clear, and it was trying to have a conversation with him.

His mind was foggy. Migraine was in full swing. He had to do something. He needed a nap; sleep would clear his mind and hopefully the headache. It didn't take too long before he fell asleep on the sofa. He didn't bother to change his clothes; it required too much of an effort. The jeans and his sweaty t-shirt were no barriers to a sound sleep.

It was evening. His headache was better. He felt fresh. That was not the case with his home. It needed tender loving care, which he was unable to provide due to lack of motivation. He lived alone. He had a detached home with a two-car garage and a finished basement. It was plenty for him. He bought the house at the right time before the boom in the Canadian housing market. He had to take a mortgage of 150,000 dollars. The house was worth well over 500,000 dollars after fifteen years of use. It was a nice return. He had paid off his mortgage. It was a big deal for him, yet he overlooked his achievements. He could have rented the basement to boost his income. He lived in Waterville, a university town. The house was on a bus route. There was always a demand for student housing, but he didn't want any hooliganism. He valued his privacy. He hardly knew his neighbors. In fact, he avoided them. He had an aversion to social small talk. He would have happily lived on an island as a lone resident. If he was an inmate, he would have pleaded to be secluded from the rest. He would have preferred summons from a court over a marriage invitation. No wonder he was alone.

There were rumors about his sexuality. He had never been in a relationship though he enjoyed female company, from a distance. He was in love once, sort of, more like an infatuation. He tormented himself over several weeks on how to express his feelings to his love interest. Presenting a rose was cheesy, presenting a ring was premature, and asking for dinner was lame. Finally, when she was sitting in the library, he asked her if she would like to go to a movie. She said, she was busy; it was a polite no. But it hit him like a brick. He said, "Oh!" And that was that. His ego was wounded and left a scar that was still visible decades later.

It was time for supper. He thought of having baby cereal again for supper, but it was too monotonous even for his own liking. He decided to have something non-vegetarian: a free-run brown egg with toasted whole wheat bread. He made a two-egg omelet. He examined the food label to check its saturated fat content. He wondered why on one hand he was worried about getting blocked arteries, but on the other hand, he was exploring various ways of dying. A contradiction of sorts. Dying in sleep would be palatable, which could be accomplished with a massive heart attack. But things could go terribly wrong; a debilitating stroke would not be welcome. It was not worth taking a risk; hence he strived to follow Canada's food guide to the letter; at least that was the resolution he made on New Year's Day and like all resolutions, it faded away by the time Christmas came along. He loved chocolate but it was hard to find a chocolate that was low in fat and sugar. He tried to limit the portion size, but a sweet tooth soured his plans for a modest sugar intake.

He was not a drinker but a sipper of wine. He was intolerant to hard liquor. It came out, the way it went in; spontaneous reflux. He wouldn't drink a glass of hard liquor even if he got paid to do it. The same was the case with beer. The wine was the only thing he could tolerate but only in modest amounts. It conferred natural protection against alcohol abuse. It did not discourage him from collecting wines. He liked the packaging and the calming effect of the wine. It was a placebo effect as a sip of wine was enough to induce it. He hoarded wines from various parts of the world. Local LCBO store had a huge collection of exquisite wines. He opened a bottle of prosecco. It was too bitter for his liking, but he needed to relax, and so he gulped it. He felt calm and a little drowsy.

"You should try wine tasting at Niagara-on -the- Lake."

Sadeep was not startled this time. Alcohol had numbed his senses and he was getting conditioned to the voice.

"Who are you? A tour- guide?"

"I am your self -conscience. I want you to be aware that you should consume more local stuff."

"Rubbish. I don't believe you. My petty little self-conscience has no voice left in it. You are an intruder. You better tell me who you are or there will be consequences."

"What are you going to do? Slap yourself?"

"Don't tempt me, I have done that too," Sadeep said.

"In that case, go ahead and help yourself," the voice said.

"Just get out of my head. I don't want any more trouble in my life."

"It's your lucky day. I am here to help you."

"Really, how so?"

"The days of your self-created misery are over. I am going to be your companion."

"Like a voice assistant?"

"I am not a gadget."

"So, are you going to be a side-kick?" Sadeep asked.

"That's insulting. I am no Dr. Watson to Sherlock Holmes. I am no Birbal to Akbar. I am no vice-president to a president."

"Then who the hell are you?"

"I don't know how to put it gently, but I am like a soul-mate; what you humans call a ghost."

"A ghost?" Sadeep laughed nervously. "I think I have had too much to drink. There are no ghosts. There are only monsters and I see them on television every day."

"I prefer the term WIMP. Ghost has become a pejorative term."

"What the heck is a WIMP?" Sadeep asked.

"I don't know how much physics you know. WIMP stands for Weakly Interacting Massive Particles. I know it's a mouthful. If you prefer, you could call me a creation of dark matter."

"A ghost talking about physics! The world has gone crazy, or I am hallucinating."

"I know, prejudice is ingrained in the human mind. You behave as you are told."

"Aren't ghosts evil? You can't help anyone."

"There are more shades of morality than there are shades of grey. Good and evil are like colors of a chameleon, which hide away human instincts. I believe in action and reaction. It's fair and objective."

There was no reaction from Sadeep. He was snoring and his hand was tucked underneath his back. He was lying on the carpet. The wine bottle and the partly eaten dinner were lying on the table. The light in the drawing-room was still on but the voice in his head had gone.

It was not his first brush with the supernatural. He was in grade five when it first happened. He still remembered it vividly as it left a lasting impression on him. His mind was like clay, it could be molded in any direction. He was being constantly molded by competing forces. On one hand, there was science with its logical and rational explanations; on the other hand, there was magic with its enchanting tales. Science seemed to be Mr. Know it all. It could explain why the sky was blue, why apples fell to the ground and where did babies come from. It quenched his thirst for curiosity but only after putting a burden on his shoulders. Science had to be learned and later tested. The homework had to be done. The exams had to be passed. It took the fun out of science. There were no such quibbles with magic. It was exciting. It was wrapped in layers of fairy tales, occult, and religion. But he was more intrigued by ghost stories. The dark side of magic was like dark chocolate, less sweet but more fulfilling. His childhood was spent in India; there was a tug of war going on in the Indian society between superstition and scientific evidence. It was not an abstract question for Sadeep; it manifested itself in the intricacies of life.

"Sadeep, what's on your eye?" his mom said. She was the doctor in residence. She did not have any medical degree, but she was well-versed with home remedies. She aptly recognized the eye lesion as a stye. It had happened several times before. She had a novel home remedy for it. She would tie a black thread around his big toe. He was no anatomist, but he did wonder how on earth it worked?

His mom would get upset at any suggestion to question the validity of the treatment.

"It works every time. You will see for yourself when the stye is gone."

He had no choice but to oblige. It was a harmless sort of treatment, but he was careful not to show his bare feet in public. He did not want to be a laughingstock. Eventually, stye did resolve and his mom took full credit for it. He was not a statistician who could argue about the concept of spontaneous resolution and inherent bias which was embedded in anecdotal evidence. He was just happy to move on from the annoying problem.

He knew where her beliefs came from. His maternal

grandmother was a step ahead. She ensured that no one left home when the minute hand of the clock hit 45 minutes. It was *apshagun* (bad omen). He was not allowed to be in the same room as his maternal uncle if there was any chance of lightning. The relationship was apparently magnetic. If a crow sat on the roof, it meant a visitor was expected. The beliefs were passed on to successive generations.

Giving exams was a high-stakes affair. His mom would give him sugar-laden yogurt as a performance-enhancing drug. Under no circumstances should a cat cross his path. If that happened, he had to return home and start all over again. She had a special spiritual book in which each page was apparently written to get the desired outcome. There was a page for getting good marks; there was a page to heal the sick; there was a page to make money. They were supposed to be recited to get the desired wish. Even genie stopped at three wishes but there was no such restriction here. Surprisingly, she did not believe in astrology. "It's superstition," she said. If asked, why? "Scripture says so," she opined.

His dad was left leaning and had left God way behind. He was averse to what Karl Marx described as the opiate of the masses. He would rather study electrical circuits during his spare time. His only non-academic interest was in cricket. He was an avid fan of Gavaskar. He did not pray for Gavaskar to get a century, but he did switch off the television when Gavaskar was batting with a score in the 90's. Apparently, it was good luck. He facilitated Gavaskar to complete his century. How could a rational person come to terms with it? He did not believe in the occult, but he did believe in correlation. "If switching off the television can help Gavaskar get a century, what's wrong with it?" he said. This was the only time when irrationality got the best of him. Otherwise, he was a flag bearer of logic and reasoning. He had a hard time reconciling with the faith of others. It made him distant and cold. These divergent points of view could have led to marital discord. But Sadeep's parents had developed a rapport that kept the peace, even if it was fragile. Their relationship was like that between Reagan and Gorbachev.

The school was no different. Computer classes were mandatory. So was the daily morning prayer. During exams, the prayer was extra-long. Teachers fulfilled their curriculum requirements diligently. They rarely drifted from the script. But when pressed on existential questions, "Do ghosts exist?" the answers were all over the place. Those who said no were further probed. "If God can exist, why can't ghosts?" They would change the answer to I don't know or maybe. Those who said yes were more likely to point to someone else who had seen one. Due to the paucity of clear answers, children were left to choose their own path. Sadeep was in a dilemma whether to follow the herd or take the less-traveled path. His friends had various theories about ghosts and company. He knew Dracula was afraid of the cross, but he didn't know if he was real or fictional. It was also not known if that knowledge could be extrapolated to Dracula's Indian cousins. He had to find a local solution for a local ghost.

Sadeep could recite God's name as fast if not faster than a bullet coming out of a machine gun, which could come in handy in an encounter with a ghost. He knew certain ghosts had their feet pointing backward. But ghosts could take any shape or form. Even a snake could take the human form. A detailed description was available in multiple blockbuster Bollywood movies. He was told not to utter its name after 7 pm, IST. The best thing he could do was to keep on guard. He and his friends had made a special file where they recorded what was known about the ghosts. After a while, they lost interest as there was no actionable intelligence.

His life as a child was full of dreams and there was plenty to dream about. One day he was a karate master, another day he was a chess master. He would enact those dreams in his backyard after he was done binge-watching movies, TV shows, and comics. The backyard was huge. Most of it was used to plant vegetables and flowers. There was a row of trees on the perimeter. He used to walk under their shade on a dirt path. His footprints would stagger all over the place. It was during one of these escapades that he noticed a set of footprints were following him. They were tiny in comparison. They resembled the Greek letter psi. They were definitely not human. Maybe a bird or an animal. It was a plausible explanation. There were lots of footprints. It wasn't clear if they belonged to a two-legged or a four-legged creature. But why were they following him? He hadn't seen any-one following him. Could there be a more sinister explanation for the incident? After all, he was loitering around the trees which were known to harbor ghosts. Maybe his mind was play-ing tricks on him. He decided to let it go.

The next day, the same thing happened. He was con-vinced that this can't be just a coincidence. The correlation was too strong. He was terrified. He asked himself, "Did I do something wrong?" He remembered cheating in a carrom board game. He was a bad loser. But was it enough to punish him for his deeds? He could stop his daydreaming trips and the problem would be solved. It was not that simple. There was no guarantee the footprints won't follow him elsewhere.

He decided to use his first line of defense. He prayed to God. It should have worked but it didn't. The footprints con-tinued to follow him. He felt haunted. Who should he turn to for help? The options were not great. His mom would overreact; his dad would ridicule; his friends would laugh; no one would sym-pathize. It was his problem and he alone had to solve it. Maybe a little bit of detective work could help. But the problem was not elementary. He took inspiration from Sherlock Holmes. He had to pursue the path of truth. He decided to carry out surveillance. He prepared like a commando. He had a banyan stick in one hand and binoculars in the other. He had a picture of deity in one pocket and a string of prayer beads in the other.

He had a good look at the target area. There were no plastic bags or pots filled with sinister stuff to indicate black magic. *Jadu Tona*(sorcery) was a common ploy to seek revenge and set-tle scores. It was time for him to lie in wait. He saw a couple of pigeons moving around. He sneaked in on them. To his relief, the footprints were made by those damn pigeons! But why were they following in his footsteps? As he closed in, pigeons flew away. He decided to look closely at his own footprints. There were tiny pieces of bread littered around. He had an epiphany: he was snacking on bread that day. The inquiry was complete. The resolution was satisfactory. The emotion was triumphant. He did it. It worked. The path of reasoning had opened for him. But should he credit it all to logic? Maybe God listened to his prayers, and it was His way of helping. As he thought of it more, he was confused again. Questions were many, answers were few. He became ambivalent on the matter of ghosts, which was in keeping with his agnostic beliefs. All of it was about to change.

CHAPTER THREE

Lost Dreams

Sadeep was in a frenzy. He was terrified. His right arm was paralyzed. "Did I have a stroke?" The thought reverberated in his head. It was too hideous to contemplate but the signs pointed to that eventuality. He blamed the ghost. "Those things are evil. I should not have engaged with it."

"Don't worry, it would get better," the ghost said.

"You are still here. Did you do this to me?"

"Typical human. Blaming others for his mistakes."

"What did I do?" Sadeep said.

"My dear, you had too much to drink. You slept on your arm all night. What did you expect? It's typical Saturday night palsy. Shake your hand. You will be fine."

He shook his arm; the strength gradually came back. He had tingling feelings all over the arm. He was still worried, but the explanation made sense.

"I must thank you for your insight. I know ghosts pay unsolicited visits, but unsolicited medical advice is a first."

"Very funny. When humans can search their symptoms on the internet and come up with a medical diagnosis, I can too. I have had the luxury of dealing with human bodies for hundreds of years. It's a piece of cake."

"Piece of cake! Do you have any intentions of eating me?"

"I know English is your second language but don't act smart. You know what I mean."

"I must give credit where it's due, but don't get cocky. I will see my doctor and get a proper diagnosis."

"Are you also going to tell the doctor that you are hearing voices?" the ghost said.

"Should I?" Sadeep asked.

"You have to be honest if you want an honest opinion."

"You are right. I have a request, please don't tag along to the doctor's office. I need privacy and besides no visitors are allowed in the exam room."

"Don't worry. I hate the doctor's office. I can't stand the smell."

"Have ghosts been festooned with the sense of smell?"

"There are many things you don't know."

Sadeep called the doctor's office and was given a litany of choices: If this is an emergency, please call 911 or go to the nearest emergency department; if you need a prescription refill, please call your pharmacy to fax the prescription; if you need to book an appointment, please stay on the line – you are caller number 3 – thank you for your patience– did you know flu shots save lives, please get flu shot at your nearest pharmacy or at one of our designated flu shot clinics – you are caller number 2 – thank you for your patience– if you are above 50, please talk to your doctor about screening tests for cancer – you are caller number 1– thank you for your patience.

"Dr. Banerjee's office, may I help you?"

"I need to see the doctor. I couldn't move my arm in the morning. The strength came back on shaking it, but I am still having pins and needles sensation in my arm."

"It could be a stroke. You should go to the ER."

"I don't think it's a stroke. I slept on my arm last night."

"Do you have other symptoms of a stroke like slurry speech, facial deviation?"

"No, I feel fine otherwise."

"Alright, what's your name?"

"Sadeep Singh Pardesi."

"Health card number?"

"10011001BA."

"Next available appointment is in two weeks."

"That's too long. I should be seen today."

"That's what everyone wants. Dr. Banerjee is away on vacation next week. Routine appointments are all booked. We only have same day spots left."

"Give me the same-day spot then."

"I am not authorized to fill the spot. Let me instant message the nurse. Stay on the line."

"Okay."

"I have a ten 'o clock appointment this morning. Would that work?"

"Yes, wonderful."

"Please be on time and bring your health card."

"I will."

The doctor's office was in a strip mall with an attached pharmacy. It was convenient for the patient and lucrative for the pharmacy. The prescriptions went straight to the pharmacy from the doctor's office; an ethically questionable but financially brilliant proposition. Space was well utilized but it was still tight. The rooms had no windows. The ambiance was dull and depressing. The grey paint, the brown furniture, the posters warning about horrible diseases, the containers full of discarded syringes, and the air that had never seen daylight brought gloom to an already anxious mind. Getting into the rooms was not easy; there was waiting involved at every step. The waiting room was full: patients with coughs and colds, crying babies, restless toddlers, walkers, wheelchairs, and grumpy receptionists. Sadeep was on time for his appointment but still had to wait for his turn. The typical wait time was one hour.

He was relieved to be called. He had to wait again in the room for the doctor to arrive.

"Hello Sadeep, how are you?" Dr. Banerjee said. Sadeep was surprised Dr. Banerjee remembered his name or it could be that the good doctor glanced at his name on the computer; either way, he was happy he was called by his name, not by some number.

Sadeep stood up to greet the doctor. Dr. Banerjee was of the same age as him but looked older. His hairline was receding, and he had plenty of grey hair. Sadeep looked like a model by comparison, but it was Dr. Banerjee who was a role model for him. He looked at the doctor not for inspiration but for regret; the things he could not achieve in life: the Rolex he can't afford, the Swiss holiday that's beyond reach, and the medical career that never was.

"I don't know how to answer that doctor, but I am here to see you. You look tired."

"Yes, I am. It's been crazy busy. I need a break."

"I can understand, doctor. You get sick of healing the sick."

"It's not that. I love helping patients, but you know, we are all growing older. The energy level is not the same. Never mind, it's about you not me. How can I help you?"

"I woke up with a paralyzed exam. I shook it. It's better but there is this tingling feeling."

"Did you sleep over the arm?"

"Yes, I did. I had a glass of wine last night."

The doctor did a brief neurological exam; strength and feeling in the arm were intact.

"It's Saturday night palsy. The nerve function is preserved. Your symptoms will get better. Don't worry but be careful in the future."

"Thank you, but can I ask another question?"

"You know the rule: one problem per visit."

"But doctor, the real reason for making the appointment was something else. It was too personal to tell the secretary."

"Okay, go ahead. I will make an exception, but I can't give you a lot of time today."

"Thank you, doctor. I have been feeling depressed for the last few months. I am frustrated with life. I have very little hope that things would get any better. I sometimes think, why to carry on?"

"I am sorry to hear that. I want you to fill two questionnaires. I will be back in five minutes."

They were self-screening questionnaires. He scored high on the screening tests. He wished if he had scored high on the entrance tests, he would have been a doctor in Canada. The doctor was back after twenty minutes.

"You have clinical depression. Is there anything going on in your life?"

"That's the problem doctor, nothing is going on in my life. It feels empty. I am so disappointed with life."

"Are you suicidal?"

"To be honest, yes, it has crossed my mind, but I don't have the courage to go through with it."

"Do you have any plans to take your own life?"

"No, I do not."

"That's good. I don't want you to do anything stupid. If you feel overwhelmed and suicidal, I want you to promise me, you will seek help."

"I would." Sadeep was getting teary-eyed.

Dr. Banerjee offered him a tissue. He had already made a suicidal contract with the patient, which meant he had done his due diligence. He felt safe allowing the patient to go home. It would make him sleep well at night. Keeping his medical license safe was critical to his own survival. His financial well-being and reputation depended on it. Getting a divorce was less traumatic than getting a disciplinary warning from the medical licensing body. He could always marry again but he was never going to get a second shot at his medical career. He practiced defensive medicine: ask questions, order tests, make referrals, keep patients happy, and document everything. If it wasn't documented, it didn't happen. He always had a chaperone when doing a sensitive exam. The medical licensing body had a quarterly magazine, which highlighted disgraced doctors and their behavior. It was a nightmare to read through for the doctors. Some of them read it during Halloween to get scared.

"Are you interested in taking an antidepressant?"

"Would I feel any better?"

"Yes, you would, but it takes time to feel better. You got to be patient."

"I will take it if you say so, but I don't know how it's going to change my situation. I have been a failure in life. You know I did my medical degree in India. I passed all my licensing exams, and yet I could not secure a residency spot. All my education went down the drain."

"Don't lose hope. Keep trying. I know many people who got into residency after years of trying. They have increased the spots for foreign graduates."

"It's too late now. I have been out of touch with medicine for over ten years. I have forgotten most of it. I don't think I can go through the rigor of residency. I am done with medicine."

"You are too harsh on yourself. You have a successful car driving school. You are not a failure." It was not that Dr. Banerjee was friends with Sadeep or he remembered all his patient's details, but it was the magic of electronic medical records and well-documented social history, which he kept referring to during the patient encounter.

"Thank you for the kind words. As a doctor, you have respect, authority, prestige. It must mean something."

"To tell you the truth, it doesn't feel that way anymore. The level of anger and rage among patients has gone up many folds. I get cursed on by patients. Burnout rate among doctors is high."

"I guess everyone is stressed out. One more thing, is it normal to hear voices during the depression?"

"What do you mean by hearing voices?"

"I don't know if it's in my head, but I hear a voice that talks to me. It says weird things."

"Like what?"

"It says, it would help me."

"Do you see anything that others don't see?"

"No, I am not hallucinating."

"Drugs? Alcohol?"

"I don't do drugs. I had a glass of wine last night. That's about it."

"Well, it can happen in depression. I would add a mild dose of antipsychotic."

He wrote a prescription of 2.5mg olanzapine to be taken at night.

"I am running late. I must leave now. Call me if you don't feel better."

"Thank you, doctor."

He felt better after meeting the doctor. His concerns were validated, and he felt better in knowing that he was not alone who was miserable and fed up with life. He had been envious of Dr. Banerjee. He wanted to be in his place. He listened with pleasure, the frustration, and the anguish of his doctor. He had put doctors on a pedestal. It was a reality check for him.

The pharmacy was next door. The pharmacist gave him the spiel on the side effects of medicines. It was scary to listen to what could go wrong while taking the medicines. It was a comprehensive list of adverse reactions, which was burdensome for the patient, but the legal burden was lifted off the drug companies. Sadeep did not have a drug plan. The pharmacist offered him the cheaper generic versions, but they were still not cheap. He had no choice. He could only hope that the cost was worth it.

He had no other appointments for the day and came home.

"How was the doctor's visit?" the ghost asked.

"You are still here."

Sadeep was not home alone but alone with a ghost. He had doubts if the ghost was real or if dopamine receptors in his head were playing tricks on him.

"You didn't answer my question," the ghost said.

"It's none of your damn business," Sadeep said.

"Yes, it is. I am your guest and I need to know the health of my host.

"I am doing alright, thank you very much."

21

"That's an oxymoron. You don't go to a doctor's office for a social visit."

"You already know. Why are you asking me?"

"You are right. Let me guess what would have happened. You must have scored high on PHQ-9 and GAD-7 questionnaires. Your affect was enough to make a diagnosis of major depression. If you were bold enough to mention that you hear voices, a psychotic modifier was added to your diagnosis. If I am not wrong, you got an SSRI along with an atypical antipsychotic."

"That's impressive as well as spooky. You spoke like a true doctor, full of jargon," Sadeep said.

"Thank you," the ghost said. "I have an inherent desire to show off and get validated. In that sense, I am almost human."

"I don't know who you are, but I am sick. I need these pills to get better."

"I don't mind, but you won't get rid of me by blocking dopamine receptor surge in your brain."

"We shall see."

Sadeep was ready to call it a day. Before the medicines knocked him out, he checked that the doors were locked, the garage was closed, the lights were off, the car keys were in his pocket, the phone was charged, and the alarm was on. His fear of ghosts was receding, but the fear of home invasion was elevated to a red alert. The recent surge in burglaries around the city was worrisome. That worry was compounded by his habit of listening to local radio and newspapers, which made the city look like the wild west. He couldn't rely on a gun; there was no second amendment in Canada, only onerous regulations on guns; he couldn't rely on his luck, which had always favored others; he couldn't rely on courage when he didn't even have the courage to look himself in the eye; all he could rely on was fear because even if he couldn't put up a fight, he could certainly muster a quick flight.

CHAPTER FOUR

The Road to Nostalgia

S adeep had enough reasons to be sad. He had put all his eggs in one basket, which turned upside down when it was time for the eggs to hatch. He was reaching a bittersweet milestone. Let me ask you a question that would help you understand Sadeep's dilemma. What are the most memorable moments of your life? It's a question that crosses everyone's mind. You don't have to be a celebrity to answer it. The responses are predictable. The birth of a child, the death of a loved one, first job, first love etc. are obvious answers. The ones who have unique answers are likely to become authors. Immigrants are in the same boat, but due to their unique journey, they have a slightly different repertoire of memories. The landing date is a memorable moment for them. So is the citizenship ceremony. An immigrant greeting is incomplete without asking the length of time one has been in Canada; a time tracker that every immigrant keeps: an immigrant standard time.

It struck Sadeep that soon he would have spent more time in Canada than his country of birth. It was an important milestone for him; it reminded him of his broken dreams, and it was painful. Coming to Canada is an exciting time for any immigrant but it's soon replaced by the anxiety of the ground reality. Most professionals are inflicted with the fear of losing their careers. Their hard-earned degree becomes just a piece of paper to stamp rejections. A buyer's remorse sets in. Resentment is not a good feeling. Lack of amenities that were once frustrating in the home country, suddenly don't seem too bad. They rationalize it by saying that if the amenities were less, so was the stress. As they say, nostalgia is best served late! It's obviously not true of refugees fleeing persecution and war, but for most economic immigrants, it fits the bill.

As a Punjabi, Sadeep was introduced early to the glamorous life in Canada. The returning immigrant relatives painted a rosy picture. There was heaven on earth where you get paid in dollars. The conversion factor against Indian currency was a huge bonus. You got paid even if you were sick or unemployed, that too by the government. It felt too good to be true. He had never seen snow in his life. It was something exotic; the more the merrier. He was given a picture book of Niagara Falls and its parks. He couldn't believe nature can be that beautiful He was amused by the lifestyle of the returning immigrant relatives. They stood out in their tracksuits and the smell of their exquisite perfumes filled the air. He waited for their arrival every year. They did not disappoint. Like Santa Claus, they brought toys, video games and clothes, which were not available locally. The Indian economy was shaped by socialistic principles. Socialism had created barriers, which promoted inequality; strange isn't it.

The Canadian passport inferred a VIP status, and it was officially recognized. Non-Resident Indians (NRI) had special incentives and laws to facilitate their arrival and stay in India. Every relative was keen to entertain them. Every host had just one question for them: when can I go to Canada? Hosts were oblivious to the rules around immigration. NRI's would dangle the carrot and enjoyed the perks.

When Sadeep's uncle sent a sponsorship letter for a visitor's visa, the excitement in his household was palpable. The idea to take a jet across the oceans and above the skies to reach Canada was nothing short of a dream. But there was a small problem, he still needed a visa. The Canadian High Commission was an eight-hour drive with congested highways and chaotic traffic. The High Commission was in the diplomatic enclave. It was a beautiful area of New Delhi with imposing buildings, lush green trees, and numerous gardens. It was a far cry from his rustic hometown. There was no appointment system to get a visitor's visa. It created a nightmare of sorts. Applicants would line up the evening before the opening time of the Commission. There were always hundreds of people in the lineup.

Getting in the queue offered no guarantee of entering the High Commission. Only a certain number of applicants were allowed daily. The exact number was a mystery. It was a nerve-wracking time for those in the queue. His family also got in the queue the prior evening. Some people had hired replacements to stand in line. But Sadeep's family was naïve and decided to wait in line all night. There was a festival-like atmosphere outside. People talked to each other and shared tips about the visa interview and the application. Anecdotal evidence on how to impress the visa officer was shared along with the wonderful life back in Canada.

The imported cars of career diplomats would occasionally enter the High Commission. Everyone stared at them. They were like royalty. There were vendors of soda and chips, who were selling items at exorbitant prices. When questioned about price gouging, the standard reply was, "Once in Canada, these prices will be peanuts for you." It was a clever moral boosting statement that preyed on the psychology of the applicants. Most obliged. Beggars also made their presence felt. They used different tactics outside the Commission, "May God fulfill all your wishes. May God give you a multi- entry visa." It was amusing to listen to their customized pleas. They did get the bang for their buck.

The morning arrived and the officials started letting people in. Just when Sadeep's turn was to come, an official halted the queue. He wondered if that was it. A disaster to put it mildly. How could he spend another night in the queue? But they let few more people in, and his family got through. He thanked his lucky stars and felt it was a good omen. There was another round of waiting. All eyes were on the windows of visa officers: how they reacted, how were applicants treated. It was a guessing game. Applicants speculated if a short or a long interview was a sign of success. There were long faces along with some smiling ones.

A typical visa interview went on like this:

"What's the purpose of your visit?" the visa officer said.

"I want to see your beautiful country," the applicant said.

"You won't come back."

"I will."

"You won't."

"I will, I will, I will."

"You won't, you won't, you won't."

"Please......"

"Sorry...... Next."

The visa rejection rate was very high. Sadeep was envious of those who got the visa. His expectations were high, his dad had a decent job, and they had a sponsor. What more would a visa officer want? Their turn came and the officer went straight to the point. He was not impressed with their financial ability to pay for this trip and within seconds said, "Sorry." The interview barely lasted a minute. The window was closed, and they were unable to mount any defense. An anticlimactic and disappointing finish.

The family was stunned. As they sat in the autorickshaw, Sadeep started crying. He was a young kid who had his first and only dream crushed by an unreasonable bureaucrat. His parents were more concerned about how their relatives would react.

Times changed. Point-based immigration system was introduced by the Canadian government. His dad applied under the skilled category. Another waiting game began. Sadeep prayed every day and asked for good news from the High Commission. None came. Maybe there was a delay in the postage side of things. He was ready if and when the delivery was made. Long behold, someone rang the bell on the door. He ran to answer the bell. He was elated to find a postman on the door. It was a registered post. He signed the papers. He tried to reign in his emotions in front of the postman.

But the postman couldn't help himself, "Good news!"

"I don't know," Sadeep said.

"Come on, I can see excitement in your eyes," the postman said. "It warrants a baksheesh."

A tip was in order. Sadeep had no choice but to fulfill the request. He didn't want to be in the bad books of the postman. He expected a prompt response from the postman in the future who enjoyed a certain authority. There were no alternatives for official letters. The postman had a permanent job and a secure pension. Customer service was usually an afterthought.

"I will get the baksheesh," Sadeep said.

"Mom, please give me 100 rupees."

"Why?"

"The letter has arrived, and the postman is asking for baksheesh."

His mom reluctantly gave him 100 rupees. She knew what was at stake.

"Best of luck!" the postman said as he was more than happy to pocket the note.

The letter had a nice smell to it. It could only mean one thing: an official letter from a foreign country. It was a letter from the Canadian High Commission. The letter was an invitation for an immigration medical. Sadeep's prayers had been answered. He was confident he would get through. His dad, Zor Singh was a teacher of mathematics, which was an in-demand profession. He had published several papers in international journals. His chances to get the point-based immigration were high.

Sadeep had been pushing for immigration. He was desperate to get out of the country. He was in grade 12, a make-or-break time for any teenager. He had been nurturing dreams to go abroad. It was not a surprise. It was a favorite pastime in Punjab.

The diaspora pulled like a magnet. These snowbirds came calling in the winter months and upset the local ecology. The clothes, the fashion, the smell, the style, the gadgets. He was mesmerized. So were his parents.

His elder sister, Rajni, was even more eager to go abroad. She was remarkably discreet for her age. She kept her cards close to the chest. As she was getting older, she found her freedom getting restricted. There were restrictions on her clothes, who she could meet, and where she could go. She needed a security detail if venturing outside alone. It was stifling. She was told that these restrictions were for her own good. She did not rebel. She somewhat bought into that narrative. She was fed up with eve-teasing: the whistles, the stares, the chases, the remarks. She felt like a prisoner on an assault row. Her outings were sanctioned by the parole board, headed by her parents. Her rights were only on paper. She saw those rights more often breached than observed.

A caged bird could also dream. She dreamt of a window of opportunity. She dreamt of a successful career. She dreamt of independence, personal and financial. She saw her mom asking for money from her dad. She felt it was demeaning. She wanted to be in a relationship of her choice. She was allowed some freedoms but with restrictions. If constitutional rights were not absolute, how could she get a free pass? The word reasonable worked like an ankle bracelet, restricting her freedom. She could pursue a career, but not any career. She couldn't join the military or the police. Becoming a fashion model or an actress was prohibited. She was encouraged to become a doctor, non-criminal lawyer, or computer engineer. Even then, she couldn't apply anywhere. It had to be vetted for safety. She wanted to leave all that behind. She saw Canada as a beacon of freedom.

"Mom, medical has come," Sadeep said. "But it's in Delhi. We need to schedule an appointment. I am going to call Dad."

"Have lunch first!"

Sadeep told the good news to her sister as well and they did the happy dance together.

His mom, Dildar Kaur, was a homemaker. She took her

responsibility seriously. She had the support of a housemaid. Even then she would supervise every detail. The home was thus immaculate and welcoming. It was not a role she envisioned growing up. She was finishing her bachelor's degree in arts when one day she arrived late from college. The tire of her cycle had punctured. She reached home late by a few hours. It put an end to her college career. Her ultraconservative parents took no chance. She finished her degree studying at home through a correspondence course. Her marks were not good. Officer class jobs were out of reach. Her father was a class I officer and didn't want her daughter to do clerical-level jobs. The class system was as rigid as the caste system. Father's wish was an edict. It was desirable to marry a class I officer or a government employee of equal repute, that too was selected by her parents. It was an arranged marriage where only pictures were shown before tying the knot. No meeting, no dating. That was the end of her career dreams.

She was not resentful. She adjusted to the role of a homemaker. She now wanted her children to excel. She did not want the same fate for her children, especially for her daughter. She provided support but she was also fiercely protective of her children. She made sure that Rajni spent more time on the study table than on the kitchen table. Rajni on the other hand belonged to a new generation: young, restless, and full of dreams. Nothing could come between her and her dreams. The world was flattening, and she was ready to slide across.

The appointment was at a private clinic in Delhi. Immigrant physicals were a big business. Only certain designated physicians had the authority to do them. With authority came power, and with power came money. The fees were enormous. The queues were relentless. They had to wait. As their turn came, it was a fairly standard procedure.

It started with a general physical exam and a questionnaire.

"You have a good job," the doctor said. "Why do you want to go to Canada?"

"Ahh," before Zor Singh could finish, the doctor interjected.

"I know it's for your children's future. I would have done the same. Anyways, you are done with me. Please go to the lab for blood work and then for a chest x-ray."

"Is everything ok, Doctor Sahib?" Zor Singh asked.

"No problem from my side," the doctor said. "But the test reports are sent directly to the Canadian High Commission."

The phlebotomist was amusing, "Sir ji, don't worry. It will cause some pain. But once in Canada, you will forget all the pain and suffering."

It was a code word for another baksheesh. Zor Singh was a pro and he obliged. After the chest x-ray, it was finally the end of a long arduous day.

Another wait, another bell, another baksheesh, another letter. Sadeep was suspicious as it was a small-sized letter. This couldn't be a visa letter. His mind ran amok. The worst-case scenarios came to his mind. What if they had found something terrible like cancer, TB, HIV? He did a prayer and opened the letter.

To determine the medical eligibility of Dildar Kaur, we have asked for further testing. Her chest x- ray showed a borderline cardiothoracic ratio. It requires cardiac investigations. After the investigations, we will determine her eligibility for the immigrant visa.

Sadeep had a sinking feeling. He was not sure what it meant. He was a bit reassured that words like regret and unfortunately were not there. But he did not see congratulations either. He immediately ran to a cybercafé. He spent the next few hours searching for the meaning of an enlarged cardio-thoracic ratio. It meant an enlarged heart. The reasons were many, ranging from heart failure to cardiomyopathy. If any of these conditions were diagnosed, an immigrant visa could be denied. The Canadian taxpayer didn't want to take the onus of welcoming a sick patient. He was angry at God. It was strike two for Canada after the visitor visa debacle years ago.

"What's the point of praying? No good ever happens to me."

The next target was his mom.

"Why didn't you take your health seriously? Why should I pay for your negligence?"

His mom was wise enough not to react to a teenager's rant.

"Don't worry. God is kind. What's the worst that could happen? I will not go to Canada. So what? I can always withdraw my application."

Rajni kept mum. She was equally disappointed but was more levelheaded. Sadeep had no such intentions. He threw away the letter and locked himself in the room. The boat of empathy sailed right in front of him. The fear was overwhelming. He apologized to God as he needed more favors from Him. The rest of the evening was spent with his parents, who listened to him like professional therapists.

It was time for a whole battery of tests. Electrocardiogram, holter, echocardiogram, and stress tests were done. Needless to say, the bill was huge. But more agonizing was another waiting period. This momentous time was spent worrying about the future. He had a list of questions which he jotted down on a piece of paper to ponder over.

"How would I live without mom?"

"What if she is really sick?"

"What if the whole application is denied?"

"Should I go abroad on a student visa?"

"How would I face my friends?"

The wait was getting unbearable. Another bell rang. It was Rajni who answered it and she was ready with the baksheesh. The letter was small again. Sadeep snatched the letter from her. He was panting as opened the letter. The letter was full of bureaucratic jargon.

It's in response to our earlier correspondence regarding the medical eligibility of Dildar Kaur to grant the immigrant visa. The borderline cardiothoracic ratio has been determined to be due to rotation during imaging. Her ejection fraction is normal and there is no evidence of cardiomyopathy or heart failure as per the cardiolo-

gist's report. The chest x- ray report was a false positive. Her eligibil-
ity thus remains intact. We will inform you to collect the visa papers
in the next six to eight weeks.

He was elated. But his anxiety had taught him to be cautious. He asked Rajni for her input, but she was of no help. Decoding bureaucratic jargon required special skills. He wanted to run it by his dad, who was well versed with the bureaucratic language. Zor Singh reassured him that all was well. Sadeep was ready to start packing. He had to say goodbye to his friends. He had to tell them how lucky he was. He had to work on his Canadian accent. He had to develop a taste for Maple syrup. All roads were leading to Canada.

He hugged his mom, "Mom, you really have a big heart."

The visa came, tickets were bought, and the flight took off. He enjoyed every bit of it. The flight was long, but he kept himself busy. He got the window seat. He kept looking down: he saw the Himalayas, the desert of the Middle East, the cities that looked like a bunch of lights. It was cloudy over Europe, but it cleared on approaching London, where there was a layover of four hours. Heathrow was busy and the pilot had to keep roaming around London, which was fantastic for Sadeep; he got the mesmerizing aerial view of London. He saw the sea of buildings and the Thames River dividing the city. He saw the bustling Heathrow terminal, which was like a city in itself. The duty-free shops incited him, but he had no money. He was happy just to be a part of it.

The final leg of the journey was at night. He had a good night's sleep despite the bumpy ride. He never felt unsafe; he was busy knitting his dreams than worrying about his mortality. The arrival was a smooth affair. The officials were friendly and kept repeating, "Welcome to Canada." He also heard sorry and thank you a dozen times. He was proud to be in such a civilized society. His aunt was there to receive them. He was hoping that she would come in an Aston Martin; she didn't. She had an old rusty minivan. It was a disappointment, but he let it go. He saw the multilane highways; traffic was smooth, and everyone was driving in their lanes. What a disciplined bunch of drivers, eh! he thought. It was a sharp contrast to free for all driving style back home. The high-rise buildings, the Victorian-style homes, everything looked charming. His aunt lived in a two-bedroom apartment. It was a problem; it was too overcrowded for two families to live together. She was blunt with Zor Singh, "You need to find your own place brother. I can't keep you for too long. This is Canada. Everyone is on their own."

It was boom time: the economy was superb, the internet had arrived, the stock market was high, so was the enthusiasm. The unemployment rate did not reflect the reality of finding jobs for immigrants. Zor Singh applied for teaching jobs; the result was zilch. He did not have enough time; he had taken a short leave and he was in no mood to resign from a well-paying job. Rajni got into university as she was pursuing computer engineering and there was a frenzy to train as many computer engineers as possible. Jobs were plenty too. The internet was poised to take over the world and computer engineers were being offered insane starting salaries. She was in the right place at the right time. The same could not be said for Sadeep. He attended school for one day and came back in tears. The counselor told him that the road to medicine was long and arduous and full of misery. Getting into medical school in Canada for an immigrant like him was as hard as becoming an astronaut with NASA.

Sadeep had already gotten into medical school in India, which was no small achievement. He had to make a choice: stay in Canada and forget about medicine or go back to India, finish medical school, and come back as a doctor to try his luck. He was unable to make a decision, but his dad took the decision for him. It was marching orders for him, he had to return but it was not that simple. He had to apply for a returning resident permit to leave Canada for studies. Without the permit, only 6 months in a year were allowed outside Canada. He got the permit and started his medical school. His mind was fixated on Canada. Then came an additional complication, a new immigration act was introduced in the Canadian Parliament. If it got rid of the returning resident permit, it would be a disaster. He could lose his immigrant status. It was too hideous to contemplate. He did some digital advocacy and shot off angry emails to the immigration minister under pseudonyms. He did not get any response, not even an automatic reply; e-mails probably landed in the junk folder. All he could do was pray. His prayers were answered; the requirement to maintain landed immigrant status was eased; immigrants could stay out of Canada for three years in a five-year period, which was plenty for Sadeep to finish medical school.

It was ultra-competitive to get into medical school in India. It was a game that required a mastery of tests, not necessarily a mastery of knowledge. Entrance tests with multiple-choice questions required a certain skill set that was not taught in schools. Coaching classes filled the gap; attending school was a formality but attending coaching classes was a necessity. What is the length of the small intestine? The choices were 20-25 feet, 21-24 feet, 18-22 feet, or none of the above. It was essential to know the length of each part of the human body to the last mm. It required cramming the entire medical encyclopedia. The scoring of exams was equally onerous. What is the lowest score possible in an exam? If you answered zero, you are wrong. There was negative marking and no minimum passing marks were required. It was possible to get into medical school by leaving the answer sheet blank! The mark-sheets were accurate to two decimal places. Between the score of 65.50 and 65.49, there were hundreds of students, whose careers were decided by the rounding error. The competition was cutthroat, which was a worthy challenge to the budding surgeons.

Sadeep got into medical school even after the quota for religion, castes, domiciles, sports, and the like scooped most of the seats. It was no doubt an achievement; a morale booster for any young man. It was short-lived. "Hey freshie, I need your dignity, your self-worth, and your self-respect," a senior said to him on the first day of medical school. Seniors called it a get-to-know moment while others called it ragging. It was banned, but only on paper. He washed the clothes, polished the shoes, did the scutwork for seniors. It was a rude reality check for him. The world was cruel, and he could either be at the receiving end or at the giving end. He had no choice but to obey orders, but he did have a choice whether to give orders or not. He did not seek revenge when he became a senior.

He did not excel in medical school, but he was not a failure either. He barely got through, which was enough for him. He kept the bar quite low; he only had to get through medical school without failing any exams, which he did. He did lose the art of lowering the expectations later on in life, which cost him dearly. He was happy to say goodbye to the medical school once for all. A burden had been lifted off his shoulders; he was ready to fly, literally as well as figuratively. He expected a reward for enduring years of humiliation. He expected a fairy tale ending, but all he got was a bona fide Greek tragedy; what Kurt Vonnegut would describe as a story arc that falls to negative infinity.

The title of International Medical Graduate was conferred on him on entering Canada. The title offered no privileges, only prejudices. When asked about his qualification, he would say he was a doctor. Invariably, the reaction was, "Wow." The supplementary question was, "Where did you go to medical school?" When he answered that he was an international medical graduate, the reaction was, "Oh." The change over from envy to pity was hard on Sadeep. He would skip the medical school part and told people that he was looking for a job. It had a more neutral reaction. He could not escape from the taunts of his relatives, who were only too happy to rub his medical credentials on his face. They gave unsolicited career counseling advice to him, "Drive a taxi, a lot of foreign doctors do, it is good money." He listened, nodded, and ignored.

The exams were expensive, lengthy, and hard. He barely passed them. It was not enough. The entry into postgraduate residency was the only way to kick start his medical career in Canada but it was easier to break into Hollywood than to enter the minuscule spots available to international medical graduates. It was an officially sanctioned discrimination, where Canadian medical graduates were ensured residency, but no such guarantee was available to international medical graduates. Canadian graduates called it fair as the government had spent thousands of dollars training them; they should have the first go at the coveted training spots. It was a fragmented system, and each province preferred its own domiciles. There were competitive exams where only the chosen few were selected and Sadeep missed out each and every time.

He realized his mistake; he flunked the clinical exams. The actors played the role of patients and they had to mark the candidates based on their clinical competency and bedside manners. He didn't say the magic phrase, "It must be hard for you." It was mandatory to show empathy on demand. When Sadeep realized what he had to say, he went overboard, which looked insincere. It was like acting, both under and overacting irritated the audience. The game was over for Sadeep. It was strike number three for Canada. He seriously looked at leaving for greener pastures in the US, UK, Australia, and New Zealand, which accepted foreign medical graduates, but he was in the wrong place at the wrong time. 9/11 had just happened, and the student visa was under attack, among many other things.

Sadeep had no choice but to find an alternate career. He drove taxis but did not like public dealing. He worked in factories, only to get a bad back. He found a niche in driving school and stuck to it; it provided him the money to live off, but the taunts and indignation never left him. Going back to India was a non-starter. He had changed and so had India; both were strangers to each other. He had to live in Canada and had to come to terms with it. His sweet Canadian dream was over, and a bitter nightmare had started which continued day and night.

CHAPTER FIVE

The Yellow Light

S adeep had to carry on with his life despite the ghost that was haunting him. It was a freaking ghost, not a genie, so there were no perks associated with the haunting. He had to carry on with the mundane things in life, including taking care of his business. He was ready to head out. He bowed in front of a rising sun, "Oh God, let it be a bright and sunny day. Please protect me from any and all problems that may be coming my way."

"That's quite a comprehensive list of demands from God," the ghost said. Sadeep had mumbled the prayer, but it was loud and clear to the ghost.

"A ghost should not come between me and God. I expect a ghost to be fearful of God and not be condescending."

"I have no fear of God. I am intrigued by the concept of God, and you can't stop me from thinking that way."

"Point taken. I am going to work. I don't want you any-where near me."

"Don't worry, it won't be me who gets you into trouble."

"What does that mean?"

"I don't need to explain myself. You go and do your job."

Driving was a part of his identity. He considered it a right, not a privilege. He was aware that driving was a weapon of mass momentum, which could destroy lives. He had learned to drive on chaotic roads of India. Obeying traffic rules was an afterthought in those days. He used to go with his uncle to the market. His uncle considered red light a signal for others to stop so that he can go through. It made Sadeep nervous. His uncle encouraged him to be brave, nothing bad would happen. Nothing bad happened to him and Sadeep on their travels. His uncle carried on with his transgressions, until one fateful day, he was struck by a truck that was also working under the same principle. Beparvah Singh died on the spot. It was a shock for Sadeep, and he took driving with utmost seriousness from thereon. He learned to drive two-wheelers first. It was through trial and error; driving test was needed but only on paper. Touts outside the licensing office could provide any category of driving license, the only requirement was their commission. He learned car driving in Canada, which helped him avoid bad driving habits from back home. Left-hand drive felt natural to him, unlike his immigrant friends, who had driven on the right side for years and found it hard to adjust their driving to Canadian conditions.

It was natural for him to gravitate to driving school as a career once he had given up on his medical degree. His car driving school was a success. It was due to his hard work and professionalism. It was also due to his obsession with all things driving. Despite his propensity for bad luck, Sadeep never had a motor vehicle accident. Touch wood. That's what he would have done. He wouldn't take a chance on his luck. His insurance premiums were low, and he was determined to keep it that way. It didn't make him happy though. It added extra pressure on him to maintain his driving record. Driving for him was akin to performing delicate surgery. There was no scope for making mistakes. It was not by accident but by design that he had a stellar driving record. He was anal about all things driving. Backing up a car required care and attention. He had reverse cameras, but they were for assistance; he couldn't rely on them entirely. His eyes would keep scanning the surroundings as if he was in a war zone looking for snippers. He did not live in a war zone but living in a school zone made driving a matter of life and death for him. There were plenty of stop signs around his neighborhood. He stopped at each one of them for full three seconds.

He kept his distance from the cyclists. A school bus coming his way would elevate his heart rate. His mind was fixated on the flashing yellow lights of the school bus. He had to be prepared to stop instantly at the first sign of flashing yellow lights. Sometimes a school bus driver would start flashing the lights even when the bus was moving, much to the annoyance of Sadeep. He didn't mind school children making faces at him; he would gladly ignore them. If given a chance, he would rather take a turn than face a school bus or a cop car. He kept music in the car at a lower decibel so as not to miss an ambulance or a fire brigade siren. He took his time to make a turn even if it was a right turn; pedestrians always had the right of way and he ensured that they were well out of his way. That's why he hated driving at night. Pedestrians, unlike cyclists, were not wearing high visibility jackets, which made for a nervous driving experience. He could have bought a night vision camera as an option in the car, but the technology was expensive, and he didn't have the Mercedes S class money to avail all that was available in the car safety systems. Lane departure and pedestrian detection systems were slowly trickling down to affordable cars, but his sports car was too old for that kind of tech. He had to choose between the mind and the heart, and he went for the heart. He had to rely on his sharp driving instincts to make up for the lack of technology.

He had kept a high standard of driving for himself. It didn't mean he was perfect. He was far from it. He had his transgressions. The speed limit was a suggestion not a rule in his mind when driving on remote rural roads. But even then, he kept a limit of 20km above the speed limit as a red line for him. He was annoyed by a slow driver or a slow-moving vehicle; he was itching to overtake them, and in that process, he sometimes came closer to breaking his red line, which made him regret his decision to overtake. It lasted a few minutes only till the next annoying vehicle came along. It was not the only thing that annoyed him. There were rule-breakers everywhere, and the only thing he could do was to shake his head and honk. He was one honk away from road rage, but he channeled his rage into curse words that were audible only to him.

He was a hard taskmaster when it came to his driving school. He considered his driving school the crème de la crème of driving schools; not anyone could enroll. The applicants had to fill a questionnaire before he could accept them. Are you a bad driver? If yes, please elaborate. If no, then don't bother. Have you made any driving mistakes? If yes, please elaborate. If no, then don't bother. You get the point. He selected the ones who were humble. He hated the arrogant and the overconfident types.

Shanti was his only client for that day. She was in her 50's but looked much older; she walked slowly due to bad back and arthritis in her knees. Nevertheless, she was determined to get her driving license. She had no choice. She had been in Canada for ten years and all this time, she relied on her husband to drive her to places. She had always been a homemaker. She was set in her ways. She saw the world through the lens of her husband. Her English was limited but she improved her language skills by watching daytime television. Her husband had a stroke last year and he was not capable of driving or even taking care of himself. Their kids were too young to drive. Taking a taxi was expensive and taking public transport was inconvenient and cumbersome. She had to get a driving license. It was a matter of survival for her.

Sadeep picked Shanti up from her apartment. She was wearing a sari and walking shoes. Her face was like that of an Olympic athlete, nervous but determined.

"Hello, auntie, ready for some driving."

She nodded and mumbled something, which Sadeep couldn't make out. She was in the driver's seat. Sadeep went over the checklist: seatbelt use, adjusting the mirrors, explaining the controls, and last but not least, knowing the difference between the accelerator pedal and the brake pedal.

"I want you to keep your eyes on the road and follow my directions."

She nodded without saying a word.

"Please ask me any question. No question is silly."

She nodded without saying a word.

She was driving on city streets with the urgency of a snail. There was a beeline of restless drivers, who were stuck behind her. But she paid no attention to them; her sole attention was on the traffic ahead. She would occasionally glance at the speedometer. She was driving a hybrid car. The odometer had given up on counting the miles, but Sadeep hadn't given up on the car. It was cheap to run and maintain and it did the job; what more could he want? It kept his overhead low and if an accident happened, it could be written off without giving him a panic attack.

"Take a right turn. Please don't hit the curb."

She nodded and took a wide turn as if she was driving a lorry. It was an unsavory site but the driving school logo on the roof prevented drivers from honking at her.

"You forgot to use the turn signal."

"Sorry, sorry."

"Now let's practice parallel parking."

"I hate it."

"But you still got to do it. Use that car over there and remember to do it step by step."

"Ok."

She followed the steps meticulously but couldn't manage to park cleanly.

"Try again."

She did, a total of ten times. She got fed up and so did he.

"I can't do this."

"Don't say that. Many drivers can't do it either. It's a matter of practice. You'll get it eventually."

It was time to move on busy city streets. She was about to turn right but was cut off by a speeding SUV. Shanti was startled for a moment. The car shuddered as she put on the brakes.

"Be careful," Sadeep said. "You see, you not only have to

make sure you drive sensibly but have to look out for stupid drivers and there are plenty."

She nodded but didn't say a word.

It was time for another obstacle: the dreaded intersection, with no left turn signal. The intersection had a red-light camera; the signage warned drivers to be careful, a traffic ticket may be coming your way. Shanti hated left turns. "Why can't I keep taking right turns?" she wanted to say it but didn't.

The intersection was upon them.

"Light is green. Go in the middle and wait for the gap."

She nodded without saying a word.

She was waiting for the gap, but the traffic was heavy. No one showed any consideration. Everyone was keen to take advantage of the green light; they were keen to go to the jobs they hated. The countdown had begun; the vanishing seconds were visible on the sidewalk. Pedestrians had gone across. The traffic signal went from green to yellow. It was now or never for her.

"Should I take it?" Shanti said softly.

There was no response from Sadeep.

She panicked and took the turn. There was a loud honk and squealing of brakes. Another car had also decided to squeeze through the yellow light. It was speeding through the intersection. It had the forward-collision warning system, which applied the brakes. It worked; the cars were a few inches from each other. No one was hurt except some egos.

"Are you stupid?" the driver shouted from his car.

Shanti was stunned. The angry car driver took a sharp turn and was gone after showing the finger to her. The traffic on the other side was on its way. Sadeep woke up from his daydream and was baffled at what was going on.

"Don't panic, drive straight ahead."

She pulled out of the intersection. She was driving even more slowly.

"Turn right into the plaza and park anywhere."

She was relieved to park the car. "I can't do this anymore. It's so stressful. I almost killed someone today."

"It was not all your fault. That driver was stupid. He knew you were a novice driver. There is a freaking driving school logo on the top of the car. He should have given you the right of the way. It was partly my fault as well. I got distracted by my own thoughts."

"Still. Bad things always happen to me. I did not ask for this. I was happy living my life in the confines of my home. It was and still is a safe place to live. My husband's stroke has upended my life. Why is God so cruel?"

"Who knows why God does what He does. What I know is that you can get a driving license. I promise you that. If it takes more than one try, so be it. I got my license in the third try. You hang in there. I won't charge you for extra lessons. Have confidence in yourself."

"Thank you for the kind words. I needed to hear that. My husband thinks I can't do it. My children think I am no good. I know I can but it's not easy."

"If it was easy, I would not have a job," Sadeep smiled.

She responded in kind. "Please don't tell my husband of this incident."

"I won't. He calls me after every lesson to assess your progress. I always give a glowing report."

"He has become pessimistic. I don't blame him. It's too much for him, to go from a sole breadwinner to a person who can't even take a bath without help. He can't let go of the control."

"I can understand. Let me drop you off at your apartment. I would not be available for the next few days. I will call you to reschedule the lesson."

"Thank you, you are so kind."

Sadeep came home with a headache; his second one in a week. It was a bad one. He went straight to the washroom and stayed there until he was exhausted from retching. His eyes were hurting and so was his neck. He had to blame someone, and it was the ghost, who had been the common thread in both the migraine episodes. He felt better after blaming someone else for his woes.

"Why don't you take some preventative medications to quell your headaches?" the ghost asked.

"Again, unsolicited medical advice. I had a bad day. I am in no mood to argue with you."

"I care for you. I need you to be strong and healthy."

"Where have I heard it before? I know, in political speeches. You care for me because you care for yourself."

"Don't be so cynical."

'Why don't you get out of my life?"

"You don't get to choose who comes and leaves your life."

"You are right. You pretty much summed up the story of my life."

CHAPTER SIX

The Proposal

The sunlight was reflecting off the dressing table and onto his face. It was a signal from nature, get up and feast on a beautiful summer day. He sat on the floor and took on a yoga pose. He kept on repeating God's name with each exhaled breath. His breaths were fast and deep. He sat quietly in meditation. A smile appeared on his face; it was brief like Canadian summers.

"You look cheerful today," the ghost said. "Sertraline did its trick. It's pretty quick if you ask me."

"I just had an amazing realization," Sadeep said.

"What? That ghosts are real?"

"Yes, if ghosts are real, so is God, so is religion. I don't have to be an agnostic. I can go full steam ahead on the religious path. I have found the ultimate answer to life. I feel lucky. I feel privileged. What more do I want? I would like to thank you from the bottom of my heart. You saved my life."

"Sorry to burst your bubble but I have one or two things to add. The premise of your assertion is only valid if the preconceived notion of a ghost has been affirmed."

"You are not presenting oral arguments in court," Sadeep said. "Please speak in plain English."

"If what you thought of a ghost is not true then what you

thought of God cannot be true either," the ghost said.

"That was not an improvement. I am still confused."

"Let me answer your question with another question."

"Like a politician?"

"No, like a pragmatist. What do you mean by a ghost?"

"I don't know the exact definition. I have to search it or find it on Wikipedia."

"Why don't you use your brain? It doesn't cost anything."

"Don't be condescending. I get your point. A ghost is a soul with PTSD."

"Is that part of DSM-5 diagnosis?" the ghost posed a rhetorical question.

"A ghost is a disturbed soul that seeks revenge," Sadeep answered. "Something bad had happened to it in the past."

"That's the myth. The technical term for it is utter nonsense."

"Why don't you enlighten me?" Sadeep asked.

"I will. My blood boils whenever I hear this kind of nonsense. By the way, I don't carry blood. It's just that if I say my particles flip up and down creating ripples in the spacetime continuum, it doesn't have the same punch line."

"You can't blame me for my half-baked knowledge about ghosts. It's not part of the academic curriculum you know."

"I concur. The prevalent narrative about ghosts shows the human desire to be immortal. There must be something beyond the mortal body. When the soul leaves the body, the consciousness must stay alive forever. It implies a judgment day. Everyone must answer for their sins. If someone escapes answering for their deeds in life, the soul is always there to answer for it in perpetuity. The contrast between good and evil has to be sharp. Ghosts have been condemned to the latter. We have been made caricatures of human perversion."

"Then what is the truth?" Sadeep asked.

"I am not an arbitrator of truth. My humble submission is if you don't know then don't guess. Immortality is a fantasy. There is nothing wrong with fantasizing, but one must come back to reality."

"So, what's the reality?"

"Reality is quantum mechanical, which implies it's incomprehensible. The information is hidden. Nature values its privacy. Nature is a one-long movie trailer. It never shows everything it has got; we are left with a longing for more. You are a quantum configuration stuck in a four-dimensional space-time; I am a quantum soup suspended in an extradimensional loop."

"You sound intelligent when you use technical mumbo jumbo, but I have a sneaking suspicion it's all crap."

"You are what you know and between you and me, there is a big gap that can only be overcome by a quantum leap. The jump requires both faith and knowledge. Knowledge comes from information, which cannot be lost. A book could be burnt, but its information cannot be destroyed. Bigots and fascists have tried that to their own peril."

"Thank you for an unsolicited sermon, but where do you come in?" Sadeep asked.

"You want to know who I am, right? What I am saying is that nature believes in recycling. The human body is consumed by the earth and the soul percolates into the extra dimension giving us life."

"It's not that much different from what we know about ghosts. Whose ghost, are you?"

"That's where you are wrong. Distinctions are gone. Only probabilities are left. I am what is called a singlet state. It means you could have full information about who I am, but you are completely uncertain of what I am. Let me give you a familiar example. We know there is going to be a president after a US presidential election. That fact is certain. But we are uncertain as to who it might be, a Republican, a Democrat, or a Plutocrat. What I am trying to say is that there is no one-to-one correspondence between a human and a ghost."

It was turning into a question-and-answer session. Sadeep was longing for his morning tea. He was a tea person and not just any tea, it had to be loose Assam tea, which he brewed with cardamom and sweetened with raw brown sugar. It was served in a teapot. Teabags were the last resort. He had tea only at home; Canada was a coffee nation; other beverages were not their cup of tea. He prepared the tea and dipped English biscuits in it to soften the texture. It was an exercise in precision and self-indulgence. He skipped his traditional baby cereal breakfast. It didn't feel right to eat it in front of the ghost. He had to make an impression. He sipped the tea and focused his mind on grilling the ghost.

"Do you have a name?"

"I have a quantum configuration, but that cannot be used for name-calling. You can call me Qubit Preet."

"Very funny, you are emulating a Punjabi name."

"I like Punjabis; they are free-spirited. No pun intended."

"Gender?"

"We are gender-free but for you, I am a male ghost. I think you would be more comfortable with that."

"Do you age? How old are you?"

"It is a tricky question. Time runs differently in the extra dimension. We move close to the speed of light in the extra dimension; time is frozen for us. We don't get older. We could last millions of years from your frame of reference. Only when we reach your space realm, time passes for us like everyone else."

"Why would you bother entering our space; it literally kills you."

"Yes, time is a bomb that keeps on ticking; that's life. It has to be this way, otherwise, you're not living but merely existing. It's like saying that you would live longer in sleep. That doesn't mean that you spend all your life sleeping. It's not worth it."

"At least give me your approximate age."

"We go by the half-life. I go back and forth between dimensions, but I have been around since the Renaissance."

"You must have been witness to a lot of history."

"I don't get the human fascination about the past. When the past is present, it is seen with disdain, but when the present becomes the past, every effort is made to cling to it. A worthless and fruitless exercise if you ask me."

"Could you go back in time?"

"Time travel is pure fantasy. The number of possibilities always increase. In other words, the entropy goes in one direction only, creating the arrow of time. It is the second law of thermodynamics. It has never been violated."

"Bummer. I know you can hear me but what about vision and sense of smell?"

"A sensation is an interaction between two systems, so the answer is yes. We don't need nose and eyes to sense things."

"What about language?"

"Language is information. We exchange information in qubits. And for your benefit, they could be translated into English."

"How do you know all this?"

"How does a baby learn to walk and talk? Practice, motivation, and instincts, not in any particular order."

"Fair enough. Are afraid of death?"

"Who isn't? Those who pretend otherwise, are liars. Consciousness is special. When a bunch of particles get together and ask a question, 'Who am I?' It's a true miracle. To fathom these atoms would eventually disintegrate and lose the ability to feel, perceive and ask questions is worth shedding a tear over. I would die by dissipation of my particles through radiation; a predictable conclusion to a random process."

"What about your brethren like genies, angels, and the devil himself?"

"The devil is in the details; it's everywhere from consumer contracts to tax code. I pity angels and genies. They believe in granting wishes. I wish they had better sense. Their utopian fallacy has failed like communism. Who cares about a flying carpet when a Boeing 747 is at your service?"

"It's all well and good, a fascinating insight into the world of the supernatural, but how do I come into all this?" Sadeep asked.

"Because you're the chosen one."

"Please don't patronize me. It's a cliché if ever there was one."

"I chose you, that's what matters. Our fates are entangled to each other. We can communicate instantly, what Einstein called spooky action at a distance. Our tastes match: you are witty and so am I. You would be my spitting image if I had one."

"What do you need from me?" Sadeep asked.

"I need your help," Qubit Preet answered.

"How can I help when I can't even help myself?"

"You are so self-effacing. Change your attitude. You are destined for bigger things."

"I hope I am not being scammed. I can't even report you if I get duped."

"Relax. Have some faith."

"In a ghost?"

"Yes, and for once, in yourself."

"What do you have in mind?"

"Details will come later. To be perfectly honest, I am still working on them. But I need to give you some background; I need to lay out the landscape that we need to navigate together. In short, we are in trouble. When I say we, I mean we the ghosts, not we the people."

"You are in trouble with whom, God?"

"Listen carefully, it's serious business. We thrive on fear. It's our lifeline. It's our mission. It's what keeps us going. What do humans want? Happiness and satisfaction, right? What do ghosts want? Screams and terror. It was easy to achieve. It was easy to exploit human fears. Ignorance and superstition ignited the flames of fear. We thrived. We dominated the culture, religion, and social life. Those were the hay days. We kept a low profile, staying out of the limelight, staying behind the scenes. We wanted to maintain the mystique of the ghostly phenomenon. We had a good run from the Arabian Nights to the House of Usher, but then came the digital age, the age of viral videos, the age of plenty, the age of skepticism, the age of fake news."

"Sorry to interrupt but there is still plenty of fear; what's the problem?"

"Yes, there is fear but it's not a fear of ghosts. Those who believe in us get ridiculed; those who don't, laugh at us. Humans have become experts in creating fear, whether it's reality or fiction. We are remembered only during Halloween. We are binge-watched on streaming services. People dress up as ghosts for parties. It's ridiculous. It's demeaning. There is no use for ghosts anymore. We have gone into hibernation. It has made us lazy. It has caused disuse atrophy. We have become an endangered species."

"So, what are you going to do? You can't turn back the clock. We are what we are."

"I am not blaming humans. Change is inevitable. It's our fault that we have failed to evolve with the change in human tastes. With time, everything becomes stale. Millennials have little interest in Charlie Chaplin. Fashion and tastes change on a dime. Attention spans are shrinking. The lifespan of a viral video is less than that of a fly. It was bound to happen."

"Now what?" Sadeep asked.

"I have a plan," Qubit Preet said.

"What sort of plan."

"A cunning and sinister plan."

"Out with it."

"I need help from fellow ghosts and patrons like you."

"To do what?"

"To create fear of course."

"How?"

"Have patience," Qubit Preet said. "Let it sink in. A good plan is like a good meal; it needs time to digest."

"Speaking of digestion, I have to go to the washroom, I would be right back."

He wasn't. Constipation has a mind of its own, the relief doesn't come easy. His anxiety worked as a laxative sometimes, but it was short-lived. He never worked out why he was constipated. He had learned to live with it, the same way he had learned to live with knee pain, headaches, and acne scars; but he never came to terms with the emotional scars. They could neither be hidden under the make-up nor washed away with tears. He tried both and failed. The made-up smile only showed his crooked teeth and so he gave it up. The poker face suited his personality better. He smiled, and like a leap year, it was an event. The tears too had dried up without moistening his heart. Doing therapy required him to speak, but words like his smile were hard to come by. He had trust issues and opening his secret emotional vault to someone required more than a few empathic words. He agreed to take medicines only when he was at his wits' end. How long he would remain compliant was an open question.

"Where were we?" Sadeep asked.

"We were making plans that were put on hold by a call from nature."

"Before we go any further, I need to put a face to your voice, otherwise it sounds creepy."

"I don't have a set shape; I only have data and it's quantum data. It's up to you what you make of it. Let me think about how we are going to do it. Okay, got it. We will do a double-slit experiment."

"We are at home, not in a science lab."

"We don't need any fancy equipment. We'll improvise. Take cardboard, carve out two slits in it with a knife. Then get an aluminum foil and place it one meter from the cardboard. You have to wear polaroid sunglasses. You have to shine pulses of light on the cardboard, that will go through either of the slits. When the light strikes the aluminum foil, it would create flashes of light that you will see through your sunglasses."

"It won't work. The set-up is too crude."

"You are right it won't work if you are on your own; the light is polychromatic; it's made of particles with many frequencies. It will create a lot of artifacts. But my presence would make it work. You just wait and watch."

Sadeep's eyes were beaming with anticipation. He was rubbing his hands with excitement. The last time he was that excited was when he got his Canadian immigrant visa. It resulted in regret. Opportunities were hard to come by and failures were hard to shake off. "Why don't you go back to India?" a friend once told him. It was not friendly advice; going back would have been humiliating. Punjabi immigrants called Canada a *mithi* jail (sweet prison). It was difficult to get in and even difficult to get out. Putting up a pretense of success was a necessity. Immigrants were Canadian brand ambassadors by default. They had to show their relatives how much they were better off living in Canada. Racism and other problems were kept under the carpet. Only the good side of Canada was exposed. It meant telling lies to relatives back home. Sadeep was fed up with the lies and stopped calling friends and relatives back home. It was deemed snobbish, and he parted away with them. He was left lonely and sad; not a good combination. He had learned his lesson: never trust happiness. He was wary of getting excited again, until now.

The results of the experiment were anticlimactic. He saw random dots appear here and there on the foil.

"I can't make out any pattern," Sadeep said. "I don't get it."

"You need to increase the frequency of pulses of light," Qubit Preet said. "Press faster."

"Okay, I am beginning to recognize something; there is a bigger bump in the center with tiny bumps on the side. My fingers are tired. I can't do it any longer. This is disappointing, to say the least."

"Don't give up too soon. Take a permanent marker and connect the dots on the foil."

Sadeep marked the dots and a clear pattern emerged. He had a smile on his face.

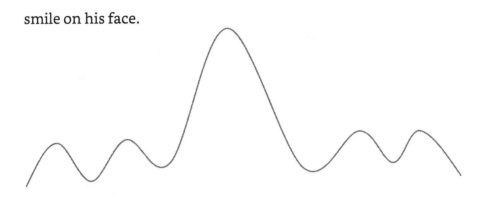

"So, how do you picture me now?"

"I can visualize a ghostly robe that covers your head, there is a torso in the middle and your waving arms on the side. Only eyes are missing."

"That's interesting. Humans have the most fertile imagination. They look at stars and see crabs and scorpions."

"How would you like to be viewed?"

"It's like asking artists about their work. Their viewpoint is irrelevant. The audience is always right. To me, it's just a graph of my probability distribution. I am more likely to be found in the middle and less likely to be found on either side. It's like a bell curve. Nothing more, nothing less."

"I would still take it, at least it gives me something to look at. It makes your existence more tangible."

"You could say the same thing about Artificial Intelligence," Qubit Preet said.

"But AI is not scary," Sadeep said.

"Stephen Hawking would have disagreed with you, and I would too. It could pose an existential threat to the human race.

You wait and see."

"You are scaring me."

"What else do you expect from a ghost? Let me make one thing clear, you cannot divulge my existence to anyone. You have to take an oath of secrecy."

"Like taking an oath of office?" Sadeep said.

"Yes, power comes with responsibility and all responsible people keep their secrets," Qubit Preet said.

"What power? I don't see any upside."

"You would in the nick of time. One more thing, we can't be seen talking openly in public."

"That's easy. I could use earbuds. People use them all the time. It's a cool thing to do. We would slide under their radar."

"Good. Did I mention that you need to take a leave of absence from work? I need your hundred percent attention and devotion."

"That's impossible. Who's going to pay my bills?"

"That's a million dollar question but I have an exponential answer. I can break any password or encryption."

"How?"

"Can you factorize the number fifteen with only prime numbers?" Qubit Preet asked.

"Of course, the two prime factors are three and five," Sadeep answered.

"Ditto. That was an easy one. Can you factorize 2^{2048} ?"

"No, I can't. I have to use a calculator."

"You could use all the computers in the world to factorize it, but you won't get anywhere. It would take thousands of years to factorize. You see, prime factors are unique. That's why the 2048 bit is the standard encryption. Now if you have access to a quantum computer like I have, it could factorize the number in seconds."

"How would that help me?"

"It means I could access any bank account or credit card. You tell me the amount; it would be deposited in your bank."

"I don't know if I should feel excited or scared."

"Are you scared to be rich?" Qubit Preet asked.

"I am scared to commit a crime," Sadeep said.

Sadeep lived by the book. He felt guilty if he threw a straw in the organics bin. Recycling was a religious experience for him. He over-reported his income and under-billed the expenses. He had an entire room full of receipts and bills; he kept them forever. He had never broken a line; whether it was to get a coffee or to go to the washroom.

"I could hack a criminal or a mobster's account. That's a moral thing to do. That's what created the folklore of Robin Hood."

"No sir, it's not. You are going to financially link me to those criminals. I would receive proceeds of a crime. It would only make things worse."

"What about fleecing a cent here, a cent there? If done on millions of accounts, you would get a substantial amount and they wouldn't even notice it."

"I am sorry. It's still not acceptable to me."

"You are not easy to work with. Let me think – what about day trading?"

"I don't know anything about stock trading. I don't want to lose whatever money I have."

"Relax. It's not about the investment thesis. It's about the computing power. That's what high-frequency trading is all about. Powerful computers are programmed to find the tiniest of trends in the stock market and they try to squeeze profits from a hypercompetitive marketplace. We could play that game much faster and make much more money."

"I don't think that's fair," Sadeep said.

"I have run out of ideas," Qubit Preet said.

"But I haven't. I would take a loan. That's what Canadians do."

"Do what you have to do, as long as you do what I tell you to do."

Sadeep got busy binge-watching his favorite movies. He

wanted a distraction. He wanted a holiday. A home holiday was all he could afford at present. It was cheap and he had the control. He watched movies that made him smile. It was worth it to pay for streaming services, where he could choose the silliest of the comedies. He was in the mood to watch Ghostbusters today. He especially enjoyed the zapping of ghosts; it provided a cathartic release for him.

CHAPTER SEVEN

The Journey to the Graveyard

I t was pouring rain outside. Sadeep didn't like rain. He didn't like snow, flurries, freezing rain, fog, and clouds for that matter. He longed for bright blue skies with interspersed white clouds. Canadian weather was a bummer. It contributed to his seasonal blues. The leafless trees felt like lifeless skeletons to him. Summer was short and a cool rainy-day during July was cruel. He, like many Canadians, wished to be on a Caribbean island in the winter, drinking Pina Colada on a white sandy beach. There was one problem: it was not money but a fear of flying. He knew the fear was irrational. He knew the safety record of planes; it didn't matter. He couldn't think straight. His thinking got cloudy in the sky. It made each bump on the plane, a call out of death for him. He became religious on the plane; to hell with evidence and science. His anxiety would reach heights that even the plane couldn't match. He had confined himself to taking road trips locally, which made it especially painful to have bad weather at the height of the summer.

It was ten 'o clock in the morning; he was reading a newspaper. It was a real newspaper made with authentic Canadian paper, not a digital one. He didn't pay for the newspaper; there were several free promotions; he moved from one promotion to another. He didn't mind being a freeloader. It was essential to have a hard copy of the newspaper. It kept him well informed and regulated his bowel habits. It was easy on the eyes and soft on the hands. He noticed something sliding over his arm. He peeked and screamed. He yanked away the thing on the ground. He regained his composure and looked at the damn thing. It was not an insect or a spider, but it was his smartphone that had melted and slid on the floor.

"What in the name of God is this?" Sadeep said.

"It is art," Qubit Preet said.

"It's you. Let me tell you one thing, you are no Salvador Dali."

"It was a prank, cheer up. I am glad you are a connoisseur of art."

"I can recognize fakes. Please, can I have my phone back? Can I have my life back?"

The liquified phone came together but it was frozen. He had to charge it to put life back into it.

"Our journey begins today," Qubit Preet said. "Get ready by eight o'clock at night, we are going to meet a friend."

"Where are we going?" Sadeep asked.

"To a cemetery. It's deep in the Mennonite country."

"Do I need to carry anything, like a knife or a pepper spray?"

"Just carry your brain."

"Hey, show some respect," Sadeep said.

"I am sorry, but I like dry humor," Qubit Preet said. "You have to put up with that."

"Humor is fine, but humiliation is not."

"Point taken."

Sadeep was hungry but he was a terrible cook. He could make a two-egg omelet which was barely edible. He relied on frozen Indian food. It had a shelf life longer than the term of the current Congress. His freezer was full of frozen Indian buffets. The cupboards were full of baby cereal and corn flakes boxes. He bought them in pairs; it was a choice between two for seven dollars or $3.99 each. It was a no-brainer. They had long expiry dates. It made sense to hoard them. He was now comfortable in sharing his food eccentricities with Qubit Preet.

"Baby cereal with probiotics, hmm," Qubit Preet said.

"Please, don't be judgmental."

"I am not, it's an observation."

"What do you know about food?" Sadeep asked.

"That's judgmental as well," Qubit Preet said. "I see pure desi ghee over there. There is more sodium in your food than it's in seawater. It's like running a marathon only to chain smoke at the end."

"I try to control the portion size."

"It's not working, man. Look at your belly. Your shirt doesn't stay in your trousers. Get yourself together."

"It's hard to maintain discipline when you are not in love with your life."

"You want to die by overeating?"

"I don't overeat, but my lifestyle is sedentary. I don't have the motivation to go for walks or exercise. I get muscle aches with physical exertion. It's no longer fun; it's torture."

"I could make you see worms in food as you see in horror movies. That would do it."

"Yuk. Please don't. I prefer to be a vegetarian."

"A practical suggestion: buy one thing at a time. Park your car farthest from the grocery store. It will make you walk more and avoid scratches on your pretty car which you so adore. Buy eggs one day, milk the other day, vegetables another day, and so on. You could finish a marathon in a grocery store."

"I tried that; it only resulted in a huge gas bill."

"Then go for walks, bike to stores. Don't make excuses. And who told you to buy a sports car? Why can't you get an electric car?"

"There's no soul in the electric car. It hums, not sings, and I can't deal with the range anxiety."

"There's no winning with you."

The interior décor of the house was depressing. There was beige everywhere. There was dust, there were spider webs, there were insects. For a ghost, it would have been a paradise; maybe that was another reason Sadeep was chosen by the ghost. It was not that he didn't make any attempt to warm up the home. Besides setting the thermostat at 25C, there were many flowers in the house: tulips, roses, sunflowers, but they were all artificial. They were low maintenance, and he had no motivation or incentive to clean up his act.

"Could you clean up the house for me?" Sadeep asked.

"I don't specialize in vacuum cleaning. I could grant you money. Money can't buy happiness, but it can buy a good housekeeper."

"It's not a question of money, but of trust. I can't allow anyone to come to my house and have access to everything inside it."

"You are not hiding any treasure or dead bodies, are you?" Qubit Preet said.

"Money could go missing," Sadeep said. "Clothes could go missing."

"Loosen up. You get something, you lose something."

"I have lost enough. I want a partner who could do that for me, with love and affection."

"That's a fantasy. The expectation is a steppingstone to misery. You ought to know that by now."

"I hope you don't mind but you are getting on my nerves. I need some alone time. I would be right back."

"By all means. Take your time."

Sadeep went to the basement. He stored his valuables there, which for him were his childhood memories. He loved to go through the past. It was the only treasure he had. He took extraordinary precautions to protect his memories. He had scanned old pictures; stored them on a USB and in the e-mail and on the backup disc. But there was no substitute for the printed photographs, which were meticulously arranged in chronological order in the family album. He had the enthusiasm of a stalker as he browsed through the pictures. He recalled the excruciating details of each picture in which he alone was interested.

He paused at one picture. He caressed the picture of his grandfather. He closed his eyes to go back in time and remember everything he could think of about his grandfather. It was the sort of mental gymnastics, which kept his memory cells active. It was important for him to remember the details as only then he could recollect them later. His fondest memories were with his maternal grandfather, Major Khush Singh, who had the habit of asking a perceptive question to others: "Is he dead?" The question was fired like a bullet. There were no fatalities or spillage of blood, just some wounded egos. The question was hard to dodge; some nevertheless tried. Pleading ignorance was the favorite trick but it came with a price. A sorry figure had to be cut. Answering the question was even more precarious. It meant the prey was trapped, the time had stopped, the story had begun.

Sadeep visited his grandparents during vacations. He went with his grandfather for morning walks daily without exception. Mornings were beautiful: the grass was embellished with dew; the fragrance of jasmine filled the air; the birds chirped in excitement. Kids played hopscotch, a group of adults practiced laughter yoga, others took a leisurely stroll. Scores of avid walkers would descend on the lush greenery of the railway colony, like a swarm of bees. It was like an oasis for them, in the midst of a concrete jungle. But there was a danger lurking around; a pair of eyes in search of acknowledgment, a smile looking for an admirer, and hands that were ready to hold and fold. The major could have been mistaken for a cunning salesman in front of the Colosseum in Rome. If someone avoided eye contact and tried to sneak by, he did not hesitate to ask, "Excuse me, what's the time?" It was a rhetorical question that landed many in trouble. He was not looking to deceive or make a quick buck. He needed something far more valuable: empathy.

Major Khush Singh was already in his 80's when Sadeep was a kid. He was decently fit for his age. He walked like a Gandhian, fast but not furious. He had bowed knees that made his gait a bit unstable. He carried on despite his propensity for falls. He had a bamboo stick to prevent an unscrupulous fall and to fend off stray dogs. He wore a sandy brown kurta pajama, which matched with his curved tip slip-on. He had an elongated face, which made his rhinophymatous nose stand out like Pinocchio's nose.

If wrinkles on his face, a thinned out white beard, and bags under the eyes didn't give his age, then his turban surely did. He tied a small muslin fabric turban with crowded symmetrically arranged folds. He belonged to a bygone generation. He was the last of his cohort. He longed for their company, but communication was a problem. He never had a car. He gave up his scooter after a fall. Cycling was torture for his arthritic knees. He could only do some walking. His trips were limited to daily morning walks. He had a landline but the phone numbers in his diary were outdated. His memory was failing him. He could remember old stories but couldn't tell what he ate last night. Whereabouts of his friends and colleagues were unknown.

Talking to him meant a curfew would be imposed. People were not allowed to go anywhere unless and until the major was done with his sweet talk. Some would pretend to look busy and ignored overtures from the major.

"Sharma ji, good morning," the major said to his neighbor. His voice had a certain sweetness to it. It felt cruel not to respond.

"How are you, Major Sahib?"

"I am alive. What more can be expected. It's nice that you are keeping up with morning walks. Nothing like a scent of fresh air to start your day."

"Sure is, Major Sahib."

"Do you know, 50 years ago this was all shrubland. We used to have our drills in here. Col. Brooks was a hard taskmaster and we had to go through strenuous physical training. It was a deserted area. There was a dirt path that crossed it. I used to ride across it on my cycle. It was dangerous, not only because I had to reach my in-laws' village but there were gangs of dacoits that were active in the area. On one such journey, when I was returning along with my wife, we were stopped by a band of dacoits. We were terrified. A dacoit asked us, 'Where are you coming from?'

'Daulatpur,' I said.

'Who lives in Daulatpur?' the dacoit asked.

'It's my in-laws' village.'

The dacoit had a smile on his face. He said, 'It's my grandparents' ancestral village. The daughter of that village is like my sister. Are you newly married?'

'Yes,' I said.

'Take these 5 rupees, it's a small gift from a brother,' the dacoit said.

I was stunned. I did not dare to refuse it. It was a miracle."

"That's an amazing story," Mr. Sharma said.

"Even dacoits had morals in those days," the major said. "The crazy part is 5 rupees was a big amount in those days. You could buy an entire month's grocery with it. Let me tell you the other things you could buy with 5 rupees."

Mr. Sharma was getting restless, "I must go now. I am getting late."

The major was hard of hearing, so the request was politely ignored.

"I knew Mr. Alok Goyal in your department. He was the head clerk when I was in service. Is he dead?"

Mr. Sharma ignored the question and repeated his plea again and started walking away.

There was a quick exchange of goodbyes. Mr. Sharma walked away rather briskly. It was not the time to look back. Sadeep felt bad for his grandfather, but he was learning a valuable lesson of life: do as you please, ignore the subtle indifference shown by people.

The major was happy that someone listened to him. He then indulged himself in the collection of twigs of the Kikar tree. The datun made from them was used as a substitute for toothpaste. He offered datun to others for free, but the offer was often refused as time was more valuable to them.

It was time to head home. The major was a disciplinarian. He got up before dawn. He took the bath first and then recited the morning prayers. He had memorized the scripture, but due to his failing memory, he would often forget it in mid-sentence. Rather than reading from the scripture, he would recite from the start and tried to roll through the lines. Sadeep would also join him and learned a few rhymes, which were forever ingrained in his memory. After the walk, morning tea was ready along with the newspaper. The major had a rather odd habit of reading the newspaper aloud.

"Twenty people died in a bus accident. Many were children. It was a head-on collision with a truck. The cause of the accident is under investigation."

His flow of news was interrupted by his wife, "Please stop reading it aloud. Other people live in this house. I don't want to hear gory details in the morning."

"Don't pay attention then."

"How can I, when your loudspeaker is on!"

"I met Sharma this morning. He was delightful. I told him about Col. Brooks. I even told him about our adventure with the dacoits. He was amused."

"No one is amused. They just want to be over and done with your stale talk. Col. Brooks is dead. Dacoits are dead. Your friends are dead. I don't know how long it would take for you to be dead."

"Why don't you give me some poison!" the major said.

"Don't you drink it every night in the form of your brandy", his wife said. "You have made my life poisonous. I am tired of looking after you, preparing meals for you, doing laundry for you. Your urine leaks like a baby. You have to wear some diapers. I am done with you."

"Why don't you send me to a nursing home?"

"Things are looking that way", his wife said, as she stormed out of the room.

Major was enraged and started slapping himself, "Why am I alive?"

It was not their first fight. Sadeep hated when they fought. He learned another valuable lesson: the burial of dignity precedes that of the human body. Sadeep's grandmother, Dard Kaur, was ten years younger than his grandfather, but she looked older for her age. She was declining and couldn't keep up with the same daily routine. The major had been nice to her, but he dominated during their younger years. Tables had now turned. They had six children who were busy with their own lives. She had no help. The major lived in the past, leaving the present to her. Children would come once a month to get the canteen card from the major. As an ex-serviceman, he had the privilege to buy everyday essentials from the military canteen at discounted rates. The most important item was alcohol, which was available at a deep discount. They would get their monthly quota of alcohol and leave a bottle of rum for him.

Dard Kaur hated his habit of taking alcohol at night. She had seen enough alcoholics in the family and was wary that the major was one fall away from becoming one. His children were indifferent to his drinking habits and to his military service, which was for the British colonial army. He retired soon after India's independence. He was proud of his military service; a nameplate with the army rank was posted outside the house. Like many statues of prominent men, the nameplate was embellished with bird poo, which no one cared to clean. His military service was short but sweet. He did not see any action as he was far more suited for the bureaucracy. He moved into government service and held important positions for the state govt. His children resented his gentleness and honesty, "Your colleagues made so much money. You left us peanuts."

"At least, I didn't go to jail. No one can cast any aspersion on my character in service," was his standard response.

He was reminded of a time when honesty was appreciated, hard work was rewarded, and dedication was acknowledged. He was well regarded by his peers and superiors. He was looked upon by his juniors. He had connections with top bureau-crats. There were always visitors at his home; people asking for favors. He shined like a sun on everyone who came. But in the twilight of his life, his home was more deserted than a cemetery. He would often brag that so and so got the job because of him. He considered himself a gardener, who planted careers. "I have planted an executive engineer. I have planted a professor. I have planted a superintendent of police." It remained to be seen if trees remembered who planted them.

Mr. Gill once took him for his word. He needed a favor from a police officer. If the major recommended him, the job would be done. He went to the police headquarters and asked for an appointment. He gave the reference of Major Khush Singh. The only response was, "Major, who?"

The major was a creature of the past. He had no interest in the present. He had a glow on his face which the younger generation couldn't match. He had a collection of black and white wartime photographs. He had a bunch of military medals conferred to him during the reign of King George VI. He had pre-served them with meticulous care. It was the only way for him to relive his youth. He flowered praises on his British officers. It was a faux pas in modern India. He had a son settled in Southall, UK. He dreamt of seeing London someday and visiting his erst-while British officers. He was too proud to ask for a sponsorship visa. He expected his son to make the first move. He consoled himself by saying that his health insurance would be onerous. Why take such a risk? Where would he find those officers? Maybe they were already dead. He knew his time was coming too. He was not afraid to die. He had his innings. He was fascinated by death, he read about death, asked about death, thought about death and in a few years, he was dead.

Morning walks were never the same. People carried on with their walks. There was a voice missing; an absence was felt; some eyes were searching for a gentle soul, but no tears were shed. If their minds were to be read, many would have said, "Is he dead?" Sadeep regretted not spending enough time with his granddad and wished he had listened to the stories that no one gave a hoot about. He had no video recording of the man, only some black and white pictures. He carried the family album in his hand as if he was carrying a baby. The album was not heavy, but his heart certainly was.

"Do you want to see the treasure I have?" Sadeep said.

"It better be good," Qubit Preet said.

"This is my family album. The most precious thing I own. I don't know how I will cope if I ever lose it," Sadeep said.

"Nostalgia is not my thing," Qubit Preet said. "All family albums are the same. This is my grandpa, and he is dead. This is my grandma, and she is dead. Here I am and someday I will also be dead."

"You are like my mom. She always shrugs it off whenever I want to show her our old family album. She says it's painful. I get teary-eyed, but those are the tears of happiness, and I can't get enough of them. Wouldn't it be wonderful if we could go back in time and just observe, not take part, not distort history, not create paradoxes, just relish their presence, the culture, the times?"

"You could watch an old movie or a historical drama, that would quince some of your thirst for the past."

"It's not the same thing," Sadeep said. "It's like saying that I could get the same enjoyment and experience by watching a sandy beach on television than actually going there."

"It's coming," Qubit Preet said. "It's called augmented reality."

"I really hope it fulfills its ambition. At present, it's not there. It's confined to drive and shoot video games for teenagers. It's like driverless cars, all talk but no execution. I dig for a pause button which would hold the wonderful moments in life so we could live them a little longer."

"You have to remember that the moment you consider wonderful could be tyrannous for someone else. That's why laws of nature are such an equalizer. A dictator cannot hold on to a moment any more than a peasant. There is only one way where a moment can be held forever: on the event horizon of a black hole. If your loved ones manage to reach the event horizon, they would be frozen forever on the horizon, never quite entering the black hole as seen by you. You can relish that moment for eternity. But from their point of view, they would fall into the black hole and pay the ultimate price for your desire. Anyway, I do have a question: I can't help but notice that you had beads on your neck in one of the photographs. What were these for?"

"It is to pray; you keep a count of how many times you recite God's name. When I was in grade four, I was fascinated by all things religious. I wanted to be a saint. I thought it was a profession. If I kept on reciting God's name, it would manifest itself before me."

"Sounds pretty narcissistic," Qubit Preet said. "You were after power, not God. But you could say that about a lot of people."

"I was naïve," Sadeep said. "It didn't last long. I have since been disillusioned with religion. I want to believe in it, but I crave evidence. I don't want to waste my time. I thought your existence was direct evidence for the existence of God but your scientific explanation behind the existence of ghosts dimmed my enthusiasm."

"God by definition means everything there is and more. How could you think that you or anyone for that matter could ever know everything that there is to know?"

"You are right. What I know is that it's time to go and meet your friend. I better get ready. It won't take long."

He was ready in five minutes. There wasn't much imagination to his fashion choices, it was as generic as it could get: a t-shirt with blue jeans, sneakers, and a baseball cap. He trimmed his beard to hide grey hair. He cut off grey hair at strategic places. They were not numerous to need coloring and the baseball cap was enough to hide away the unruly hair.

"Your closets are full of clothes, but I have seen you in the same jeans and t-shirt," Qubit Preet said. "What a wastage."

"I know I get carried away with shopping sometimes. It comes in waves. I regret it later but by then I neither have the receipt nor the time to return them; I am stuck with them like I am stuck with my life. I have a protruding belly, which has messed up my physique. I can't wear skin-fit and custom-fit t-shirts. I am selective with jeans as I can't find the right fit. Most of the jeans are low rise with skin fit. They look good on teenagers but not on middle-aged men. My crotch gets squeezed in tight jeans. I prefer an extra stretchable fabric that provides room in the groin."

"You have so many hang-ups. I didn't need to know your anatomical details. I am not a tailor. And besides, who cares if you don't look like a model. In North America, every other person is overweight; you hardly stand out."

"You are right. I am thin-skinned. I can't take any criticism. I want to be invisible. I want to go unnoticed, but my ego instigates me to be famous."

"You only want to be admired. You want everyone to like you all the time; a feat that even the holiest of men have been unable to achieve."

"What should I do?" Sadeep asked.

"You need exposure therapy," Qubit Preet said. "I want you to do the opposite of what your mind tells you to do."

"I would try."

"That's the spirit; I mean the attitude. You know what I mean."

Sadeep checked the pressure in the tires and pressed the ignition button to awaken the beast, which made a loud mechanical sound that mellowed as the engine warmed up.

"It's important to check tire pressure, you know," Sadeep said. "My car doesn't have a spare tire. It's to save weight and weight is everything in a performance vehicle. I don't want to be stuck with a flat tire in the countryside and that too at night."

"Are you scared of getting stuck?" Qubit Preet asked.

"It's not a question of being scared. It's about the inconvenience. And I don't know if you can fix a flat tire. I can't."

"If I can melt your smartphone, surely I can seal and inflate a tire."

"Good to know. Even if you can't, I have a CAA membership."

He was humming along with the songs on the stereo. He had a collection of his favorite songs stored on the USB drive. The car was winding down the single-lane highway with the Grand River on one side and cornfields on the other. It wagged its tail around; a rear-wheel-drive dance choreographed by the limited-slip differential. Farmhouses were scattered around the landscape. They looked like miniature toy houses in the vastness of the fields. He had to share the road with horse carriages as he drove deep into the Mennonite country. The absolute distance between the city of Waterville and the Mennonite country was small, but the cultural distance was huge. Waterville boasted itself as a digital hub, and the Mennonite country was the epicenter of a unique culture and heritage.

"These songs are from the '90s; the cheesy boy bands and the formulaic Bollywood songs," Qubit Preet said. "It says a lot about you."

"It does," Sadeep said. "These songs belong to my childhood. Songs are the best way to go back in time. They remind me of what it was like when I first listened to them. You would never understand."

"I have a different taste in music. I have listened to Mozart when he was alive."

"Music is not just a matter of taste, it's also about experience and emotions it evokes. Mozart's music feels cold and distant to me. I am not ashamed to admit that the so-called trashy boy band songs put me to tears."

"I didn't say that I like Mozart. To me, music is nothing more than wave packets that transform through Fourier series. I am more interested in their effect on humans. Screams, that's what I want to hear. That's what makes me a human and you a ghost."

"Fair enough."

Sadeep had glee in his eyes as he clicked on the shift paddles mounted on the steering wheel. They made a clunky metallic noise, which was music to his ears. He was in love with his car. It had never disappointed. It followed his command; he only had to press a button. There was no judgment involved; the car didn't tell him to slow down. It didn't tell him that he was looking shabby. It didn't tell him what he was doing with his life. It was better than man's best friend; he didn't have to clean up after a stroll. The maintenance costs were reasonable, and the car hadn't broken down thus far.

"We are getting close to our destination," Qubit Preet said. "Let me bring you up to speed with the formalities of meeting a ghost."

"Are you sending me alone?" Sadeep asked.

"I will be around, but you must know that ghosts mark and defend their territory. I don't want any confrontation."

"I would love to see some punches being pulled."

"You don't understand. We are made of dark matter that is millions of times heavier than regular matter. When dark matter collides, particles can annihilate each other, releasing enormous amounts of energy. Recall that $E = mc^2$ and if m is large enough, simple processes can release a lot of energy. A punch is equivalent to thousands of tons of TNT. You do not want to be near that explosion."

"That's scary, but I see a silver lining, an answer to our energy crisis. All you have to do is to rub your hands or whatever you have, and you could supply energy to half a city."

"That's why we make every effort to hide. We don't want to be fossil fuel or become weaponized for human interests."

"You have suddenly raised the stakes. I can hear my gut rumbling. I have an urge to relieve myself."

"Hold on to your overactive bladder. You would be fine. It's safer than you think. I would be worried if there was a beware dog sign. Ghosts don't bite you know, and they don't give rabies either."

"If you say so. I have a request: when you are communicating with your fellow ghost, I should be able to understand it. Plain English please."

"Don't worry, it would at a level of ESL."

"I scored 60/60 in the Test of Spoken English. It was the only exam I aced. I may not be a native speaker, but I could form sentences vigorously."

"I wouldn't call it vigorous," Qubit Preet said. "Those who can write and speak well rule the world. You can devour your enemies with words. Read novels. Read Hemingway."

"I have an attention span of a fly," Sadeep said. "I get bored if a joke gets longer; do you think I can sit through a novel?"

"Read a short story then. You forgot to ask the most important question."

"You are right. How would the ghost recognize me?"

"Good question. We have a password. What is e to the i pi plus one?"

"I don't know. I was never not good at math."

"It's simple. In fact, it's elementary. $e^{i\pi} + 1 = 0$. It is the most beautiful mathematical equation in the universe. It is called the Euler's identity."

"What's so beautiful about it?" Sadeep said.

"Beauty is in the IQ of the beholder," Qubit Preet said. "What's beautiful about Mona Lisa? When intelligentsia said it was beautiful, it became beautiful. You would be glad to know that I was a witness to its discovery."

"Really. How so?"

"I was haunting Euler's friend. He asked for money from Euler. A gold coin was handed over by Euler by rotating his arm in a semicircular arc, which is represented by the imaginary axis, $e^{i\pi}$. His friend got one coin and Euler was left with zero coins. That pretty much sums up $e^{i\pi} + 1 = 0$ equation."

"That's the nerdiest story I have ever heard. Is it true?"

"I am not going to certify it. You better believe it as hearsay evidence."

"Who else have you haunted?"

"That's for another day. We are almost there. Pay attention to sensory stimuli. Good luck."

They were traveling on a gravel road. He cringed as stones continued to hit the car. It was pitch black. There were no streetlights. Moon was nowhere to be found. High beam light was cutting through the darkness like an icebreaker cutting through the Arctic ice. The cemetery was located on higher ground. There were no houses around. The cemetery covered an area of half a block. There were no flowers or garlands anywhere on the tombstones. It was an old and deserted cemetery; there were no loved ones left to remember the lost souls. He turned off the car; the headlights were off after 5 minutes. Parking was no problem. He walked for a hundred yards inside the cemetery under the watchful guidance of the headlights. As the headlights died, he couldn't see anything. It took time for his eyes to accommodate to the dark surroundings.

It was a clear night with astrological signs hovering in the sky. He stared at the sky with amazement. He had not seen so many twinkling stars since his childhood. It reminded him of the summers in India, where he used to sleep with his grandfather on the roof with foldable beds. They counted stars and recognized their patterns. He missed those days. He had missed the stars. He was glad to see his old buddies after a long time. They hadn't changed but he had. He was still staring at the sky when he saw a flash of light go by.

It was like a bolt of lightning. There were repeated bursts of lightning as if someone was circling around him. He followed the flash of light with every available attention at his disposal; he could see the outline of a person, probably a woman in a white robe. The flashes of light stopped, and a woman was standing 20 feet ahead of him. He was looking at her back. She was at least 6 feet tall. She had long black curly hair that slid on the ground like a wedding dress. She was glowing like radioactive material. His heart was in sinus tachycardia. He was going through a real-life cardiac stress test. He had shallow breathing; sweating was guaranteed on a humid night. A fine tremor was passing throughout his body.

He took baby steps towards the woman. If it was a horror movie, the audience would have been at the edge of their feet cursing the dumb protagonist to get the hell out of there. He was putting his finger in a beehive, thrusting his head in a lion's mouth, chasing a rabid dog. It was the bravest thing he had ever done. He was at arm's length from her, so he reached out with his arm. Before his hand could reach her shoulder, he fell backward as she rotated her head 360 degrees. It was a jump scare that he had seen in countless horror flicks.

He was disoriented by the face of the ghost. One half of the face had protruding white eyes, absent nose, crooked teeth, wrinkled green skin, chameleon tongue; the other half of the face had sharp eyebrows, dark brown eyes, pointed nose, puffed lips, and red cheeks. Her head started rotating at high speed. It produced a draft of air that was strong enough to issue a wind warning by meteorologists. It wasn't a bad thing. On a hot and humid day, it was rather desirable. He couldn't help but glance at her feet; they were pointing backward. His heart rate had come down from the panic mode. The air draft had dried up the sweat. He was not afraid anymore, but it was bad manners in front of a ghost. He decided to do a customary scream. He wanted to be on good terms with the ghost. She went all in to scare him, and obviously expected validation.

He screamed loud enough for the ghost to hear but not enough to raise an alarm. The ghost went quiet and static. Tears in the form of pus began to flow.

"You are faking it, isn't it?" she said.

"I am sorry if I disappointed you," Sadeep said. "I swear I was genuinely scared, but it didn't last long as I was expecting you."

"I am not an expectant ghost."

"I realize I am uninvited, but it's not like I could call to book an appointment."

"Before I use your jugular vein as a straw to suck all your blood, you better tell me why are you here? It's hot today and I am thirsty."

"That's high-risk behavior. You don't even know if I carry blood-borne diseases."

She was not amused. Her nails were long and sharp, and she rubbed them like samurai swords. It produced electric sparks but more than that, it elicited an uneasy feeling in him as if she was scratching her nails on a chalkboard.

"Please, don't shoot the messenger. I am here on the suggestion of a fellow ghost."

"Password please."

Sadeep wrote the password equation on the ground with his finger.

"It must be something important. No ghost gives out the password to a human. It's like voluntarily handing over your email password to hackers. You can get up from the ground. Feel free to sit on any of the tombstones."

"I am alright. I don't want to offend any sensibilities."

"Don't worry, you are not spitting on them. By the way, the tombstones are empty."

"How come?"

"Since you are in, there is no point in leaving things out. Their bodies were rented out."

"To whom?"

"To interested parties, mostly ghosts."

"What would they do with the bodies?"

"I didn't sign the end-user agreement. They could do whatever they want. From the feedback I received, they were looking for a sensual experience. Many animals have senses that are many magnitudes more developed than humans, but it's the quality of perception that is unique. Consciousness makes all the difference. To touch a trembling hand, to feel the warmth of blood, to smell fear; it's orgasmic."

"What about pain and suffering?"

"That's part of the deal. It's no different than drinking alcohol; it gratifies the senses, but it comes with a hangover. We are interested in pain and suffering and fear. The trifecta is fodder for us. Humans have a never-ending ability to create pain, suffering, and fear for themselves and others. I'll tell you: the worst type of suffering is a feeling of worthlessness."

"You should have saved yourself the trouble by taking a course in psychology."

"It's not the same thing. Becoming a marriage counselor does not give you the same experience as getting married. Having said that, the trend is changing. The new generation of ghosts have no interest in having blood on their hands. Taking on a human body is considered clumsy and old fashioned."

"Why not haunt humans that are alive?"

"They put up resistance. They want their freedom even though many of them are used to living under tyranny. It's stressful and just not worth it."

"What about hauntings, paranormal activity, exorcism, and the like? They are part of human culture. Are you suggesting that there is not an iota of truth to all this?"

"It's a well-carved-out narrative. That's what it is. It took us generations to infiltrate arts and culture to create an image of a ghost that suited both us and humans."

"Why would we create fear for ourselves?"

"Why shouldn't you? You need someone to blame for your problems, the sins you commit, the darkness that exists within you. God is the default choice, but Almighty is all-powerful. You can't just pile everything on God. So, we help you out. We create a rumor mill. Products are well received. There is a receptive audience; the rest is easy. There are collaborators of course. They do our bidding, from authors to priests."

"Do you mean to say they were once haunted?"

"I shall say no more. Let sleeping souls lie."

"So, what happened?" Sadeep asked.

"Humans have moved on."

"Why don't you? Why are you still here?"

"That's rude. How would you feel if I told you to go back to your country?"

"How can you compare an immigrant with a ghost? There is a difference between a taunt and a piece of advice. By the way, how did you know I am an immigrant?"

"Please, you can't fool anyone with your made-up Canadian accent. Every word you utter screams South Asian."

"You haven't answered my question."

"*Tempora mutantur, nos et mutamur in illis.* Times change and we change with them. Evolution is not a prerogative of only the natural world. Humans may not fear ghosts anymore, but they do fear the law; not the law per se but the consequences of breaking the law, and that's where I strike. I publish a newsletter: I have grave news for you. It has a well-established audience among ghosts."

"You have all the bells and whistles of a ghost: long hair, ugly face, backward feet, and rotation of the head would freak anyone out."

"Thanks for the compliments. I wish that was the case. I have to be careful. People get startled for a second but that's about it. After that, they see it as an opportunity to make a viral video and upload it on social media. It's not them but I who gets scared. I only show them a trailer, not the whole movie. I don't give them time to click selfies."

"You scare us with the law? I don't get it."

"It's simple. When I see a distracted driver, I come in front of the car and then disappear. The fear on their face is pure gold. It gives them nightmares, and I can bet they would never use a phone while driving in the future."

"That could be dangerous. It could result in a horrible accident."

"I know what I am doing. I give them time to respond. I know typical human reaction time. Touchwood, no accidents have happened so far."

"That's an ingenious way to create fear and change behavior. You are the spirit of the law."

"There are certain rotten souls that refuse to budge. They drive right over me. Rather than slow down, they speed up. I am almost tempted to report hit and run on them, but I can't."

"You can't expect everyone to behave alike. There is always some variation. It follows a bell curve."

"Enough talk. What do you want from me?"

"I was sent by Qubit Preet."

"What kind of name is that. I don't know anyone by that name."

"I am not familiar with your nomenclature, I am not privy to his quantum configuration either, but I can describe his qualities. He is charming with an inflated sense of self-worth. He has ideas, he calls them original ideas, ideas that would change the world, for both humans and ghosts. He is witty with a dark sense of humor. He is scholarly and a showoff. He gives different vibes at different times. I hope you are getting the picture. He has no shape but has a probability distribution."

"I know who you are getting at."

"Good. Pardon me but I didn't even ask your name?"

"You can call me Chudail."

Their conversation was interrupted by a gust of wind. It was a calm night; leaves were quiet and so were the insects. The localized wind marked the arrival of Qubit Preet. He made quite an appearance. There was a squeaky sound as if someone was walking. The rustling sound of leaves provided the eerie background music. Chudail went silent. Sadeep was suspicious that things were happening, and he was being left out. He looked at the white sclera of Chudail and saw Boolean numbers dispersed across it. He was perplexed. He wanted to be part of the action.

"Madame et Monsieur, I crave your attention," Sadeep said. "Please speak in English. If that's not too much trouble for you."

"No problem," Qubit Preet said. "We were clearing up certain misgivings which had developed between us over the centuries."

"Did you get what you wanted?"

"Yes, I did. I was looking for the whereabouts of my compatriots."

"How come she knows, and you don't?"

"You don't have to go into the nitty and gritty of our workings. The distinguished lady keeps a repository of ghosts, who stay below the radar."

"What are you going to do now?"

"I have finalized my plan. It's a work of genius. I am struggling to find superlatives to express its magnificence. There's no going back now. We have to take it to its logical conclusion."

Sadeep kept a poker face. He had a certain disdain for braggers. He however gave Qubit Preet the benefit of doubt. Maybe the ghost was telling the truth.

"What's the plan?" Sadeep asked.

"The plan is to cast the spell of truth on you."

"That sounds scary."

"It better be. That's the intention. The spell would make you speak the truth and nothing but the truth. It would be achieved without the unnecessary inconvenience caused by an oath. Humans have gotten used to lies, big and small. It has become their default setting. I want to convert them to their original configuration. It would give them a jolt, unnerve them, scare them to death. If I, as a bona fide ghost can terrify humans once again, it would be a moral victory. That's the mission and it has to be accomplished."

"It's not a novel idea. I have seen it in movies. I have seen it in real life. There are interrogation techniques, which extract the truth after injecting unbearable pain. What would you do differently?"

"You forgot about the tale of Raja Harishchandra and Mahatma Gandhi's experiments with truth. I am familiar with human history. The idea of truth never gets old. The execution matters, the details matter. You wait and see how this idea catches fire."

"I don't see that happening. You are setting yourself up for failure."

"Don't be defeatist. That's your fundamental problem. You

have to believe in the plan. It's an act of faith. There are always variables that would determine the outcome. Nothing is foolproof, only probabilities could be derived. We start small and then go big. We learn at each stage. I can't do it alone. I need you. It's a mammoth exercise. You are going to be subject number one. Even to let you only speak the truth is a daunting task. Truth is like grease; it's sticky and difficult to wash off, except with a lie. Humans have an abundant supply of lies to pressure wash the truth. My task is to make the truth slippery, so it escapes the onslaught of lies. Once I am successful, I am hoping other ghosts would join the movement as well."

"Wouldn't that make me a traitor for hobnobbing with a ghost to subvert humankind?"

"How so? Speaking truth is not a sin. Honesty is the best policy, and we are only going to enforce it."

"You speak with a religious zeal. I am ready to help but I am not ready to be a guinea pig. Why don't you cast the spell of truth in such a way that anyone who speaks to me only speaks the truth? That would spare me a lot of misery and still meet the mission objective."

"That could work," Qubit Preet said. "It needs a lot more effort, but I am willing to do it as a favor to you. The relationship must be mutually beneficial for it to last. Okay, it's a deal."

"Good," Sadeep said. "What do you think Chudail? You are keeping very quiet."

"I reserve my judgment," Chudail said. "If it works, that would be wonderful. You have my support but not my enthusiasm."

"I have a request: please keep the whole thing under wraps for now," Qubit Preet said. "I don't want our fellow ghosts to get the whiff of it. You know jealousies run deep even amongst us."

"Discretion is my second name," Chudail said.

"It's time to say adieu," Qubit Preet said. "Thank you for your help."

"Thank you," Sadeep said rather meekly.

Chudail offered her hand, not for matrimony but for a

goodbye kiss. Sadeep was hesitant and understandably so. It was a courteous thing to do even if it involved a certain degree of risk. He bowed and held her hand; it was ice cold. The skin was wrinkled but it was hard like carbon fiber. He pretended to kiss and before he could raise his eyes, she was gone. It went dark again. There was pin-drop silence. He looked around and realized where he was, in a cemetery in the middle of nowhere. He doubted his reality, "Am I hallucinating? Am I in a dream?" He had heard not one, but two voices. He saw a ghost; he bloody well kissed a ghost. It couldn't be just his imagination. He couldn't ask anyone to clear his doubts. It was up to him to make sense of it all. There was only one way to find out: he pinched himself hard and winced in pain. The pain was real; he felt better. His next concern was to get back home safely.

He kept his eyes on the road on the way back home. No tinkering with the volume knob, no trying to adjust the temperature controls, no fiddling with the air vents. He drove within the speed limit for a change; he was outside his comfort zone; night driving was not his thing. He saw lights flashing at a distance. As he approached nearer, the flashing lights were coming from police cruisers, not one but five of them. Was there an accident? He couldn't spot a wrecked vehicle, neither there was an ambulance or a fire truck. His worst fear came true; it was a ride check to nab drunken drivers. His spontaneous reaction was to hide and run. It was too late; if he turned around, it could make the situation worse.

Cops had laid their eyes on him, and a police pursuit would be the last thing he wanted. He had to face the cops. His heart was beating fast, his bowels were making gurgling sounds, his hands were holding the steering wheel tightly. He said to himself, "why should I be scared?" He had taken no alcohol. He had no drugs on him. He was driving under the speed limit. His papers were in order. In other words, his hands were as clean as a scrubbed surgeon. But they were cops and he was a person of color, so there was that. They could strip-search him on the flimsiest of grounds. They would go through his driving and insurance records and make him take the alcohol breathalyzing test. He couldn't refuse the test.

The law was clear and draconian and much scarier than the ghosts he had encountered earlier. What if he failed the test? What if it was a false positive? No test could be perfect. His license would be suspended, his car would be impounded, his insurance premiums would go through the roof, he would have to pay a humongous fine, and last but not the least, he would go to jail. That would lead to a new set of ripple effects: having a criminal record, may have to close his business, default on loan payments and bills, go broke, go homeless. The thoughts were reverberating through his mind and exposing his innermost fears. The thoughts came in waves, hitting his self-confidence repeatedly. He was like a sandcastle in front of powerful tidal waves.

His last encounter with a cop was pleasant. It provided some solace. He was caught going over the speed limit. He was about to get a speeding ticket, but he pleaded with the cop that he never had any speeding ticket, and if he could be forgiven. The cop let him go and said, "Merry Christmas." It was the miracle of Christmas, but he could not rely on the festive spirit anymore. He had to play nice. He had to get himself together. He could not afford to appear nervous. A nervous driver would be a red flag and the only flag he wanted to waive was a white one.

The other pressing issue was his whereabouts. He was bound to be asked, what he was doing on a country road late at night? He was a city lad, and he was not expected to roam country roads late at night. He had to come up with a reasonable answer. There wasn't much time left. He was trying to rein in his sympathetic nervous system, which was flooding him with unwanted stress hormones. He took deep breaths and prayed to God. It was all that he could do. He slowed down as he approached the cops. A cop signaled him to pull over. He rolled down the driver-side window and activated the flashing lights.

"Hello sir, where are you going?" the police officer asked.

"I am going home to Waterville," Sadeep said.

"What are you doing here?"

"I went for a drive."

"This late at night."

"I like night drives. It's relaxing."

"I don't buy it. Do you have any alcohol or drugs on you?"

"No sir."

"Did you drink any alcohol today?"

"No sir."

"I need to make sure you are telling the truth. Please give me your driving license, car registration, and insurance papers."

He opened his dashboard to find the papers. It was full of clutter: old bills, parking receipts, and outdated insurance papers. He was struggling to find the right papers. He kept throwing the irrelevant ones on the floor. He would sort out the mess later. He finally retrieved the papers and handed over them to the cop. His hands were trembling a bit; a fine tremor that he didn't want to be confused with alcohol intoxication. The cop went to his car and cross-checked the authenticity of the documents. He took several minutes to search the database for any previous infarctions. Sadeep was sitting still, but his mind was far from being stationary. He was awaiting his fate, like a person under trial awaiting the judgment.

"Would you please step out of the vehicle?"

"Sure, officer." It was bad news but there was no time to analyze the repercussions.

"Please go to that officer over there and do an alcohol breathalyzer test."

He took brisk steps to show he was sober and to demonstrate a persona of confidence. It was a real-life performance with real-world consequences. He was a lamb in front of a lion. He was relying on the lion not to follow the law of the jungle. He blew into the breathalyzer, and it read zero. It lifted a whole lot of burden off his head. He took a deep breath without showing any emotions.

"You can go back to your car," the police officer said.

He went back to his car as fast as he could. The officers had further discussions amongst themselves, and the verdict was due any moment.

"You can go, sir," the police officer said. "Be careful out there."

"Thank you very much," Sadeep said. It was an insincere thanks but a necessary one.

"Phew," Sadeep said aloud. "Where is the stupid ghost? His bravado is all a facade."

The response came a few seconds later.

"I am here, I was here. You should thank me that I used discretion and left you alone. I didn't want to confuse you. You would have panicked if you had heard my voice. You did well. You need to fight these tiny battles on your own. It boosts your confidence. It gets you ready for what lies ahead."

"Perhaps you are right. I can only listen to one person at a time and now I need to listen to my body. It was a long day and an even longer night. I am dead tired. I need to sleep. Goodbye and good night."

He parked the car in the garage, locked the doors, put on the alarm, washed his face, brushed his teeth, flossed his gums, did the night yoga, and slept on the yoga mat. His eyes were fluttering; he was in REM sleep and dreaming. He had taken a U-turn at the ride check and was involved in a police pursuit. He was going at breathtaking speeds, sliding, and burning his tires on twisty roads. The cops had to abandon the chase as he was too fast and too good for them. He was snoring and smiling in sleep. It was short-lived. He realized that even if he got the better of cops, they still had his license plate number; he would be caught sooner or later, and he was. A police raid with the SWAT team took him down. There were shot fired which missed him. He was caught and handcuffed in full view of his neighbors and taken to the police station. He had his mug shot flashed all over the news. A sweet dream was turning into a nightmare. His rational mind was fighting the nightmare in sleep," It's couldn't be true; I passed the breathalyzer test."

The nightmare carried on; he was transferred to a maximum-security prison, where he found a classmate of his. Jimmy was his best friend in elementary school. They had many adventures together. They once ripped windshield wipers off a neighbor's car and were caught. It was Jimmy's fault, who under the influence of guilt, gave away the secret to his parents. They were humiliated in front of their parents, but it didn't leave any scars, they laughed it off. They were carefree and mischievous and loved every bit of it.

"What are you doing here?" Jimmy asked.

"I got caught speeding and running away from cops," Sadeep said. "What about you?"

"I work here," Jimmy said.

They had met after decades and recognized each other instantly; it happens in dreams. Jimmy was short but sharp, like a squirrel, and with an expression of a salesman. He could sell jail time as an incentive. He lacked guts and chose convenience over conscience most of the time.

"When did you come to Canada?" Sadeep asked.

"I came two years ago," Jimmy said. "I had trouble finding jobs. I saw the job offer in a newspaper. They were looking for people with diverse backgrounds. I took a shot and got the job."

"Lucky you."

"It's ok. Pay is good, so are the benefits, but getting cursed at is not. It's a thankless job."

"You tell me who's troubling you, I would make him straight as a ruler."

"You see the guy over there, 6 feet 5-inch, 300-pound monster. He is a gang leader. He is a troublemaker; he has made my life hell."

"Why are you scared? Law is on your side."

"That's the problem. He has no rules to follow but I have to follow a manual."

"Don't worry, I will take him on. I may be weak, but my

resolve is strong."

Sadeep got behind the man's back and poured a glass of cold water on his bald head. The man was furious and began chasing him; there began a race between a tortoise and a rabbit. The man was throwing punches in the air and Sadeep was hurling insults at him. The other prisoners and rival gangs got involved, and a brawl was underway. The maximum thrust of the punches fell on the flimsy prison wall and long behold, the maximum-security prison was breached. It had a remarkable effect on the prisoners; the fighting stopped, and a sprint began to get out of the prison. Sadeep was the last one left.

"Should I run?" Sadeep asked himself. "It's against the law. I am already a prisoner. Law didn't treat me fairly. What the heck?" Sadeep was the last one out. It was not an end to his problems. Law had been hard on him, so had been the weather; there was freezing drizzle and running was a perilous affair. However, his immediate concern was his bladder, which was full and at risk of overflowing. He didn't want to wet himself. He was looking for a washroom; there was none.

He was reminded of his bedwetting days as a child, the embarrassment he had to face, the restrictions he had to endure, the sleepovers he had to miss, the clothes he had to discard, and the pills he had to swallow. He couldn't hold on to his sphincter any longer, so he got up; there was darkness all around, but he could still see. He was going from the bedroom to the washroom; it was a few steps away, but they had to be taken with utmost care. Many had fallen in taking this short journey to the washroom and ended up breaking their bones or even worse. He realized that he had woken up from a bizarre dream and before he could apply Freud's psychoanalysis of dreams, he had forgotten all about it.

CHAPTER EIGHT

Mapping the Thought

Sadeep was neck-deep in a swamp of melancholy. He woke up at 4 AM and couldn't go back to sleep. Early morning awakening was a classic symptom of depression, but he disagreed vehemently. He said, "I am not depressed, I am just unhappy." Depression was a label, and unhappiness was a state of mind. The former needed therapy and the latter needed empathy. It was not the first time he had encountered the state of despair. His thoughts were laden with existential questions and self-doubt. He felt like a mediocre writer struggling to free himself from writer's block. He felt his work was meant for the dustbin. No one needed it, no one wanted it, and no one cared about it. He couldn't blame others for this predicament when he himself looked at it with disdain. He was good at nothing. When God was distributing talent, he somehow missed out. Whether it was his karma or a random act, it didn't make any difference. He didn't make progress in life; he kept moving in circles; the only thing progressing was his age.

Why should one bother with life? was the motto of his existence. Mundane was what had remained in his life. He didn't cry but he was one lacrimal duct away from shedding a tear. He was lying on the sofa flipping through the tv channels: there was an inauguration of a president who appeared no different than the former president; some stocks had gone up while others had gone down; some couples had broken up while others were drafting new prenups; rich were getting richer while poor getting poorer; none of it interested him; he was only interested in himself.

"Get up young man," Qubit Preet said. "We have a long day ahead of us."

"Don't call me young," Sadeep said. "It stings. It's an insult. It reminds me of my age. I don't want to celebrate my birthday anymore. When friends wish me a birthday only after getting prompts from Facebook and WhatsApp algorithms, it seems fake. Fake like an e-mail which claims a long-lost uncle has left a fortune for me."

"I was not giving a compliment. I was merely stating a fact. As compared to me, you are an infant."

"No one wants to die young but dying old is not fun either. Life is not fun; death is not fun. What should one do?"

"Crack a joke," Qubit Preet said.

"Life itself has cracked a joke on me," Sadeep said. "I feel worthless. My existence is as futile as someone trying to move Mount Everest."

"It's not futile. Do you know nature itself is trying to push Mount Everest? It's getting higher and higher, slowly but surely. Quantum mechanics tells us nothing is improbable. If you push on Mount Everest, there is a non-zero probability of it moving a tiny bit."

"Balderdash. I want my life to mean something. I want people to remember me."

"I get it now. You want to be famous. You want to be a celebrity. Let me tell you, fame is relative and inconsequential."

"That's what I have been telling myself. It's a defense mechanism. It's sour grapes."

"Fame is like a Venn diagram," Qubit Preet said. "Fame is local and cultural. Global celebrity is a misnomer. It's a marketing technique. Tell me, who was the president of the United States in 1900?"

"That's ancient history," Sadeep said. "I know who's the current occupant of the White House."

"I can bet not everyone in the world knows about the US president. I'll give you another chance; who won the Giller Prize this year?"

"What's a Giller Prize?" Sadeep asked.

"Never mind," Qubit Preet said. "Who won the Nobel Prize in Economics?"

"I don't know. It's a technical field, only economists would know."

"My point exactly. Let me make it easy, can you tell me the name of anyone who has won the Nobel Peace Prize?"

"Mahatma Gandhi."

"Wrong. He missed out on the Nobel Peace Prize."

"Really. He was probably the most deserving person for the prize."

"Who told you that only the deserving get prizes?" Qubit Preet said. "And who decides who is deserving?"

"Then who gets it?" Sadeep said.

"A person whose time has come."

"When will my time come? When will I see happiness?"

"Happiness is not seen but felt. Highflyers don't get the first shot at happiness. In fact, their fall is particularly painful as it's steep and relentless."

"You are right. The happiest people I ever saw were in the hinterlands of Punjab. The folks who sat below the Banyan tree all day. They had all the time in the world. They played cards, cracked jokes, engaged in gossip, stared at others. They had never heard of New York or Paris. They would not be able to tell the name of any Hollywood celebrity or even what the word Hollywood meant. Names like John Lennon and Michael Jackson meant nothing to them. They laughed at those questions. Their laughter was genuine and infectious. They could name every young and old in the village. They could name every bird, animal, and tree in the area. Their footprints were all over the muddy streets of the village, but their carbon footprint was nowhere to be found. Those folks are fast disappearing. Whenever I go back, I get disappointed. It's not the country I left. I can't recognize the streets, the cities, the people, it has become a foreign country."

"The past is like an alien planet. You can watch it from far away, but you don't get to visit it. A British novelist said something similar. Do you know who that was?"

"I don't know," Sadeep said.

"L.P. Hartley, another famous person who you probably don't know."

"What I know is that I need a bit of ignorance and carelessness," Sadeep said.

"I am glad you got the point," Qubit Preet said. "It's time for another excursion. Get ready, we are going to The Institute of Exciting Physics."

Waterville was a university town, bestowed with not one but two world-class universities. It kept the town young and energetic. There were street parties; many of them were unsanctioned. Student housing was a big business. Students paid high rent for speculative condo buyers. They also paid exorbitant university fees. They provided a talent pool for software companies. Some enterprising students started their own companies. Some companies made it big, but that was not enough to secure their future. They had to compete globally and fight for their survival. Above all, they had to adapt to changing times. It's capitalism. Waterville was not Silicon Valley, but it didn't need to be. That was its selling point. It was a small city, relatively. It had its own charm and problems. If it had to compete with Silicon Valley, it had to be smart, and the best way to become smart was to attract smart people and the smartest of them all were physicists. That's what Waterville did as it rolled the red carpet for physicists.

The world of physics needed reinvention. It was the granddaddy of all sciences and sought answers to the most fundamental questions. The field had been stagnant for decades. The major discoveries in theoretical physics were made in the early part of the 20th century. Nothing had come closer to the success of the theory of relativity and quantum physics. There was a time when physicists like Einstein were as popular as celebrities like Charlie Chaplin. Later Stephen Hawking was the only one who came closer to that kind of fame, but for most people, physicists were out of sight and out of mind.

People cared more about the fate of their favorite soap opera than the fate of the universe. Physicists tried to market themselves by using exciting terms like dark matter, dark energy, and the theory of everything. It was in the same vein that the Institute of Exciting Physics was established in Waterville. Donations came from university alumni and provincial and federal governments. The building was state of the art and was shaped like h bar, the Planck's constant. The value of this constant is quite small, and we should be thankful for it. The small value spares us from experiencing the weird nature of quantum physics. It also puts a limit on how small things could get. It has big implications. It was an appropriate symbol for the new institute. It was critical for physics to get the young and the bright to choose physics as their preferred career. It was not easy; it had never been easy. Even Einstein had a hell of a time getting a job in the field of physics. He had to work in a patent office to pay the bills and developed the special theory of relativity in his free time. It was difficult to convince a student to pursue a career with limited job opportunities and even limited pay.

The Institute of Exciting Physics promised a lifestyle that was akin to a Silicon Valley campus minus the weather. The atmosphere was informal: there was a gym, pool tables, badminton court, and a bar for relaxation. The favorite hangout of physicists was the boxing ring, where string theorists served as punching bags. There were no exams, only projects. Collaboration with industry was encouraged and making money was not frowned upon; what was frowned upon was wearing a tie and that too a bow tie; casualness was encouraged over pretentiousness. The idea worked; bright and illustrious physicists from all over the world came to work at the institute. They were still frustrated by the lack of progress in theoretical physics but their lifestyle and the generous research grants more than compensated for it.

There was progress on the quantum computing front; there were no practical applications yet, but the promise was enough to get the venture capitalists excited. It meant money flowed in; some of it trickled down to the physicists. They were driving BMW and Mercedes and Tesla cars and were paying off their mortgages faster than the pace of their work. The public benefitted as well. The outreach program of the institute was a hit. Public lectures were sold out. It was heartening to see people line up for a lecture on string theory. Ed Witten and Juan Maldacena were household names in the vicinity of the institute. Coffee shops and restaurants around the institute offered menus to cater to their clientele. The meal orders were taken and delivered slower than the speed of light, and it was probable but not certain what was ordered was in fact delivered.

Sadeep was not amused at the chance of visiting the institute. It was in the heart of the downtown, which he desperately avoided. One-way streets, metered parking, construction, and temporary road closures made it an unnerving experience for him. However, he did not show his disdain overtly. He wanted to impress the ghost and put on a brave face. He searched google maps, saw the street view, and checked the latest construction updates on the city website. He checked the parking regulations and where to find the coveted parking spot. He wished the appointment to be after hours, and it was. Qubit Preet was not stupid to rush in during the rush hour. Time was not of the essence for him. Sadeep drove along University Avenue and turned right on College Road and then left on School Street to reach the institute. He was amazed at what he saw: an empty parking lot. A lucky sign. The building was modern, which it had to be. Modern physics cannot be taught in a castle. The color scheme was dearie, but official buildings came in dearie colors. Doors were closed and surveillance cameras were watching.

"Now what?" Sadeep asked.

"We go across to Waterville park," Qubit Preet said.

The park was across the pond from the institute and it was busy. Sadeep found an empty bench on the side of the pond and waited. The park had many amenities including a small zoo, a kids' playground, and a steam engine. Kids were playing on the slides; couples were taking a leisurely stroll; some folks were busy feeding the ducks and others were mesmerized by the calmness of the pond. He was not impressed by the calmness of a water body. His mind dwelled into the unknown: what lurked under the impermeable water; a dead body perhaps. He had the mindset of a horror novelist, but his feelings were ego dystonic. An affliction of the miserable kind. His character was well suited for an Anton Chekov story.

He stared at a homeless man who was a stone throw away from him. Sadeep passed a judgment on the man: he must have done something in life to deserve it; he must have made mistakes in his life; he must have ignored good advice; how can a rich country like Canada with a strong safety net have homelessness? Sadeep had seen worse back in his home country: lepers, limbless beggars, and crushing poverty. It always made him feel fortunate despite his tendency to nit-pick his misfortunes. What if he was in this poor man's place? How would he survive? He was feeling miserable living in a two-car garage home and driving a sports car; what a display of selfishness and snobbery. He was being too harsh on himself. Determinants of health were not the sore arbitrators of misery. The homeless man looked at him; Sadeep immediately turned away. He did not dare to make eye contact with the man. He expected questions to which he had no answers. He had empathy to give but not on demand. He was fearful of rejection and thin-skinned to absorb a snide remark or a curse word. He pretended to look busy. It was not too hard; a smartphone could get anyone busy. He felt awkward sitting alone on the bench. He needed validation from others that they didn't care. He looked around; no one was staring at him.

He felt better.

"Where's your friend?" Sadeep asked.

"Hold on to your minutes and seconds," Qubit Preet said. "We are early. He is never late. He runs on an atomic clock. By the way, his name is Professor Pi Off."

"What kind of name is that?"

"He is a Pi Phanatic. He has calculated the value of pi to the trillionth decimal place. He can recite the value of pi to you till you die."

"What a useless preoccupation."

"Don't say it in front of him. The value of pi is a thing of beauty. Writers love their words, painters adore their creation, actors relish their performance, and nerds fantasize about irrational numbers."

"Whatever," Sadeep said. "That homeless guy is still looking at me. Is he suspicious?"

"Don't worry about him," Qubit Preet said. "There are so many voices and images in his head that it's a stampede. Here comes the professor."

"Guten Tag," the professor said. "It's a pleasure to make your acquaintance."

He looked like an absent-minded professor: double-pleated trousers with suspenders, a bow tie, a wrinkled full sleeves shirt, reading glasses with lanyard, uncombed curly hair, and a pencil mustache. In other words, he was in full academic uniform. His image was blurry, like watching 144p videos on internet.

"Pleasure is truly ours," Qubit Preet said.

Sadeep nodded.

"What can I do for you?" the professor said.

"I need information," Qubit Preet said.

"You have to be more specific than that. What do you want to know?"

"I want to know what you know."

"Please come to the point."

"I am trying to," Qubit Preet said. "You know we can come

closer and closer to a point but never actually reach there without catastrophic consequences. Gravity becomes infinite at a point creating a black hole, isn't it?"

"Yes, it does," the professor said. "It's a Newtonian point of view and it's outdated. Einstein's view was different, but it still led to black holes."

"My point exactly. Let me be specific: have physicists resolved the conundrum of point masses?"

"Yes and no. They have resolved the issue by stepping it aside. At the core, the reality is nothing but quantum field theory. Many infinities are lurking around in the theory. To make sense, physicists ignore the unwanted infinities by renaming them, a procedure called renormalization."

"Can I interject?" Sadeep said. "Why are we having this pointless discussion? Most of it is passing right over my head."

"I want to know the extent of human knowledge," Qubit Preet said. "I want to know the facts. Truth is nothing but facts arranged in a chronological sequence. Once facts are known, we will know the truth, our most potent weapon. Physics forms the perimeter of human knowledge. I want to know how fast this perimeter is expanding."

"Not very fast," the professor said. "Nothing much has happened in the field of physics in the last 50 years."

"You say that but words like extra dimensions, dark energy, dark matter have entered the human vocabulary," Qubit Preet said. "Aren't they close to making another quantum leap in understanding the universe?"

"Far from it," the professor said. "Naming something doesn't mean you know about it. Humans have named God in so many ways and for so long. Do you think they are anywhere near finding out about the Almighty? The predicament for humans is the flawed mathematics that underpins their theories. Let me ask this human friend of yours, can you add $1 + 2 + 3 + 4 +$ million $+$ billion $+$ trillion $+$ gazillion $+$ ......?"

"I don't know," Sadeep said.

"Take a wild guess," the professor said

"A very large number."

"Good guess but it is incorrect. It's not even close. The answer is -1/12."

"Really."

"Isn't it crazy," the professor said. "It is this kind of math that is used to give twenty-six dimensions to the string theory."

"Unbelievable," Sadeep said.

"That was the reaction in the physics community as well," the professor said. "M-theory cut down the number of dimensions to eleven, but still, they remain far too many. That's where physics is stuck. I call it M for mad. It has caused polarization in physics. There are physicists and then there are string theorists. Each has their own belief system."

"Let them fight, but don't underestimate them," Qubit Preet said. "They know about dark matter. If they can create it in a lab, we are screwed."

"Don't worry," the professor said. "They call it dark matter for a reason: they are in the dark. LHC in Geneva is their largest particle accelerator. So far, it has been a dud. It only produced Higgs boson. To get to the crux of the matter, they need an accelerator of the size of the solar system. It's not on the horizon any time soon. There is no appetite in the political establishment for such a level of extravagance."

"They still detected gravitational waves against such odds. Never say never."

"That's true but the probability of a dark matter breakthrough is remote. That's the fact, that's the truth. I will give you references if you wish to dig deeper into the subject. If you want to brush up your fundamentals in physics, check out the books written by the author of this novel."

"I am not going to do that. That's a conflict of interest."

"It's up to you," the professor said. "I had the irresistible itch to mention it, so I did. Do you need anything more from me?"

"Yes, I do," Qubit Preet said. "I want to know how an MRI works. I want to target my attack on the lie receptors in the brain."

"MRI is easy. Protons are aligned in a magnetic field. A signal disrupts their alignment, and they go back to their original configuration, emitting a signal. This realignment creates images and that's all you need to know. I don't know about human physiology, it's beyond my area of expertise."

"That's all right. I know a thing or two about the subject. I need access to an MRI machine. I have already lined up a volunteer."

"Hey, I am no lab animal," Sadeep said. "You need informed consent from me."

"Consent is implied," Qubit Preet said. "You signed on to collaborate with me. Besides, doing an MRI is no big deal. You get into the machine and close your eyes. It's not difficult."

"We shall see," Sadeep said.

"You can decide on the validity of consent later," the professor said. "If you need an MRI machine outside of hospital premises, you have to go to the Waterville Brain Institute on Columbia Street. There is no one there at night. I can grant access to you. I know the security codes. Rest you have to do."

"Wonderful," Qubit Preet said. "You have been of great help. Thank you for your time."

"No worries. Do you want to know how far I have reached in calculating the value of pi?"

"I would love to, but some other time," Qubit Preet said with the sincerity of a politician.

The professor accepted the thanks with a smirk and teleported himself inside the institute. He made scribbling noises on the blackboards, which had been heard by people in the institute from time to time, but they kept mum. The fear of embarrassment and ridicule was a potent threat to their careers. A physicist believing in ghosts would be accused of blasphemy. They made their own excuses to explain the phenomenon, and all was well.

The park was getting deserted after the sun said goodbye. Few shady characters were loitering around. He felt unsafe but not alarmed; he had a ghost at his disposal, who at his request could be unleashed on the miscreants. He went over to the parking lot. He inspected the car carefully for any scratches or graffiti. It was a part of his habit. He had given up trying to rectify his annoying habits. He was a firm believer in a couplet written by an eighteenth-century Punjabi poet Waris Shah:

> Pieces of the body if someone did,
> Habits still can't be gotten rid.

He defended his habits by arguing that it's better to be safe than pay high insurance premiums. It was for obvious reasons that he avoided parking near a big pickup truck or a two-door sports car. The only time he would let that go was on Boxing Day when parking lots were full, and he had to keep roaming around the lots till an empty parking spot was found.

Waterville Brain Institute was fifteen minutes' drive from the park in regular traffic, but the traffic was minimal, and the drive was over in less than five minutes. Sadeep parked his car not at the institute but at the adjoining strip mall and walked. He was essentially trespassing which would be followed by a break-in and enter, hence the need for elaborate precautions. He had an intense urge to search the legal repercussions of break-in and entry but decided not to pursue it. It would have made his anxiety worse to the point of panic. He counted his breaths. It was a time-tested strategy for him. The distance to the main entrance was completed in one hundred deep breaths. The building was no bigger than a public library. He counted fifteen cameras on the outside premises. There were welcome signs: please smile, you are on camera; this building is under 24-hour video surveillance; trespassers will be prosecuted. He had to go for it no matter what.

He reluctantly put his hand on the door latch and prayed, "God, please, no alarm activation." The door opened without resistance, and there was no alarm.

"Thank God," Sadeep said.

"Why are you thanking God," Qubit Preet said. "You should thank me and the professor."

"No, I will thank God only. If it weren't for you, I wouldn't be here in the first place."

"Yeah, I know, you would be checking out on another date with death."

Sadeep kept quiet. It was an acknowledgment of truth, which as usual was bitter. He surveyed the foyer of the building. Various parts of the brain were displayed as pieces of art. He didn't find it appetizing. The walls had large portraits of famous figures in the world of neurosciences.

"Look, there is an old white guy, there is another one and another and another," Sadeep said, pointing at the portraits.

"It's not surprising," Qubit Preet said. "It's a reflection of the demographics of those times."

"You can't be oblivious to the omission of people of color."

"What do you expect? If it was your alma mater, I am sure you won't find many white guys."

"That doesn't negate the racial prejudices that exist in the world of science; the last place you would expect to find bigotry," Sadeep said.

"I am not negating anything," Qubit Preet said. "I am merely stating the facts. I am aware of the prejudices if you doubt my motives. The problem with discussing race is that you presume others are insensitive if they oppose your viewpoint. To prove my point, I will tell you a story that is far more important than these portraits. Do you know who was Srinivasa Ramanujan? I'll tell you. He was a mathematical genius, but his genius may never have been discovered but for the letter he wrote to a Cambridge mathematician, G.H. Hardy. He had no formal education, but he had the potential that needed a mentor. He was invited to Cambridge, and it changed the world of mathematics forever. He had to face an uphill climb to prove his worth and he did.

"Are you saying people of color can't make it on their

own?"

"You are taking it the wrong way. What I am saying is that in life there are no heroes or villains, only right and wrong actions. Collaboration is the antidote to discrimination. I'll tell you another story, this time about Einstein. SN Bose, another Indian physicist had worked out how to count a certain set of particles. He couldn't get his work published. He wrote to Einstein, and they collaborated to produce remarkable discoveries including a new form of matter called Bose-Einstein condensate. Bose never got the Nobel prize but the scientists who produced this matter in a lab decades later did. Another irony for you."

"Thank you for the history lesson," Sadeep said. "This underscores my point that we must learn from history."

"History is a man's version of events, a victorious one to be specific. Sometimes you have to claim your own history."

"That's true," Sadeep said. "But how can we rewrite history? It's not technology that needs updating. How can the future influence the past?"

"You are so naïve," Qubit Preet said. "History is not a chronological sequence of events. It's much more than that. It's a mirror reflection of the present. If you don't like what you see in the mirror, you either change yourself or you change the mirror. It's always easy to change the latter."

"We better get to work, otherwise we'll be history," Sadeep said.

"Ditto," Qubit Preet said.

Sadeep scanned the floor plans. The MRI was on the first floor. He took the stairs. It was a longer but safer route. He opened the MRI room and saw the machine, clean and immaculate. He had seen an MRI machine before, but it didn't dampen his enthusiasm for the state-of-the-art technology. It reminded him of the time machine in H.G. Wells novella. The MRI had a tunnel and a giant magnet around it. The processing room was on the side with huge glass windows. It was no different than an interrogation room where a suspect would be interviewed by special agents sitting behind a glass curtain.

"Here is the MRI," Sadeep said. "Now what?"

"It's designed for human anatomy. You are the only human here. So, get in there. Remove all metal objects from the body. Wear a gown and finish the MRI screening questionnaire. I don't want any metal thing coming out of your body. It's going to hurt otherwise."

"I am a bit claustrophobic. I am not sure I can go through with it."

"You are on a battlefield, soldier. You can't run away. Close your eyes, sing your favorite song, recite a poem, do whatever you have to do. It's a tunnel, not a cave. Be brave for once in your life and going into an MRI machine is hardly a barometer of bravery."

He reluctantly obliged. His eyes were closed, his body was tense, his mind was restless, while his brain was being sliced into images by the MRI machine. It made clattering noises that would be expected from a cheap washing machine, not a sophisticated machine like the MRI. A picture of his brain was beginning to emerge. It was like any other human brain with a cerebral cortex, brainstem, cerebellum, and the like. From an MRI image, it was impossible to distinguish one human from another; a scientist's brain was no different than that of an illiterate. The complexity lied in the entangled web of billions of neurons that were interconnected. It was the ultimate Gordian knot that couldn't be sliced by a sword; it needed a careful dissection by a neurosurgeon's scalpel.

Qubit Preet had an insurmountable problem on his hand; not only he had to know what each neuron carried, but he also had to swap lies with truth. How to find the biochemical composition of truth? It was looking hopeless, but then he had a brainwave. He didn't need to know the structure of the truth. What he needed was the algorithm of truth: circuits of the brain that were activated when the truth was spoken. It was a perfect job for a quantum computer. He had to make a superposition of all the neurons that were firing during a speech, which contained both truth and lies. Once a question was asked, the collapse of superposition would filter out the lies and only the truth shall remain. Superposition meant a particle was present at multiple places at once; if an observer looked at the particle, the superposition collapsed, and the particle appeared at a random place. An observer had no idea what was going behind the scenes; maybe the particle was always there. It was a novel idea. It had to be tested. Sadeep was ready. Q and A session was about to begin.

"Are you ready to tell the truth?" Qubit Preet asked.

"Yes, I am," Sadeep said. "Do it and do it quickly. I want to get out of this machine. It feels like a bumpy airplane ride without the bumps. How come I can still hear you? Are you in the machine or in the processing room?"

"You know I can be at two places at once unless you want to see me. Don't worry about my whereabouts. Answer the damn question."

"Don't get annoyed. Fire away."

"How are you feeling?" Qubit Preet said.

"Scared, anxious. I always feel like that."

"What scares you?"

"The future, specifically mine."

"Why are you scared of the future?"

"Because I can't control it."

"Are you a control freak?"

"Yes, I am."

"What do you hate the most?"

"Making mistakes."

"Have you made any?"

"Who hasn't? Getting into medicine was a mistake, giving up on my first love was a mistake, listening to others was a mistake, not listening to myself was a mistake. My life has been nothing but a mistake."

"Try to keep it short. What's your favorite color?"

"Grey."

"What annoys you?"

"Winter, rain, people who lie, people who are rude, people

who are phony."

"What do you like?"

"Summer, blue skies, driving my car, listening to music."

"Tell me a secret."

"Once I soiled myself in my brand-new car. I had the stomach flu. I was on the road. I didn't have any spare clothes. I was hungry. I had to buy food. I entered a convenience store. The guy on the counter was holding on to his nose as I smelled of you know what. It was beyond embarrassing. And I haven't even told you what it took to clean up that mess."

"Good job, I mean in answering my questions. Now let's compare notes. I will replay your responses. How do you feel about those questions?"

"They were mundane," Sadeep said. "I felt relaxed. Only at the last question, I had butterflies in my stomach. It's not fun to remember a painful memory."

"Are all these responses true?" Qubit Preet asked.

"Yes, they are. I have not told my messy incident to anyone before. I think you did something to me. I felt uneasy when I was answering it as if I was trying to hold onto something. I think the best way to describe it would be the sensation one gets when the bladder is full. You are trying to desperately hold onto the urine but eventually, it gives away, the dam bursts, it leaks, and you feel relaxed."

"Not a clean example but it would do. I would put it differently. When you put two same magnetic poles next to each other, they repel; there is resistance and a tendency to flip to the opposite pole. That's how I felt. I put up resistance to your lie and created tension in your mind until it flipped to the truth, and you felt better. I think I got the gist of it. We are in business. You can do a happy dance. Good job."

"I don't want to dance," Sadeep said. "I want to run. Let's get the hell out of here. I don't want to stay a second more than I have to."

"You are right," Qubit Preet said. "Let's head out."

Sadeep didn't waste any time. He ran through the steps

and was out of the building in less than a minute. He was ready for another sprint across the parking lot, but he stopped with his eyes wide open and mouth full of curse words.

"Did we switch off the lights upstairs?" Sadeep asked.

"I am not sure," Qubit Preet said. "It doesn't matter, no one would know. Surveillance cameras were switched off."

"How can you be so callous? I know it's going to be me who would be going to jail."

Sadeep made a dash across the foyer and up the stairs and into the MRI room. Lights were switched off. He had to run downstairs again. He stood up at the gate, took a deep breath, went through the checklist if anything was left undone. Probably not, was not good enough for him. He took more time to come up with certainly not. Now he was ready to leave the premises. He was too exhausted to have an argument with the ghost or to run across the parking lot. A brisk walk was all he could manage. It was a lonely walk. He drove back home while repeatedly looking at the car mirror for any police sirens. There were none but maybe it was too early. He couldn't wait for tomorrow to come but he waited all night for the sleep to come.

CHAPTER NINE

A Date with Anxiety

T omorrow became today as the future brought the present. Sadeep's first order of business was to browse the local media outlets. He started with the local radio and its Twitter feed. He procrastinated about checking the Twitter feed of Waterville Regional Police. He was paranoid about tracking cookies. He eventually clicked, browsed, and exited the feed in a matter of seconds. It was a good exposure therapy for him. He searched the internet for any news about him and the institute in the last twelve hours. There was no mention of his escapade from the previous night. No news was indeed good news. This could have been his opportunity to get famous, get his mug shot out in the public, and be recognized on the street. However, he didn't want his name to be associated with shame. The situation was outside his control. He tried to console himself: when murders, assaults, and burglaries were happening all around, who cared about an MRI machine, a multi-million-dollar MRI machine.

He had a burst of anxiety. What if there was damage to the MRI machine? It could cost millions of dollars. The dollar amount could warrant the setting up of a special investigation unit to nab the culprits. He was the sole perpetrator and all roads lead to him. Should he own up to his actions? Maybe he would be treated with mercy. Maybe he would get away with community service. He was adjudicating a trial in his mind. He shivered at the prospect of going to prison. Only gang members could survive the harsh reality of prison. He presented himself with worst-case scenarios, each one worse than the other. Best-case scenarios were buried in the rubble somewhere. He couldn't see his glass half full or even quarter full. His mind was an echo chamber where negative thoughts reverberated. His mind needed thorough cleansing; only if it was as easy as cleansing the bowels before a colonoscopy. Only if he could let his anxiety go but it was stuck to him like glue on hairy skin.

"I can smell fear from a distance you know," Qubit Preet said. "Get out of your stupid thoughts. Let's scare those who need to be scared."

"You want me to go from masochist to sadist."

"That's a wrong way to put it. FDR put it correctly. You should be fearful of the fear. I would submit that fear is the basis of a civilized society. Let's restore some civility by dispensing doses of fear."

"Who are you trying to scare?" Sadeep asked.

"Let's get you on a date, a real date. Let's test a hypothesis: the truth shall set your date free."

"I am scared of dating. It's emotionally draining. It's humiliating. I am not some writer who can swallow rejection after rejection."

"You don't realize that odds are on your side. She would be speaking the truth and you would be free to lie all the way. Show some sportsmanship; it's a game. You should be in it to win it."

"It's easy for you to say. Playing games is a serious business, whether it is snakes and ladders or reality television. Dignity is at stake and humiliation is on offer."

Sadeep's reluctance wasn't without merit. He was a novice to the dating scene. Since his half-hearted effort to ask his love interest for a movie was met with an equally placid response, he had given up on dating. It was more than twenty years ago but the memory was as fresh as ever. He had learned to enjoy and admire at a distance. He used window-shopping to reign in his testosterone. Window shopping experience had taught him to enjoy materialism without spending a penny. He didn't have to worry about defective items or haggle about returns or pay interest on his credit card. The bank kept increasing his credit card limit as he was never late on his payment. How could he? It didn't cost any money to try clothes in fitting rooms.

He used the same concept for his relationships. He believed in long-distance relationships; at least 10 feet of distance was required. It provided personal space and eye contact that wasn't awkward or intrusive. He could afford to have multiple love interests without having to worry about STDs. It was safe, reliable, and satisfying. Notwithstanding his aversion to real dating, he had to first find a woman. Dating sites were ubiquitous. Many dating sites claimed to have hot women in the neighborhood who were eager to meet and ready to initiate physical contact. Many aspirants believed in the unbelievable. It kept the business booming and provided an incentive to spam the internet. Authentic-looking dating sites had more reasonable profiles. There were several genres of profiles.

I am fun-loving, adventurous, bold, and independent minded. My prince charming should be chivalrous, make me smile, and pamper me. He should have a good physique as determined by me. And he should do chores, work hard, pay bills, and hold my hand through troubles that I often find myself in. Extra points for coming on a horse.

It was a wish list than a profile and better suited for Santa Claus or a genie. Some profiles had a contemporary look with realistic elements thrown in.

I am thirty-four years old and a forensic pathologist. I like my work. I like dead bodies, but I have decided to spend more time with the living. An ideal match should be able to tolerate the smell of formaldehyde. Working knowledge of medical jargon is a must. I don't want to spend my time arguing about the difference between tumor, neoplasm, and cancer. I commit to giving my full attention to you. Taking criticism would be a bonus as I would be putting you under the microscope.

Some profiles were transactional in nature. They were often found in South Asian newspapers and marriage sites. Politically correctness was often omitted.

Parents of a Jatt Sikh doctor seek a suitable match for their thirty-year-old daughter. She is five feet six inches tall, extremely smart, and beautiful. She is a medical resident, starting a fellowship in cardiology. The only brother is starting medical school this year. Ideal math should be a doctor, USMLE cleared with minimum 90th centile marks, in residency, or eligible for H1b or J1 visa. The family should have a professional background.

Twenty-eight-year-old, permanent resident of Canada, innocently divorced, working in a fast-food restaurant. Only those need to apply who could bring the younger brother to Canada (Atta Batta or quid pro quo).

Sadeep added his own two cents. It was more than two cents as he opted for the premier membership of the dating site, which provided him access to all the profiles and their contact information.

I am thirty-eight but haven't put on much weight. I am looking for a companion who can validate and not procrastinate. I consider listening to be reassuring but don't get boring. Flexibility and reliability are the qualities I am good at, but please don't make me a doormat.

Relationships were made in heaven, so it was said. But that was not true. It was the algorithm that made the match. He got his share of suggestions and liked this one:

Forty-year-old, never married, accountant, looking for a mature and stable companion. Earns enough to meet the needs. No divorcees, please.

Profile description was not the most important thing, photographs were the key. A nice pic was worth a thousand replies. Some photographs were too handsome to believe. They were probably digitally enhanced. The profile he selected had average looks, nothing stood out. It was good enough for him. She replied promptly, which was a good sign. The meeting was fixed at the food court of Waterville Mall. The food court was huge for a mall of its size. It was a public place; safety was guaranteed, and parking was free and plenty. He got ready: shaved, trimmed his nose hair, showered, wore clean clothes, and masqueraded his body odor with a lightly scented perfume. The meeting was fixed for eleven o'clock.

Karen reached on time, and so did he. Karen was short for Karamjit; an anglicized form that rendered names like Davinderjit Pal to Dave. It was Saturday morning, crowds were thin, but she could have been recognized in a packed Olympic stadium. She wore a red salwar kameez; a bold choice. He liked that. He played it safe with shades of grey, white and black. She carried a glittery but cheap handbag; an excellent choice Sadeep thought; at least she was not a spendthrift. He glanced at her car keys: an electric car key. She made a statement without saying a word. She was wearing Punjabi jutti, a traditional shoe wear with no height support. He liked her confidence. He wore running shoes which made him look taller, breaking the six feet barrier. He greeted her with an unimaginative hi and they sat in a cubicle, which provided a semblance of privacy. Her looks had gone a notch up from the photograph, at least one standard deviation up; in other words, she looked ravishing. The redness of her cheeks matched her dress well. It was the makeup done well and money spent well. He found it hard to take his eyes off her but staring at her nonstop was not good form. He blinked in an awkward manner, which only made things worse. He had to start some small talk, but it required a big effort on his part.

"Would you like a coffee?" Sadeep asked.

"No, I would take steep tea, one milk, one sugar," Karen said.

"Anything to eat?"

"No thanks."

He was relieved to take a break from her. He got into the line to get coffee. There was always a lineup in the mall. Canadians liked their coffee especially in the morning. It got the country going. He spent his time preparing for the onslaught of questions, but there was no reason to worry; lies were on his side and she bore the burden of truth.

"Here's your tea."

"Thanks."

A couple of more minutes were spent trying to adjust the cup, dip the tea bag, and trying to cool the burning hot drink by blowing bubbles in it.

"How is it?" Sadeep asked.

"It's alright," Karen said. "Nothing like homemade tea."

"Were you able to find the place alright?"

"Of course, Waterville is not Timbuktu. I confess it's my first time here. It wasn't a bad drive from Mississauga."

"Thank you for making the effort. I would have come to meet you, but you insisted on coming."

"I wanted to get out of the GTA. It's good to leave the center of the universe once in a while."

"So, how did you like our little town?" Sadeep asked.

"I haven't seen much," Karen said. "The mall was right off the highway."

"You must see the farmers market. People come from far to see it. It's one of a kind farmer's market. If we get time, I will take you there."

"We'll see. Tell me about yourself."

"I am a man of few words, and those words don't come easy to me. I like the company of myself. I am sensitive and I hate to admit it, but I have cried watching the movie Titanic. What about yourself?"

"I talk a lot, especially when I am nervous. I love gossiping. I love meeting new people. I want to be upfront with you, I have had relationships, but things didn't work out."

"Everyone has a past," Sadeep said. "I don't hold it against you."

"That's good to know," Karen said. "I don't know how much cultural baggage you carry as you were not born and brought up in Canada, but I was."

"I have changed. When I grew up, times were different in

India, especially small-town India. We were not allowed to have girlfriends; boys and girls couldn't sit next to each other. India is different now, so am I."

"My parents had the same mindset and instilled cultural values from back home. I was a rebel. When I say I was sexually active, it was an understatement. I have had my share of warts, but nothing more."

He kept a poker face as it was a smart thing to do. A reflexive gasp would have ruined the date and sealed the fate.

"How did your parents react?" Sadeep asked.

"They were furious, but being South Asian parents, they didn't boot me out. I didn't leave them either. I was used to being pampered. I was the first child, there is a sister in the middle and there is no prize for guessing the sex of the youngest; he is heir to the throne. We were always served fresh warm food. My parents used their leverage and I used emotional blackmail. We came to an understanding; their rules would be followed inside, and my rules would be followed outside the home."

"You have lived life on your own terms, good for you."

"I have tried to," Karen said. "What about your family?"

"My parents are in India. They come to Canada once a year and stay for a couple of months only. They like it there. They have a social circle back there. They don't feel at home in Canada. I have a sister in Calgary. She is busy with her family. I don't see her much. We are not a close-knit family."

"I hope you don't mind me saying it, but I can't live in a joint family," Karen said. "Sharing space with in-laws is not my idea of a happy family. It's better to stay apart amicably than have fights daily."

"I concur," Sadeep said. "When our parents haven't stayed in a joint family, how can they expect us to do the same? I find it annoying to stay with my own parents. I can only imagine the torture one has to endure staying with in-laws."

"You seem to be a nice guy."

"Thanks for the compliment. What are you looking for in a relationship?"

"Respect and understanding are the pillars on which a stable relationship is formed, and I look for the same in my prospective partner."

"True," Sadeep nodded. "What are your plans for the future?"

"Right now, I am focused on getting the right match," Karen said. "Getting married and living happily thereafter comes next."

"And having a family and children perhaps?" Sadeep asked.

She went pale. There was no response for one, two, three, four, five seconds.

"I have endometriosis. I don't know if I would be able to get pregnant. I hesitated to get married in the first place. My biological clock is ticking. It's now or never. I have to take a chance. I have to live with the uncertainty about my fertility. It's not easy, it's worse than the physical pain of endometriosis, much worse."

She was trying to hold on to her tears as her voice was cracking under the weight of emotions.

"I am sorry, I didn't mean to hurt you," Sadeep said.

"It's not your fault if it had to come out this way. I am dealing with it and if you become part of my life then you have to deal with it as well."

He was trying to find a tissue for her when she got up abruptly.

"I hope you understand but I don't feel like talking anymore. I am too emotional right now to carry on. I will leave now."

"I totally understand," Sadeep said. "Let me accompany you to the car."

"Please don't," Karen said. "I can find my way but thanks for the offer."

She walked away briskly to the exit and did not turn back. He took a deep breath and finished his cold coffee. The date had ended in a disaster. He had a sinking feeling. He didn't know how to swim, which made it a challenge for him to navigate the current situation.

"That was bad," Sadeep said to himself, but it was over-heard by Qubit Preet, who had observed in absolute silence the deliberations that went on.

"We did good," Qubit Preet said.

"How can you be so cruel. We should be ashamed of what we did to that poor girl. Is this your idea of scaring people? She got more tormented than scared."

"She fears the truth. She is in denial. You must look at the bigger picture. We accomplished our goal. The end justifies the means."

"That's what tyrants say. Life is as much about the means as it's about the ends."

"Your assertion is erroneous. Suppose she didn't tell you and you got married. She would have felt guilty, and you would have been resentful; so much for a happy married life."

"But did it have to come out this way?"

"There was no other choice. I did a therapeutic interven-tion. It was hard work. She should thank us for it. She was consumed by the fear of not being able to conceive. She was paralyzed and unable to move on with her life. She lied and it only reinforced her obsession. I gave her a jolt, sort of like an ECT treatment, only without her consent."

"I am worried that she doesn't do anything stupid in her anguish."

"Don't worry, she would be fine. If you want, I could check on her."

"Leave her alone, you have given her enough trouble al-ready. It's time for us to leave as well."

He walked around the mall to stretch his legs and ease his mind. He was heartened to see sale signs, even though he was only doing window shopping. The option to buy goods at bargain prices was enough to cheer him up. He was ready to head for the exit when he saw a group of gentlemen in the food court. He desperately wanted to avoid them. They were senior citizens. They were his uncles, not by relation but by association. They had the habit of sticking their noses into other people's affairs. They were amused by other people's misfortunes and considered it gossip. Gossip worked like an aphrodisiac. Seniority in age allowed a certain amount of indiscretion. It added flavor to their conversations. They came, they talked, and they went every single day. They did not play cards or chess or read newspapers; their only interest was in face-to-face conversation. They had plenty to discuss.

They considered themselves lucky; time was money, and they had all the time in the world. It did not put them on the billionaires list, nor did it attract any tax scrutiny. Their favorite topic was politics. They had intimate knowledge of rural and small-town politics of Punjab but were completely oblivious to the municipal politics of their current hometown. Their source of knowledge was viral videos, which they loved to share and then argue about their authenticity. The arguments got heated, some nasty words were said but never to the point of breaking up the pack. The process was repeated day after day. It was a support system that they couldn't live without.

The leader of the pack was Dalveer Singh aka Dal. He was the senior-most, not by age but by his arrival to Canada. He came to Canada in the '70s and was thus the resident historian. He had seen Canada change over the decades. Every immigrant was asked how long they had been in Canada. The question implied whether an immigrant was well settled or still struggling, as experience mattered. He was proud to say the date of his arrival in Canada; it was as important as his date of birth. He was receiving a work pension from his job; a rarity in modern Canada. He retired from an auto parts company before it moved to Mexico. He and his compatriots and for that matter the society at large measured the worth of a human being in dollars per hour. Dal loved to share financial gossip.

"Do you know he earns thirty-five dollars an hour? He is filthy rich."

The response from his friends was one of jealousy, "It must be a hard job that no one else wants to do. Wait till he gets a bad back. He won't last long."

Dal had no hesitation in asking about the hourly wages. He received two kinds of responses: international students gave accurate figures which they sometimes hesitated to provide even to the CRA, and the rest inflated their wealth. Inflation was rampant in immigrant circles. Their perceived wealth was increasing, but the evidence was anecdotal, from fancy cars to big houses. It was the only measure of success; since economic migration was based on a move to greener pastures, what was the point of it if they didn't feast on it? Credit was cheap, banks were desperate, and demand was high. The prevalence of back pain had increased as one could carry only so much debt.

Dal resented the boatloads or rather the planeloads of immigrants that were landing each day. He was happy to be in Canada and thankful for his immediate relatives who had subsequently immigrated, but now he wished for a curtailed immigration policy. He was a member of an exclusive club: citizen of a wealthy country, but if it was open for everyone, there would be no exclusivity left. He didn't understand the macroeconomics behind immigration. Economists saw increasing GDP; he saw pollution, congested roads, and increasing rents. He saw overpopulation as a steppingstone to poverty. Canada was the second-largest country in the world, but with vast swaths of land covered in Arctic ice and every other newcomer landing at Toronto, it was not immune to the problems of overpopulation. Dal remembered the good old days when immigrant communities were small but close-knit; everyone knew one another, and it was customary to greet fellow immigrants in public even if you passed a stranger. Those times were long gone; no one acknowledged the other as there were too many immigrants. Racism had declined, which was good, but indifference had taken over. He resented vote bank politics, which painted all immigrants with the same brush, but he approved of identity politics and was proud to see a turbaned minister.

Er. Sandhu was the most educated of the lot. He didn't hesitate to impress upon this fact. He expected designations to be properly recognized; Mr. Sandhu was not good enough. He had earned his designation as an engineer and like a doctor, it had to be duly noted. The request was ignored by people, and he ignored them. He was a graduate of IIT, a premier engineering institution and like a Harvard graduate, he wore it on his sleeve. He retired as a chief engineer from the electricity department. It was a managerial position that came with perks and influence. It came with an army of subordinates that were expected to answer, "Yes, Sir." No wonder chief engineers were distressed at the prospect of retirement; they wanted extensions to continue working as long as they could; they were like US senators. How many US senators would agree to term limits? He however took premature retirement to come to Canada. He was entitled to a full pension, it worked out well.

He had many tales to tell of his officer days, but no one was interested in knowing the inner workings of an electricity department. Nevertheless, it did not deter him from explaining how to get a 100-megawatt connection. His second favorite topic was his children. His children were so intelligent that IQ tests were not apt to capture it. His children were so smart that smart money followed them. His children were so talented that it was a privilege to witness their magnificence. He could go on and on about his children, and he often did. He had a son and a daughter. His son was studying robotic engineering. He applied to MIT and Harvard but didn't get through. Mr. Sandhu explained that it was their loss; people made institutions, not the other way around. His daughter was studying medicine at McMaster. She was gunning for ophthalmology; the specialty known to mint money. She deserved it as she was the topper of her class.

Last and also the least was Prem Singh. He was the least educated, but it did not deter him from educating others. Formal education did not endow wisdom. He believed in the survival of the savviest and considered himself the savviest of them all. He had worked in farms where conditions were tough; sun scorched the skin and the back had to endure repetitive bows to pick berries. He had seen educated immigrants struggle at odd jobs. The worst of the lot were educated immigrants with mediocre skills. They could not find a job in their field and manual labor was too hard for them. He on the other hand had always done physical labor and made good money doing that. He would capture the ideal spot to pick berries and filled the highest number of baskets.

Farm work was a steppingstone to his dream job: a truck driver. He was a long-haul truck driver and minted money. His English was grammatically challenged but he made his point. It came in handy at the border where he had memorized what to say, "I go, give load, come back, 5 days." He made hand gestures to authenticate his statement. He was told to be careful with finger gestures to border agents, and he followed that advice. His two sons were also truck drivers; they lived in a joint family in a big house with a three-car garage. It was bordering on a mansion. He pitied the salaried class; what was the point of making huge salaries when more than half of it was taken in taxes? He had a corporation, and with creative accounting, the tax bill was as light as a feather. These were the three amigos. There were other flybys, but none matched their comradery . They were like brothers; each one considered himself as the big brother.

They were doing their round table conference in the food court. Mr. Sandhu was dressed like an erstwhile officer with double pleated trousers, full sleeves shirt, a front pocket to keep a fountain pen, and shiny dress shoes. He wore a navy-blue turban. His mustaches and beard were immaculately glued together; only a category three hurricane could mess them up. His mustache was curved and defied gravity. It needed a white cloth called Thati, which held together the hair until the glue dried. It was mistaken for a bandage by culturally naïve people. Mr. Singh wore the traditional kurta pajama, which was bleached to look as white as possible. He had a long and wavy beard, which was free from the shackles of glue. Dal was clean-shaven; he had a puffy face that hid his wrinkles. He had a youthful look despite having his hair as white as Mr. Singh's clothes. To embellish his youthful looks, Dal was casually dressed in a t-shirt and shorts.

"Polling dates have been announced by the election commission in Punjab," Dal said. "Who do you think will win: Congress or Akalis?"

"Look, whoever is in power loses," Mr. Singh said. "It's like a revolving door. You can't please anyone these days. People are eager to show who's the boss." It's worth noting that his English has been embellished by the power of translation for the benefit of readers.

"It is becoming the norm in every democracy," Mr. Sandhu said. "Look at the US, the pendulum keeps swinging between Republicans and Democrats. People vote with their noses pinched. Thank God, Canada has so far been shielded from this pessimism, but I don't know for how much longer."

"Don't bet on it," Mr. Singh said. "Same shenanigans happen here as well. Money is offered to secure party nominations. I have been offered money. I didn't accept it, but I am sure plenty others did. Once party nomination is secured, rest is easy; you only need a wave in your party's favor. People don't care who is running, crook or a saint; they vote for the party."

"I don't think things are that bad," Mr. Sandhu said. "Some claims of impropriety are exaggerated."

"You don't believe me. I don't exaggerate. I tell the truth." Mr. Singh stroked his flowing beard and threw a challenge to Mr. Sandhu.

"Then why didn't you call the police?" Mr. Sandhu said. Not to be left behind, he caressed his curved mustache.

"Look, I am not stupid," Mr. Singh said. "I have no desire to invite trouble. I will make enemies on all sides. I would be made a scapegoat. I have no desire to pay lawyers for the rest of my life."

"Calm down," Mr. Sandhu said. "It may have happened to you; I was only making a general point."

"You better backed down," Mr. Singh said. "I know I am right; I am always right."

"Come on guys, don't fight like kids," Dal said. He noticed Sadeep sneaking by. As usual, Sadeep was avoiding eye contact but that was no problem for the gregarious Dal.

"Doctor Sahib, come this way," Dal said. "We are not going to bite you."

"Hello uncle, how are you?" Sadeep folded his hands to acknowledge the other two uncles as well.

"We are good," Dal said. "I know young people don't want to meet old folks like us. It reminds them of tough days ahead, but we cherish every opportunity to meet young ones like you. It makes us feel young."

"I am not young either. I am neither here nor there. And uncle please don't call me doctor sahib, medical degree is worthless to me."

"It's not worthless, you can always go back to India," Mr. Sandhu said. "Jobs are plenty for doctors over there."

"Why should he?" Mr. Singh interjected. "Big shot doctors are coming to Canada, big officers like you have come to Canada, even though many have to drive taxis to earn a living. He at least has his own business. If you ask me, what you really need is a wife that can take care of you and a bunch of children, obedient and respectful."

"Do you have all of these?" Sadeep teased.

Mr. Singh had answered this question many times with glee and vigor, but he paused this time. He looked straight into Sadeep's eyes with folded hands as if he was making a confession. His tone was serious, with each word coming out slowly but clearly.

"I'll tell you how delighted my family is to see me: my wife asks me why I come home early. She wants me to get the hell out of the house and spend as much time as possible outside. She feels relaxed when I am not around. She says the air is fresher in my absence. My daughters-in-law say I am annoying, and I nit-pick at everything. My sons say I am demanding, even though it's them who demand that I transfer my property to them before I die. I am an unwanted guest in my own home. They are counting days when I will die, and so am I."

"Don't feel bad uncle. It's a story that has become all too

familiar. Even Sandhu uncle would agree that his brilliant children are prone to occasional transgressions."

It was Mr. Sandhu's turn to enter the confession box. He was not only reluctant, but he was dragged and coerced into speaking the truth. It was evident from the sweat on his face which was melting the solidly held glue on his mustache.

"My kids are smart. I am proud of them, but I don't know if they are proud of me. They live on their own. They hardly visit us nowadays. They are always busy. I found out that my son is living with someone; his girlfriend perhaps. He didn't trust me to tell this. I didn't ask him either. Why should I? The onus is on him. I have done everything for them. I came to Canada to have a bright future for them. It was a demotion for me. I lost my status coming here. Now I have lost my kids. I regret it every day."

"I am sorry to hear that," Sadeep said. "I am sure things would work out fine. You have done your best and you deserve the best."

"Thank you," Mr. Sandhu said.

"I must go now; I have an appointment with a client." Sadeep tried to get out of this situation with a lie and didn't regret it one bit. He realized how useful lies were and how troublesome truth was. Truth and lie were his two legs; if either was not available, he couldn't move on with life. He got up and walked to the exit and turned around to have a peek at the senior citizen group; the friends were quiet, staring at each other and waiting for the other to make the next move. Their silence was revealing, and Sadeep left them to their misery.

The parking lot had filled up, but it was no worry for Sadeep; he had parked way out at the end in keeping with his habit. On his way, he heard a commotion. He was not the sort of person to get involved in a fight or to even watch it at a distance. It created a bad taste in his mouth, which stayed with him for a while and produced nightmares. Today it was different; he was feeling emboldened and decided to interfere against his instincts. He saw a young, tall, and imposing man speaking loudly. On the receiving end of his rage was a thin built middle-aged woman.

"What's going on, can I help?" Sadeep asked

"You mind your own business," the young man said.

"I am just trying to help."

"Oh really, if that's so then you pay me on her behalf."

"Why so?"

"This woman slammed her door against my car. Look at the dent. Who is going to pay for it?"

"It looks bad but there is no need to be angry," Sadeep said.

"I am really sorry," the woman said. She spoke English reasonably well, but she had a thick accent. In a confrontation, those words were even harder to come by. The man sensed that, and he charged at her like a lion.

"You better be sorry," the young man said. "Do you even have a Canadian driving license? How long have you been in Canada?"

"I have been here two years," the woman said. "It was an accident. I'll pay you but I don't have the money with me."

"She hit my car and then she walked off as if nothing had happened. I happened to be passing by, otherwise, she would have left the scene. Do you know it's called hit and run? You can go to jail?"

"I am s…. sorry," the woman said. Her hands were beginning to shake, and her breaths were getting shallower.

"Do you know how much it would cost to repair the damage? It would be more than the price of the junk you are driving."

The man kept his voice loud and gained the attention of mall security. Three security guards came and tried to defuse the situation by creating a human barrier between him and the woman.

"She made a mistake," Sadeep said. "She admits it, but who gave you the right to speak to her in that tone?"

"I know my rights. You people come here and don't learn our way of living. Why don't you go back to the dungeon you came from?" The young man's hands were clenched to form a fist and if swung would have hit Sadeep like a brick.

A security guard took offense, "Mind your language. Do

you want me to call the cops?"

The young man's anger got deflated as soon as he realized what he had said. He had a lot to lose, his dignity, his job, and his freedom perhaps. Better sense prevailed on him, and he apologized. It was not sincere, but Sadeep didn't press the man as it would have been too obvious that he was extracting a confession. He didn't want this situation to be about him. He requested the mall security to help the woman exchange insurance information and report to a vehicle collision center. His job was done. He felt proud. He had put quite a few people to tears today, which had emotionally drained him. He realized that hearing the truth was hard but speaking the truth was even harder.

It was a day of high tension and drama, and it was no surprise that a tension headache was on its way. He wanted to retire early for the day, but debriefing had to be done. He took a shower, had a cup of tea, a tablet of acetaminophen, and was ready to report his findings.

"I think we accomplished a lot today," Sadeep said. "Thank you for making me a part of it."

"You change your emotions like a politician," Qubit Preet said. "You were ashamed of yourself not too long ago and now you are thumping your chest."

"Why you have to ruin everything with a caustic remark?"

"This is a debriefing. We need to understand each other. Today was just the beginning. There are many more things to come."

"I am ready," Sadeep said.

"But are you prepared?" Qubit Preet asked.

"I am relying on you. Guide me through."

"A prerequisite for guidance is familiarity with the path forward. I have no idea what the future would bring, any more than you do. We need to improvise. We need to develop situational awareness like fighter pilots. It's going to be tough and perhaps dangerous."

"Dangerous? Everything has some degree of danger. Eating peanuts could be dangerous. You got to be more specific than that."

"Specifics would come later. Take it as a motivational speech. Those speeches are vague by nature. My goal is not to get the truth out of vulnerable people in despair. I am not interested in prospective brides or a bunch of old people or a run-of-the-mill bigot. I am targeting the rich and the powerful. They resist. They fight back. Risk is high, so is the reward."

"I should be scared but I am not," Sadeep said.

"Good, you are gaining confidence," Qubit Preet said. "It puts a smile on my imaginary face, but be careful, don't bask in grandiosity."

"Whose side are you on?"

"I am on my side and so are you. Let's fight side by side. Let's focus on some practical considerations. The truth won't be handed over to us on a platter. We must work hard at it. It means you need to ask thoughtful questions. It means you can't barge a whole array of questions at an opponent. It would be counterproductive. You should ease into difficult questions. You allow them to let their guard down and then you strike. Understood?"

"Yes, Sir. But what if they refuse to answer?"

"Once a question is asked, an answer is inevitable. Refusing to answer is also an answer. Going slow creates less friction and allows truth to slip out easily."

"Basically, I need to be a journalist."

"Yes, but a reputable one; one who speaks less and listens more; one who starts with open-ended questions and wraps up with closed-ended ones."

"Who am I interviewing? Let's start with a Hollywood superstar."

"Do you have access to one? Ask any paparazzi. They bend over backward to get a glimpse of a superstar. What chances do you have?"

"Then what?" Sadeep asked.

"We need to be modest," Qubit Preet said. "Who's your local member of Parliament?"

"She is Siyasat Gill. She too is South Asian you know."

"Wonderful," Qubit Preet said. "Let's get her."
"That doesn't sound good," Sadeep said.
"Let's allow her to speak her mind."
"That's better."

CHAPTER TEN

A Relentless Ambition

The Hon. Siyasat Gill was a first-time member of Parliament from Waterville. She was also a young cabinet minister. When I say young, she was fortyish, plus-minus five years, which is considered young by political standards. She kept her date of birth private but that didn't stop others to guess her age based on circumstantial evidence. She won by a razor-thin margin: seventy-seven votes to be precise. The opponent asked for a recount, which changed nothing. She was set for Parliament for four years unless the Prime Minister called an early election; a nightmare scenario for any member of Parliament. She defeated an old hack who appeared tired and didn't bother campaigning. She, on the other hand, used every tool in the toolbox to defeat her opponent including maligning the distinguished fellow. It was easy to dig up dirt on him; he had spent years in politics and his track record was available for scrutiny. She put it under the microscope and saw all kinds of dirt. She alleged that he had misappropriated funds for his own personal use; going to the Caribbean in the winter cannot be claimed as a traveling allowance. She hammered the point again and again, from social media to door-to-door campaigning. It made the difference, and the seat was flipped.

She was lucky to be the party candidate for Waterville. She

did not have to fight the party nomination. She was nominated by the Prime Minister himself. She had earned enough brownie points with the Prime Minister to secure an automatic nomination. It didn't come easy. She had spent her life fighting for it. It required hard work, planning, and of course luck; exact percentages could be found in a rap song.

She was not heir to a political dynasty. Neither was she married into one. She was not wealthy either. But she had the desire and the tenacity to pursue her goals. Her parents came as refugees from Uganda in the 70's after the despot Idi Amin evicted South Asians from the country. Canada was generous enough to grant asylum. It was a genuine case. They had to earn a living through manual labor. They worked in factories, but her mom could not sustain that level of physical exertion. Sabar Kaur developed chronic back pain and fibromyalgia. She was only fit for a sedentary job. Her English was not good enough to get a clerical job. They took a risk to open their own business. They had saved some money as spending money on luxuries was considered a sin. Taking loans was the last resort. They opened a South Asian grocery store; the first in the area. The community was small but as the number of immigrants grew, the business became successful. It was more convenient to get Indian and Pakistani groceries and movies at a local shop than to make a trip to Toronto. Prices were comparatively high, but it was offset by the time saved and the charm of the Gill family.

Gills became well-known in the community. Her father, Taur Singh, was a founding member and president of the local gurdwara. He held that position for many years but was eventually eased out by a couple of backstabbers, who accused him of siphoning money for personal gain. The allegations were all imaginary, but the pain felt was real. There wasn't that much money generated by the gurdwara as the community was small. He had to sometimes put his own money to pay the bills, but the accusers were loud and only their voice was heard. He resigned in rage; a thankless job he thought. But the accusers thanked him for resigning.

Siyasat was their only child, and being a girl child, it was a problem: a big one. The expectation to have a boy was strong in the community. Family lineage had to be preserved at all costs. It was a different matter that most of them had no idea about their lineage beyond three or four generations. Instead of congratulating new parents, sympathies were given; better luck next time was hurled as an insult to her mom, who had spent twelve hours in labor without an epidural and had a second-degree perineal tear. How could they give up after only one girl? It was the question asked by friends and family repeatedly. It was none of their damn business, but they made it so. Some suggested natural herbs, others came with a dietary plan, and some outrageously suggested sexual positions to ensure a male child. It was humiliating. Her parents tried their best to deflect and put it all on fate. The real reason for not trying remained unknown and rightly so.

They devoted their time and energy to Siyasat. It was the only way to prove others wrong. They invested in her future. It required money. She went to a private school, which was unheard of among middle-class immigrants. It cost as much money as going to a university, but they saved every penny to afford it. They did not opt for a boarding school. They could not let their only child be whisked away to an unknown place. They were possessive about their only child and wanted to keep a close eye on her. It was a good decision. She was sensitive and shy and needed reassurance from her parents. She took French immersion. Learning French was a matter of prestige and it awarded opportunities in the federal civil service where knowing French was an asset. A career as a federal politician was also a nonstarter without knowing some French.

She was the only brown kid in her class. She was unaware of her skin color until she entered the school system. She was a novelty to other kids in the class who asked her questions, many of which were not politically correct. She was hairy and her black hair stood out against her skin like a high visibility jacket. Her food smelled funny to kids. It left stains on her clothes as curry with turmeric was not kind on light-colored clothes. She insisted on carrying sandwiches and fruits, but it was vetoed by her parents who were adamant that Indian food was more delicious and nutritious than its western counterpart. She was dropped off and picked up by her father every day. Taur Singh wore a big turban; kids and their parents were curious about it. Some even asked him, "Does it hurt?" He took it sportingly and was happy to share its proud history. Some questions were mischievous, "Do you keep it while sleeping?" He didn't take the bait.

There was no bullying policy at school. Kids were allowed to be kids, to be nasty and mischievous. There was zero tolerance for physical violence, but words hurt more than a punch to the face. She had her fair share of nasty comments. She channeled her energy into studies and excelled academically. It is not a guarantee that bullying leads to good academic performance, but it makes for a good story and there you go. Academic performance was not enough to stop bullying. She learned a valuable lesson early on in life: if no one was on her side then she needed to be on someone else's side. She worked hard to please teachers. They liked her and she made them like her. This policy paid dividends. She had a rare moment of rage when a kid teased her for an old worn-out dress. She shoved the kid, and both were sent to the principal's office. Both denied wrongdoing. It came to: he said, she said. Guess who was exonerated? She learned that impressions mattered, and the scale of justice was whimsical. She imprinted her impressions on the people that mattered like a customs official stamping passport at the airport.

Politics was not in her blood but it sure was in the air and on the table at her home. Taur Singh was a political buff. He had Canadian and international newspapers displayed at his store. Unsold ones were brought home. The dining table was littered with newspapers in English, Hindi, and Punjabi. He sometimes brought specialty newspapers, and literary journals to his store, even though clientele for such newspapers and journals was miniscule in a small town like Waterville. It was not good business, but he considered it community service. Siyasat was constantly bombarded with quotes from politicians. She knew more about Perestroika and Glasnost than Cinderella and Rapunzel. She was once asked in class: what was her favorite animal? She innocently answered, "Donkey is my favorite animal as I like Democrats."

Teachers asked kids what they were afraid of and what they would do to overcome their fear. Some were afraid of monsters; others were afraid of ghosts and wished for their favorite superhero to rescue them. Siyasat had the most original answer: she was afraid of nuclear war and wished for an end to the arms race. Teachers were impressed but they were worried that she was missing out on childhood. She allayed their fears by learning about fairy tales and enacting them in class; it was an acquired taste as her interests were somewhere else.

As she grew older, her interest in politics became even stronger. She had a poster of Margaret Thatcher on her wall; probably the first and only kid to do so. It was quite a task to get that poster as she had to request her aunt in the UK to send it to her, who was embarrassed to get it as Mrs. Thatcher was a polarizing figure in the UK. She could have gone for Indira Gandhi's poster but Mrs. Gandhi's relations with Sikhs had soured following Operation Blue Star. Another female icon, Benazir Bhutto was also out; it was taboo to admire a Pakistani leader in an Indian household. Besides, both women were heirs to political dynasties; she preferred self-made leaders like Mrs. Thatcher. She didn't like the Queen either for the same reason.

Taur Singh liked the company of politicians, especially the successful ones. He loved to get pictures with mayors, members of Parliament, ministers, and even premiers. The hallmark of pictures was the smiles; politicians had an indifferent smile, and he had a genuine one. The biggest catch was of course the Prime Minister. It was not easy to get close to the Prime Minister. The security apparatus was robust and aggressive. The only way to get close to the Prime Minister was during elections and party conventions. Another but less desirable way was to settle for former prime ministers, but he preferred the current one as being in power was everything. Taur Singh had never missed a party convention attended by an incumbent prime minister. He had quite a collection of the former prime ministers ranging from long-serving ones to flybys, who were prime minister for barely months. He proudly displayed the framed pictures in his store and home and later social media.

There was one notable exception, which was the royal family. He was no fan of the royals. He resented the annexation of the Sikh kingdom by the British under Queen Victoria and the massacre of innocent pilgrims in 1919 at Jallianwala Bagh and the bloody partition of India where Sikhs suffered the most. But was it fair to blame the current royals for their ancestors' deeds especially when their role was nominal only? He thought so; everything was fair in jealousy and revenge. He eventually relented when Queen Elizabeth visited the Golden Temple and the Jallianwala Bagh in 1997. She did not offer any apology, but it was enough for him to buy the pictures of the Queen's visit to Amritsar and sell them for a quick profit.

It was not that Canada didn't have a racist past; the early immigrants faced overt racism, but times had changed, and racism had become covert, which was an improvement. The other improvement was apologies; Canadian politicians were eager to apologize for past mistakes, perpetrated by others. It was a different matter that they refused to apologize for their own mistakes. He tried to play the same game in his marriage by not apologizing for his own mistakes, but that didn't work. He had to offer apologies to his wife when asked for; they were unconditional but not heartfelt; a normal state of affairs in any marriage. He developed a working relationship with his wife, who was more interested in a romantic one. She liked movies and he liked documentaries; she went for the gossip column and he went for the editorial; she loved gold jewelry and he loved gold certificates. Their interests were different, but their mission was the same, to care for Siyasat. They compromised for the good of their daughter. It was not a happy marriage, but a successful one.

Siyasat was exposed to the world of politics at a young age. She accompanied her father to party conventions. She saw men everywhere. It was a man's world, and she was the odd one out. What did these men want? They all wanted power for themselves. The other thing they wanted was men who could nod, colloquially known as yes men. Men were surrounded by more men, like a pyramid, which was also built by men. How could she get in? There were women in politics, but they were hardly visible. Visibility was not a problem for her; she was a visible minority after all. Most of these women were strong and pushy; she was neither. She was obedient, not belligerent. She carved out her own path and walked on it quietly. She threatened no one. It allowed her to come closer to powerful people; all she had to do was to get behind their back and give a gentle push. She was not a polarizing figure but a neutralizing one.

She realized that politicians had an incredible ability to complicate things. They had convoluted answers to simple questions. It was considered in vogue. She copied what she saw. She was often asked by teachers and family friends what she wanted to be when she grows up. She said with a straight face, "I want to be the president of the Treasury Board." She had an explanation for the bewildering faces; the president of the Treasury Board was a cabinet minister; few people knew what the job meant, so the pressure was off; and the name president had a nice ring to it. It put a smile on her face and left the others confused.

Politics was a performing art; it needed a live audience. Political knowledge was not enough, she had to act the part. She took acting lessons and did stage plays to shed her shyness. She volunteered at the local gurdwara and the community kitchen. It built her resume and connections in the community. Politics was not considered a profession despite an abundance of professional politicians. There was no professional degree in politics. She had to choose the next best thing. Her parents had their own preferences. Her mom wanted her to be a doctor; doctors were considered only next to God and like God, they didn't bother listening. Her father was more flexible; he laid out several conditions for her prospective career including but not limited to a salary which had to be in six figures, respect for the profession was desirable but fear was essential, and there should be enough barriers to entry.

She didn't want to become a doctor as doctors were lousy politicians. Engineers and scientists were best suited to be political advisors. Only lawyers had most in common with politicians; both relied on facts that were circumstantial and played an opportunistic role. Politicians were in the business of creating loopholes and lawyers were in the business of finding them. It was not a surprise that lawyers filled the ranks of politicians. She wanted to be a lawyer but not any lawyer and definitely not a corporate or a divorce lawyer. She wanted to be a human rights lawyer. Her first hurdle was to get into a law school. It meant clearing the LSAT. It meant spending years on coaching classes and writing practice exams. She aced the exam and got a scholarship to go to U of T law school. Her peers were gunning for clerkships with judges and law firms, but she chose to work with refugees.

There was another kind of peer pressure: dating. She had no romantic inclinations whatsoever. She wondered if something was wrong with her. Her peers thought there was. She went on a couple of dates and scared off the guys with her talk of sexual consent and assault. She shrugged off the guys as douchebags and gained sympathy and reprieve from her friends. She realized that she was asexual by nature. She felt ok with it; one less thing to worry about. She did worry about finishing her degree on time. She graduated and worked for a human rights law firm in Waterville. Working with a vulnerable population was rewarding; it gave her confidence and moral superiority that were essential to be a successful politician.

Getting into politics is easy but getting into power is difficult. Elections produce winners and losers. Losing sucks and losing repeatedly sucks forever. Ask any Republican in California or a Democrat in Alabama. Choosing the right party is far more important than choosing an ideology. Siyasat knew that. It was natural for her to gravitate to a party that won elections. Canada may be to the north of the United States but politically it was to the left. Canadians didn't believe in giving equal opportunity to all, especially to political parties. Unlike their US counterparts, who gave Democrats and Republicans an equal share in governance, there was no shared governance in Canada; the winner took it all.

The winner was the natural governing party of Canada, known as the Party of Power (POP). It was the default choice of Canadians and an obvious choice for Siyasat as well. It was a center-left party that represented the middle. It was not a problem for Siyasat; she was a U of T graduate and her political pendulum had already swung towards the left and stayed there. There was a right-wing party, but it had only one wing, which made it hard to fly. It was called the We Are Right (WAR) party. Whatever was left, was far left and it had no chance to occupy the center. There was an environment-based party, and it chose the color appropriate for Canada: the white party; white as snow but it was looking for a name change as the name was prone to be misconstrued.

The relationship between a political party and its leader is rather complicated. Sometimes both grow together, sometimes both shrink together, sometimes one grows at the expense of the other, which invariably means a leader grows while shrinking the party but not vice versa. A leader is more important to the party than the other way around. The logic is simple: there are bad drivers but there are no bad cars, more or less. Leaders know it and they try to build the party in their own image. Their first order of business is to build a coterie around them. It serves as an echo chamber where the leader's views are solidified through self-reflection. This sort of meditation is immensely pleasurable. Pleasure is addicting but it extracts a price: the price of winning and winning at all costs. Losers are not worth a dime and are quickly discarded.

Elections are a do-or-die battle. A leader must be ruthless and opportunistic. Grooming a successor is akin to a death wish.

A leader needs a loyalist, not a successor. A leader is suspicious by nature and demands affirmation of loyalty on a recurrent basis. Loyalists are required to nod at every speech, laugh at every joke, and be floored by every suggestion made by the beloved leader. It's a job which is not suitable for people with neck stiffness or anyone with any self-respect left in them. Should a nation be judged by its leader? Leaders think so, but we the people disagree, " Judge us only by our preamble and amendments."

The Rt. Hon. John Envy was the Prime Minister of Canada. He was third time unlucky; he had two back-to-back majority governments, but the third majority was lost by four seats. It was still good enough to send him back to the prime minister's office as at least three of the four independent members of Parliament were wooed by the charms of power. He was one of the longest-serving prime ministers in recent memory. It was not a coincidence. He deserved it and much more; that's what his loyalists told him, and he agreed with them wholeheartedly. He achieved success by the sheer will of his father, who opened countless doors for him and kept them open so he can pass through them at a leisurely pace. You see, he was a senator's son.

His father, John Envy Sr. was a Canadian senator. The Senate was the upper chamber of Parliament, where old and wise men did deliberations on important matters; at least that's what they thought of themselves. They had the best of both worlds: power, without responsibility. They were not elected but nominated by the prime minister. They didn't have the same power as a US senator but nevertheless, they could slow down legislation with procedural shenanigans. Canadian Senate was modeled on the House of Lords in the UK, where they were the benefactors of pomp and ceremony and royal peerage; dear Lord, heaven was right there for them. Some believed the Senate was a colossal waste of time and money and wanted it to be abolished.

It was wishful thinking like a Democrat's dream of abolishing the electoral college. However, perceptions mattered, and the government dangled carrots in front of the dissenters. Prominent abolitionist voices were silenced by offering them honorary Senate positions and they soon realized what an honor it was to serve in the Senate.

John Envy Sr. was a professor of economics, specializing in game theory. He was well suited to deliberate on the games that were played in the Senate, but that was not the only reason he was chosen for the coveted body; he of course was the son of a cabinet minister and not any cabinet minister, but number two in the cabinet. Oscar Envy was not the deputy prime minister but considered himself one. He never got the chance to become the prime minister. He was too ambitious for his own good. The Prime Minister felt threatened. Oscar Envy was demoted and was offered the portfolio of natural resources minister. The portfolio had a poison pill: he had to nationalize oil sands and become the most hated man in Alberta. He resigned and it was the end of his political career.

He resented it all his life. It was a self-imposed failure. He became envious of others. He had high hopes for his son, who had little interest in politics. John Envy Sr. gave the most boring speeches, full of quotes from Maynard Keynes and Milton Friedman; the kind of speeches that could cure insomnia. His fellow senators thanked him for a good nap during the pre-telecast days of Parliament, but now they dreaded at the prospect of being caught with the eyes closed in front of the cameras. He retired as a senator, which was good enough for him but not for his father, who channeled his energies towards the grandson. Oscar Envy died before seeing his grandson become the prime minister, but John Envy made sure that the Canadians remembered Oscar Envy. He named airports, museums, highways after his grandfather; there was Envy everywhere.

John Envy went to Eaton for schooling but came back to McGill to finish his graduate degree. It was essential; he could have headed to Oxford or Harvard but that would have been suicidal for his political future. Canadians didn't take kindly to snobbery in the form of ivy leaguers who rubbed their credentials at them. He didn't rub anything, but he massaged his words to soothe Canadians. He became a great orator. He kept it simple for the public but gave convoluted answers to the reporters. He was a chess player who could checkmate several of his opponents. He was not a hunter, yet he slew many political opponents with his killer instinct. He was not a medical doctor, but he could take the pulse of the electorate.

His predecessor jumped on the bandwagon of post 9/11 paranoia and joined the US war to get rid of weapons of mass deception. John opposed the war; it was unpopular at the time. He was called an appeaser, a modern-day Neville Chamberlain, and a terrorist sympathizer. He lied low and let the events play out and they did. Canadians had always stood by American friends and allies. They had marched in tandem with Americans; when America raised its right arm, Canada raised its left. Canadians were never aggressive; they were at best passive aggressive. When Canadians soured to America's wars, John claimed full credit and told them, I told you so. He fought hard and won, not the war but the election. Restoring Canada's credibility was his core message. He kept it simple: We went too far, let's put an end to this war.

He was given a mammoth majority, unheard of in modern times. The WAR party was reduced to a handful of seats in the entire country. He turned hard left: opened the borders with liberal immigration policy, expanded social programs, and created a hole in the budget which was big enough to fund his ambitious projects. He was warned about deficit spending and inflation and currency devaluation. Nothing like that panned out. He was lucky and the stars aligned for him; cheap products from Asia kept the inflation under check, the US Federal Reserve kept interest rates low and made borrowing cheap. He didn't think it was fair to attribute everything to luck, some of it and in fact, most of the credit belonged to him. He grew up playing monopoly and he had his father's favorite book: The General Theory of Employment, Interest, and Money by Maynard Keynes at his bedside. John didn't have a big brother but believed the government could play that role. It could lend a helping hand to people who wanted it and twist the hands who resented it.

John Envy kept inflation under control but keeping the dissent under control was far more important. He had his right-hand man for that: Chief of Staff Nick Dread. Nick was his college buddy. They played chess together; Nick always lost, and he was happy to lose. He was playing a long game and sowing the seeds of loyalty. He was from a humble background; his parents ran a home cleaning business. He was the right man to play dirty tricks as he knew how to mop the floor clean. His modus operandi was simple but effective: drop F-bombs to soften the target. The military called it shock and awe; he called it clean the slate and then draw. If resistance was encountered, he had a set reply, "I know your secrets." It did the trick for a paranoid politician, who had no choice but to receive the unsolicited blackmail. A call from John Envy to heal the bruised ego was enough for most dissenters to fall in line. They played good cop, bad cop, without involving any cops.

Elections are won on emotions, not on strategy. Iraq war and the war on terror were becoming a distant memory and there was a danger that John Envy would become one too. His policy advisors wanted him to run on his achievements, but he knew better. No one was going to be excited that inflation was below two percent, unemployment was below seven percent and GDP growth rate was above three percent. He was entering his golden years and it was not a matter of excitement either. He chose a singular issue: to give representation to visible minorities.

It was not a novel idea; visible minorities, especially turbaned Sikhs, who were the most visible of them all, had found representation at all levels of government, but John Envy went a step further. He wanted to have fifty percent of the elected members of Parliament from visible minorities, but that was too ambitious and created resentment in the caucus. Winnability was paramount, so he placed visible minority candidates especially women in seats with at least a 30% immigrant population. It worked, to an extent. He appealed to the moral conscience of Canadians. The opposition called it pandering and he accused them of slander. He accused the Leader of the Opposition of being reclusive, who was unable to comprehend the virtue of being inclusive. His ideas were noble, and naturally, he expected a Nobel Peace Prize for himself. But he was late; President Barack Obama took the prize. He was envious of the President, but he was also the first world leader to offer his congratulations.

His strategy had an additional benefit: he could fill the seats with political lightweights, who were forever obliged to him for giving them an opportunity of a lifetime. He saw his moral height grow and he had to look down to converse with others, which was gratifying. The candidates had impeccable credentials: lawyers, doctors, scientists, with little or no political experience. Some on the right called it an affront to democracy and questioned if they deserved to be nominated, but those voices came from the far right, somewhere in the mountains of Alberta, which mattered little politically. His political base lied in the vote-rich provinces of Ontario and Quebec, which had large immigrant populations. It was all that was needed to win the election.

Siyasat was in the chosen list of party nominees. She had many things going for her: lawyer, woman, visible minority, community activist, and a personal connection to the Envy family. She had a picture with Oscar Envy and a personal letter from him, wishing her a very bright future. It was worth in gold. She never failed to mention it in her resume and John Envy never failed to honor his grandfather's wish. She won the party nomination and the election and was made a cabinet minister straightaway; a double promotion. She was handed a newly formed ministry of wealth distribution. It was to distribute money to the needy, and the most in need were the people who had lent their support to the party. They were the first in line and they were reassured by the government that their interest would be taken care of first; they, in turn, reassured the government that the money would be passed on to others in need once their own needs were met.

Economists called it trickle-down economics, but John Envy's attitude was, if it paid political dividends, economic dividends would follow. The eligibility criteria were custom-made to fit an elephant in the room. It meant only elephant-sized charities needed to apply and the grants received were proportionately larger. The Prime Minister's Office was involved in every such contract. Getting preclearance from the Prime Minister's Office before announcing any contract was mandatory and the new rookie minister was eager to show her loyalty. Ignorance was her best defense and she signed contracts with eyes opened and mind closed.

It made for a happy ministerial experience. She never required a dose of F-bombs from Nick Dread. Her certificate of loyalty towards the Prime Minister was automatically renewed. She remained in the good books of the Prime Minister and sent thank you notes to keep it filled. Was she happy? Far from it. She had her dreams come true, yet she was a nervous wreck. She kept it all to herself. Her acting lessons helped to hide her emotions. You see, there are two kinds of worriers: those who have never made it in life, like Sadeep, who have nothing left to lose but are still worried; and those who have made it, like Siyasat, who have a lot to lose. Politics is an unforgiving profession and snipers are always in place. It's hard to distinguish an enemy from a friend and whether the shot would come from far or at a point-blank range. The threat in politics is not much of actual assassination but rather of character assassination. Her worries led to a problem of checking. She checked a lot: checked with the staff about her schedule, checked with the bureaucrats about official papers, checked with the Prime Minister's Office about her loyalty, and finally, checked with God if she was on the naughty list. She prayed to have an uneventful tenure as a minister, but God had other plans for her.

CHAPTER ELEVEN

A Rookie Mistake

The venue of the event was the public library. It was getting a grant of ten million dollars. Plans were already made to spend the money: a new parking lot, surveillance cameras, new ventilation system, soundproof cabins, and subscription to obscure journals. Whatever money was left would be spent on buying new books. It was the opening day of the new wing of the library. The mayor, city counselors, and local media were in attendance. The Hon. Siyasat Gill was the chief guest. She arrived on time and the function started with speeches that lasted an hour. The speakers thanked each other and praised each other's contributions; they were as genuine as designer handbags found in a flea market.

Siyasat was professionally dressed in a maroon suit with hair tucked behind in a ponytail. Her make-up was unable to hide acne scars on her face. She wore high heels. She was five feet two inches in height, and it made her quite conscious about her stature. She blamed her mom's side for her height, but nothing could be done about it. She felt empowered standing on high heels despite her aching feet. She had benefits for massage therapy, and she felt high heels were worth the pain.

She wore a Canadian flag pin to show her patriotic credentials. She had no choice; it was part of the political attire. It silenced her fellow members of Parliament who would occasionally ask where she was originally from. In the same vein, she attended hockey games; she had no interest in ice hockey but saying it aloud would have invited gasps. She attended barbeque parties despite being a vegetarian; her voters hung out there and she had to go to shake hands and hold babies and be a part of their selfies.

She was relieved at the successful conclusion of the event and was ready to take questions from the press. When I say press, there was one reporter from a local newspaper, whose enthusiasm matched that of a child eating broccoli for lunch. He had to ask the questions to get out of the boring event and do better things with his time.

"Madam Minister, who do you give credit to for making it all happen?" the reporter asked. It was a silly question, to put it mildly, after an hour of cringeworthy speeches that the reporter missed while trying to catch up on his WhatsApp messages; but she was happy to answer it again.

"Thanks for an excellent question, Frank," Siyasat said. It was a shameless attempt to woo the reporter and it worked; for once, the reporter was keenly listening.

"This project would not have seen the light of the day without the personal interest shown by the Rt. Hon. Prime Minister John Envy. He was instrumental in securing funds and getting the necessary permissions to make it all happen. I would again thank the mayor and the city hall staff for their cooperation. I cannot say enough good things about the library staff and of course the staff at my department to see this project through."

"When would we see the Prime Minister visit Waterville?" the reporter asked. He had planned to ask only one question but buttering by the Minister had increased his level of enthusiasm.

"To tell you the truth, the Prime Minister was eager to meet you all, but he could not make it today due to scheduling problems. I can assure you that he would visit Waterville very soon and I promise he would bring more good news for the city."

There was applause all around, there was nodding left and right and there was flash photography to mark the happy moment.

Siyasat was hoping to answer more softball questions, but the lone reporter couldn't be bothered to ask anymore. There was however another hand that was raised.

"May I help you?" a library staffer asked, who was hoping the hand was raised to ask for directions to the nearest washroom.

"I have a question for the Minister," Sadeep said.

Sadeep was sitting in the front row, which was not an accomplishment as there were plenty of empty seats. He looked dapper in a white kurta pajama. He had a notepad on his lap, a fountain pen in the front pocket, and a poker expression on his face.

"Are you a journalist?" the staffer asked.

"I have a social media channel and I cover local news of interest." It was not a lie; he had opened an account on YouTube and Twitter the day before and he was certainly interested in covering this local event. It was not a fully baked truth, but it allowed him to answer the question with conviction.

The staffer looked at the Minister, who was in an obliging mood; getting more media coverage couldn't hurt. Siyasat gave the go-ahead to ask the question.

"Madam, thank you for taking my question. I don't want to embarrass you but as a South Asian, I am so proud of your accomplishments. You are a source of inspiration to us all."

Siyasat blushed at the praise which was coated with several layers of varnish. She had taken the bait.

"Who do you give credit to for your success?" Sadeep asked.

"Hard work, sincerity, my parents, and of course the Prime Minister for giving me the opportunity to serve Canadians."

"Please no more questions," the staffer interjected. There was a danger that all this sweet talk could lead to elevated sugar levels; sugar-laden muffins had already been served at the event.

"Madam, please one more question, if I may," Sadeep said.

"It's alright," Siyasat said. She was longing for more.

"What do you dream of the most?"

"To be the prime minister of Canada."

"I wish you the best of luck. If you were the prime minister, what would you do differently than the current incumbent?"

"I would treat my colleagues with respect. I would not bully them into submission. My chief of staff would not drop any F-bombs. That would be a good place to start."

There was a pin-drop silence in the room. All eyes were on Siyasat yet she was oblivious to their gazes. Truth had slipped out and she stood exposed in the eyes of others like an actress with a wardrobe malfunction. The library staffer acted swiftly and ended the press conference. It did not end the whispers and the gossip and the speculation.

The mayor was gleeful. He was fantasizing about his chances of becoming a federal politician and to join the big leagues. He felt warm-hearted from the flames that were coming from the burning political career of Siyasat. The counselors were carving their own future paths and contemplating running for the mayoral office. Her true well-wisher, her secretary, was missing in action. She had gone to the washroom and had missed the entire press conference.

"Sorry Minister, I had an urgent call (of nature) and I couldn't be there for the press conference. How did it go?"

"It went smoothly. The local press couldn't press me enough." Siyasat was beginning to doubt herself. Something was wrong but she couldn't tell what. She couldn't connect the dots and she couldn't ask others for their feedback, which would have exposed her insecurities. She went home and made a call to the Prime Minister to debrief about today's event and her upcoming project. John Envy was like an insecure father who expected a call from her teenage daughter whenever she went out.

"Prime Minister, we are ready to operationalize the project Press Ahead. Did you see the draft proposal?"

"Good job Siyasat. Make sure there is no media outlet left

behind. It's a sensitive issue and we don't want to be taking sides. Media that's friendly to us will remain friendly regardless. But it's a golden opportunity to woo the unfriendly media. They won't admit it but getting money feels good and we want to give them the feel-good factor."

"Yes Sir, we would be distributing the money left and right."

"Don't forget the smaller players; big wins come with small margins and smaller players can help us get the marginal seats."

"No worries. It shall be done."

"How was your interaction with the local media today? Are people in Waterville happy with the grant?"

"They are elated. It's the biggest grant in the history of the public library. It's money well spent."

"Good. See you in Ottawa on Monday."

"Au Revoir."

She put her phone on silent mode. It was time to relax with the family, eat homemade parathas, listen to old Bollywood songs, and read Das Kapital for light reading before switching off the lights.

Time was of the essence for Sadeep. In journalism, first come, first served rules the day. He had made a video of his interaction with the Minister. No-one stopped him from making the video of the event; he proclaimed himself to be a social media personality and it was a part of his job. He uploaded the video on YouTube and Twitter with a catchy phrase, "Minister calls Prime Minister of Canada a bully." It was a well-planned operation with operational guidance from the ghost. It was carried out flawlessly. He was proud to have pulled out such a feat. He had some self-doubt. He had done character assassination; it was a non-violent act, carried out with a microphone, not a gun. He had no contingency plan. He was there to win and for once in his life, he did win. But it didn't make him happy as he had hoped. He couldn't smile after ruining someone's career. His hands shook as he clicked the upload button.

He was reprimanded by Qubit Preet. He reminded Sadeep that he was sharing the truth with people who deserve to know what their leaders really think. He chastised Sadeep for trying to write off someone's career based on conventional wisdom. Who knows what the future would bring for her? Sadeep got convinced by the ghost's assertions. He sent the video link to newspapers and television channels. It was a bombshell story and was quickly picked up by the media. The video went viral. He became a celebrity and so did she.

Reactions came in swift and strong. First in line to give his response was the Leader of Her Majesty's Opposition, Mr. Wright. He was in Ottawa. When other politicians made a dash towards their home constituencies, he didn't feel the urge to go back. He was a politician's politician. He liked the smell of Parliament, the company of bureaucrats, and the gossip that happened on the Hill. He was dining at the luxurious Pay & Stay Hotel across the Rideau Canal. He was with his wife, but it was not a romantic dinner. He had bailed out on his promise to go on a vacation to the south of France. He had to attend the House of Commons special session on Western Alienation, but he managed to alienate his wife as the dates clashed with their holiday plans. She had hoped for Tiffany's diamond bracelet but all he could offer was a three-course meal.

He was about to order a dessert when a staffer rudely interrupted his order. His wife was flabbergasted but did not make a public fuss. It was self-restraint at its best. She had the makings of the first lady of Canada. It was a dream that she shared with her husband along with three grown-up children. The news from the staffer was sweeter than any dessert he would have tasted. It was an occasion for a spontaneous grin; a golden smile that exposed his gold filings. He couldn't believe what he saw in the video. He was skeptical at first; could it be a deep fake video? His staffer pointed out that media outlets were running this story; they would have verified the authenticity of the video. The staffer recommended to come out swinging and give a scathing rebuke of the Prime Minister's conduct. Mr. Wright huddled for a response with his staff in the corner of the room as his wife cursed the loudmouth staffer for ruining their lovely evening. There was no time for live commentary or video response. It was decided to issue a statement first and it went like this:

"I am deeply troubled by the revelations made in the alleged video. Ms. Siyasat Gill, a close confidant of the Prime Minister has reportedly accused him of being a bully. It's a scathing indictment of the autocratic functioning of this Prime Minister. Canadians have lost confidence in this Prime Minister. He must resign."

He came back, kissed his wife on the forehead, and gave the good news, "24 Sussex Drive is not far. Get ready, we might have to move soon."

"Are you sure?" Mrs. Wright said. "She is a lightweight minister. Who cares what she says? Politicians have survived bigger scandals."

Mrs. Wright had lived through scandals. Her husband had plenty of his own. He had been a touchy-feely sort of person. His touches were sometimes misconstrued, and accusations were made about his inappropriate advances. But that was a long time ago; decade was an eternity in politics, and it was long forgotten by the media and the public, who had given him a second chance. He had learned his lesson and kept his hands in his pocket. He carried a male chaperone, just in case. He paid the price in full, to his wife who would not be fooled by a simple sorry, and to the media who would not shut up if he denied the allegations. He did not have to wear an ankle bracelet, but he agreed to random and frequent searches of his phone and surprise visits to the office by his wife. It saved his marriage. He was a battle-hardened politician who had scars to show and opportunities to seek. He had found a tactical political weapon to neutralize the Prime Minister, and he was in no mood to show restraint.

The response from the second-largest opposition party, the Far-Fetched Party (FFP), was late as the leader had gone for a hike. Dr. Green, who had a PhD. in environmental science, loved to go for long walks in the Okanagan valley. Her response got delayed due to the difference in the time zone, but it was certainly not denied. She felt an obligation to weigh in. Her response carried more weight as she was a feminist icon. She was a darling of the left; a pioneer. She fought for legalizing same-sex marriage and she was among the first legally married same-sex couples. She was also the first to seek divorce from her partner. It happened in marriages.

She was a champion of environmental rights. She refused to travel in cars with combustion engines. She had an electric car and a bike. She loved recycling including recycling of her speeches. She considered recycling a fundamental duty of citizens on par with the duty to vote. Both had low participation rates as citizens considered it a chore; they wanted unlimited refills on their cups but had little interest in refilling the recycle bins. They had all the interest in standing in line to grab Black Friday deals but loathed the lineups for voting in elections. What irked her the most was people throwing garbage in recycling bins. It was worthy of punishment. She sought a criminal penalty for the above-mentioned infarctions but was ready to settle for a hefty fine due to practical considerations.

Her harshest criticism was reserved for the corporate world. She would rename Bay Street to Pay Street and send billionaires into extinction. Criminals could be rehabilitated, but there was no cure for corporate greed. The tax was the only form of defense against them, short of nationalization. She was proud to say that she had never received a corporate donation, but she was worried about her party's finances. The party was running deficits, but they were minuscule as compared to the deficits she planned for the government if she was elected to govern. Her party had a lot of young blood who were internet savvy. They ran a brilliant campaign with few computers in a basement and trolled the other parties and got plenty of free publicity. They made a lot of noise but very little money.

Her policies were not taken seriously as no one expected her party to ever gain power. But she took herself seriously and she was dead serious about breaking two things: social norms and glass ceilings. She wanted to see women and other marginalized groups breaking barriers. She didn't mind the tokenism of promoting these groups even if it was based on political opportunism.

The political scandal presented a dilemma for her. How should she react to the revelations made by Minister Gill? She didn't want to bring down the government over this issue. That would have played right into the hand of the right-wingers who were desperate to trigger an election. It was a minority government; she was not a kingmaker, but she could shift the momentum against the government. It would hurt the progressive agenda, but things were not black and white; they came in different shades of grey. How could she support a prime minister accused of bullying a visible minority woman? But could she trust Siyasat? What if she retracted her accusations? It was a delicate balancing act that Dr. Green had to perform, so she made a statement that came not from the heart but from a group discussion.

"We want the truth from the Prime Minister. Ms. Gill's concerns should be heard. She should be given an opportunity to explain her accusations. Bullying has no place in public life. We want a full public inquiry to look into the revelations made by the Minister in the alleged video."

There were other smaller parties, chief among them were the separatists from Quebec, whose numbers had been greatly reduced in the last federal election. It was their own doing. Sovereignty was always on their agenda, but they had misread the mood of the people and lost badly. Their numbers had been reduced but their voices were as loud as ever and their threat to split Canada was as real as ever. They had lost the battle, but war was still on, and losing one referendum did not shut the door on sovereignty completely.

It was too important of an issue for them. Quebec's culture was at stake, French language was under threat from the Anglophones that surrounded them. They were not pacified by the fact that in Anglophone provinces, learning French was considered prestigious, and demand to learn French was increasing. Nevertheless, sovereigntists had to think of the worst-case scenarios and tap into the anxiety and fear of the Francophones in Quebec. They waited and looked for an opportunistic moment to strike again. They needed to be successful one time and they knew that if they kept on trying, they would get successful: it's probability theory 101.

They were excited to hear about the Minister's accusations against the Prime Minister. If it led to political upheaval and a power vacuum, they would be ready to fill it up with the sovereignty rhetoric. They were handicapped by their leader who was as charismatic as a doorknob. Mr. Dion, who by the way was not in any way related to Celine Dion, was not an aggressive leader. He was a policy man who was appointed a caretaker leader before an energetic leader could be found. He had an inherent ability to make even the most exciting things dull. When he cracked a joke, all he found was internal contradictions. He would smile at his own jokes when others failed to do so, which happened often. He wanted to spice up his speeches to wake up the audience, but the result felt like a mosquito buzzing in their ears. He was mild-mannered and got along with others quite well and thus was an ideal compromise candidate. His English was also compromised, and it was difficult to understand what he said. He gave two responses to the scandal: one in French and one in English. The French one was lost in translation and the English one was lost in comprehension.

The media broke the story and politicians chewed on it. It was social media that ignited the fire first and made it into a burning story. Traditional media no longer could put cold water on a burning story. Even if it tried, smoke would still simmer. Social media was not an arbitrator of truth, but it pretended to be, and, in that sense, it was like traditional media. In social media, reality and virtual reality were hard to distinguish, but that didn't matter as the audience had already made up their mind. The line between news and opinion was becoming blurry; the gap between propaganda and information was becoming smaller; the difference between entertainment and professionalism was becoming lesser. Traditional media accused social media of being sensational and unreliable; in turn, it was accused of being paternalistic and behind the times. Both loathed each other and yet used each other all the time.

When Sadeep sent links of the video to newspapers and tv channels, they were not opened. Who in their right mind would open a link from an unknown person? The editors knew better and so did the malware protection software; it could have been a hacking attempt. The editors waited for social media to authenticate the story, which was ironic. When the story became a trending topic on Twitter, only then the editors dared to open the links and run the story.

The government-friendly Ottawa Downhill newspaper vigorously defended the Prime Minister. "Minister betrays Prime Minister" was their headline. It was chosen after rejecting a scandalous headline: "Minister shows her true colors." It was shot down by the editor for being blatantly racist. The right-leaning Calgary Sand newspaper was less charitable to the Prime Minister: "A bully roams in 24 Sussex Drive" was provocative and effective. Other headlines like "Minister breaks ranks" and "Truth slips out of the Minister" conveyed an indifferent message. Feminist blogs were cheering Siyasat: "You go girl" was their rallying cry.

There was complete silence from politicians of the governing party. They observed moments of silence to pay homage to the dwindling career of a colleague. They knew she had spoken the truth, but she had broken the oath of secrecy. There were excuses available for breaking government secrets but snitching on the Prime Minister was unpardonable. The stars of the story were missing. There was no word from the Prime Minister, and Siyasat was sound asleep, oblivious to the gathering storm.

CHAPTER TWELVE

A Press Statement

Siyasat found herself sitting in a horse carriage. It was no ordinary carriage; it had the royal emblem. She was sitting across from the Queen. She was in a panic; she wasn't dressed for the occasion; she was in fact in a tracksuit. What would the Queen think of her? The Queen kept a stiff upper lip and made no eye contact, which was a good thing for Siyasat. The Queen waved at people who had lined up the streets in large numbers. Siyasat did the same but felt conscious about her unmanicured fingernails. She was mesmerized by the royal pageantry: clip-clop sounds of the horses and the royal guards with their dragon helmets and swords. The royal procession was underway but to where? She couldn't recognize the streets. They were too wide for London. The procession stopped behind a white building. Siyasat was escorted to a stage in front of a building with a huge white dome. The stage was packed with dignitaries: presidents, prime ministers, celebrities; some alive, some dead. There was a man in a black robe who signaled to Siyasat to come forward and raise her hand and repeat after him,

"I, Siyasat Gill, do solemnly swear that I......"

Her swearing-in was interrupted by a violent shake and a familiar voice.

"Beta, get up."

(Beta is an interesting word in Hindi. It stands for son and is being increasingly used in a unisex way like guys. Feminine nouns are being assimilated into masculine ones. Is that progress? I am getting off-topic, let's resume the conversation.)

"Why?" She tossed and turned in bed.

"You need to get up to know why."

"Mom, please let me sleep."

"Go ahead and sleep and let your career burn."

"What? I don't know what you are saying. Give me a few minutes, I will get up."

She woke up from a dream to enter the harsh reality of life. She saw lights across the street and peeked through the bedroom window to see what was going on. There were media vans camped outside her home. She was alarmed. She checked her phone and there were thousands of messages; she realized the mess she was in.

Her parents were sitting on the sofa. It was getting close to midnight, but they were not in a state to sleep. Their daughter's career was on the line. They watched the television anxiously as media pundits opined on the political ramifications.

"What happened?" Sabar Kaur asked. She was confused as people often got after watching the news for a while.

"I don't know," Taur Singh said. "*Kise di nazar lag gayi* (Someone has jinxed us)."

"What happens now?"

"She would have to resign."

"*Hai Rabba* (Oh God), she would be devastated. She worked so hard to come this far and, in a moment, everything is finished."

"God help us."

"Don't be harsh on her," Sabar Kaur said. "She is already down. Let's not push her further down."

"I am not her enemy," Taur Singh said. "I know what to do. I only have her best interest in mind."

"But you don't come across as one. She needs to be listened to."

"Do you ever listen to me? You don't know a thing about politics. Just keep quiet."

"I may not know about politics, but I know enough about human nature. You are not her mother; you would never understand." She started tapping her feet while her voice was getting louder; Taur Singh was getting into the danger zone. He had seen this movie before.

"I am sorry," Taur Singh said. "We are all under stress. Let's not fight. I know what to do."

"You do that," Sabar Kaur said. "If you make her cry, I am never going to forgive you. You better watch out."

"Please let it go. I am having a headache. Can you please bring me some medicine?"

"Wait." She bought a buffet of medicines to choose from. More than medicines, avoiding a fight was key in reigning his headache.

"I don't know why God is punishing us," Sabar Kaur said.

"Why don't you ask God?" Taur Singh said.

Sabar Kaur shook her head. It was not worth giving tit-for-tat. She would rather pray and ask God for forgiveness. She devised a prayer schedule to get God on her side. Patience was already on her side. Refugees are usually patient, it's only the government which gets restless. Sabar Kaur was born in the dark days of 1947. She was born on a train to India. Her family was fleeing communal riots during the partition of India. It was a miracle that she did not die, either from a neonatal infection or at the hand of merciless rioters.

Her mother was not that lucky; she was able to cross the border but died due to a lack of medical care. The postpartum hemorrhage went untreated. There was blood flowing in the streets, yet she could not get a timely blood transfusion. Sabar was raised by her paternal grandmother while her father struggled to make ends meet. The void left by her mother was filled a few years later by the stepmother, which didn't make things any better. She was married at a young age and responsibilities kept piling on. She was settling into married life in Uganda when she had to move to Canada as a refugee. She thought it was the end of her refugee journey; her children would never have to worry about oppression and political chaos. Life had other plans for her. A politician without a party is a political refugee, and Siyasat was on the verge of becoming one.

Siyasat was in shock. Her blood pressure was high, so was her heart rate and so were her emotions. It did not require an IV bolus, but it did need few kind words of reassurance. She was going through different stages of grief and currently was in denial bordering on anger. She couldn't believe what she had said. How could she have such a lapse in judgment? She was digging for reasons and looking for excuses. She was in a deep hole and the only thing she could do was to keep digging. She was desperate for a way out.

She was however realistic. There was no chance of leniency from the Prime Minister. It was an all or none scenario. She was on her way out and she had to come to terms with it. Her only hope was public opinion. The public was far more forgiving and it had given second chances to many politicians with far worse scandals. Time was at a standstill for her, but events were happening at a lightning speed. She came out of the room, switched off the television, and sat beside her parents.

There was silence for a moment. It was time for mourning.

"Beta, don't worry, everything will be fine," Sabar Kaur said.

Siyasat nodded while trying to fight tears that were desperate to come out.

"Come, hug your mom."

Siyasat put her head in mom's lap and felt the motherly warmth. It was unconditional, genuine, and priceless.

"Things won't get better on their own," Taur Singh said.

"I know Dad. I don't know what to do. I can't think straight."

"You have to play your cards carefully," Taur Singh said.

"What do you suggest?"

"Don't trust anyone."

"I don't."

"You do. You put too much faith in your leader. There are no friends in politics, there are only competitors. You record every conversation. Protect yourself."

"I don't know what I would say to the Prime Minister. I have no clue how and why I said those words about him. I felt I was under a spell."

"That won't fly," Taur Singh said. "You better come up with a plausible explanation."

"Could there be a medical reason behind it?" Siyasat said. "I hope not but it's worth pursuing."

"I saw the video many times. You were quite articulate in your reasoning. It didn't sound like a sick person talking."

"That's what I don't understand. It's almost spooky. What I said was true, it's just that it was not supposed to come out."

"Who was that reporter that asked you these questions? He looked desi."

"I don't know. He was a mystery man. Did he trap me into answering these questions? I am getting paranoid."

"His motives don't matter. Even if he had an agenda, the onus was on you to answer appropriately."

"Prime Minister must be angry at me. I am dreading taking his call. His Chief of Staff would call first. He is even scarier."

Her phone buzzed. She sighed. It was a call from Nick Dread, Prime Minister's Chief of Staff.

"Thinking of the devil….," Siyasat said as she rushed to the room and slammed the door behind her.

"Should I listen to the conversation?" Taur Singh said.

"Give her some privacy Sardarji," Sabar Kaur said. "She is going to tell you everything anyway. If you want to do something, pray for her."

Call from Nick was like carpet bombing by a B-52 bomber. The only difference was that F-bombs were dropped at her. She was threatened with political consequences. It was political blackmail that had to be paid in the public humiliation of

Siyasat. She had to retract her statement and issue an unequivocal apology. In other words, she had to tell the world that she lied. It was a form of political suicide, and she was being coerced into one. She listened patiently while the recording button was on. She was determined to teach him a lesson but at a time and place of her choosing.

She was reeling from a wounded ego. She knew the Prime Minister would call and offer a soothing touch. She had seen this playbook before. She was expecting the Prime Minister to offer her a face-saving measure. Past loyalties were not worth much in politics and she knew she had limited leverage. She was playing Russian roulette with a revolver pointing at her. She was in no position to bargain. She could only ask for forgiveness, and forgiveness was not something available on demand.

The Prime Minister called after fifteen minutes. She was ready as she could be, nervous but determined.

"Madam Minister, Prime Minister would like to talk to you," the Prime Minister's secretary said.

"Sure."

"Hi Siyasat, how are you?" the Prime Minister said. It was a rhetorical question.

"Couldn't be worse, Prime Minister."

"I know. We are in this together. I don't want to go into why and how it happened. Let's focus on where to go from here."

"Yes, Prime Minister."

"It's not about you or me or Nick. There are bigger issues at play: the issues we care about and the people we want to help."

"Yes, Prime Minister."

"We don't want the opposition to bring down the government over it. It would be a disaster. It's time to put aside personal agendas for the larger interest of the country."

"Yes, Prime Minister."

"The only way forward is for you to resign, and it should come from you rather than me. I know it is a difficult decision but rest assured that your sacrifice won't go unnoticed. You would be accommodated in due course."

"I would resign if that's your wish but..."

"No ifs, ands, or buts."

"If I may, Prime Minister, it's important to me. I don't want to be called a liar. If Nick would resign as well then I would be spared public humiliation."

"That's not possible. It would be an admission of guilt. The opposition would have a field day. You won't be called a liar. You had a momentary lapse in judgment."

"Let me think about it."

"You do that. Pay my regards to your parents. My best wishes are always with you."

"Yes, Prime Minister."

The Prime Minister issued a statement shortly after the conversation.

"I have full faith in Ms. Siyasat Gill. She has been an exemplary minister and a great team player. We have a good rapport and would continue to work together to serve Canadians."

She resigned the next day. It was a short letter but required much deliberation to write. She tore several papers and after three strong cups of coffee, she was ready with the final draft, which was sent to the Prime Minister.

"I am submitting my resignation as a cabinet minister. I thank the Prime Minister for allowing me this opportunity to serve Canadians."

The Prime Minister was furious. Her resignation added fuel to the fire. She did not address the allegations and her silence on the matter spoke volumes. The opposition heard it loud and clear, and they hammered the government over it. The Prime Minister wasn't going to take it lying down. He had experience and he had a plan. The first order of business was to change the channel. He had to give the media something new to talk about. He decided to cut the sales tax by a full one percent. It made the already ballooning deficit worse, but the government was in a survival mode. A balanced budget was not a priority; he had to stabilize the political situation first.

He was not finished with his plan. He announced billions

of dollars in funding to promote social housing, gender equality, and indigenous health. No one could object to such noble causes and throwing out his government would mean an end to those programs. He tied his future to the success of social programs; a smart and shrewd move, which the opposition characterized as shameful. It was not all. I haven't mentioned his most potent strategy: smear and clear; smear Siyasat and clear the Prime Minister. There was a parade of his loyalists hitting the airways and sowing doubts about the credibility of Siyasat. It was choreographed in such a way that only persons of color were chosen to directly attack Siyasat. It worked. The opposition's noise was tuned out by the media and the people, and life carried on. It was the nature of things.

You may be wondering what happened to our protagonist Sadeep. You see, when politicians get involved, they control the center stage. It's all about them. They don't allow others to share the limelight. The same is true with celebrities. Sadeep like others was a mute spectator. The situation was untenable. He was no longer an ordinary person. He had acquired power. He could extract truth and it hurt more than a tooth extraction. It made him confident and boosted his ego. His ego demanded importance from others and sitting at home was making him restless. He was itching to use his power. His conscience was prodding him to act. Truth shouldn't lead to punishment; it was no crime. He was determined to punish the Prime Minister. It meant getting the Prime Minister to speak the truth, which would automatically qualify him for punishment.

"We should do something," Sadeep said. He presumed he was talking to the ghost. Even if the ghost was not around, he would have said the same thing.

"We are doing something, in case you haven't noticed," Qubit Preet said.

"We need to do more. I am mad at the Prime Minister and

the entire political system."

"You are not alone. Many people are mad at politicians."

"Why don't they do something about it?"

"Yes, they do. They vote, at least 50 % of them."

"And yet nothing changes. I would change that. We need to teach a lesson to the Prime Minister."

"I am with you but it's not that simple. Access to the Prime Minister needs money, which you don't have."

"But I have you."

Their conversation was interrupted by a phone call. His parents were calling. They didn't call often but when they did, it was to deliver a sermon. Zor Singh had retired as a schoolteacher. He was a strict disciplinarian. He used to carry a cane in his hand when he was a teacher. It sent a shiver down the spine of students. When corporeal punishment became a taboo and it was decided to ban it in schools, he was a conscientious objector. He resented the curtailment of his abilities to discipline students. He knew what was best for his students. He was a pioneer in introducing multiple choice questions in exams. It gave him control over the answers as well. He used the same approach at home.

Dildar Kaur was submissive by nature, which was put to good use by Zor Singh; he reduced the choices to only one. When it came to career choice, he offered two choices to Sadeep: medicine or engineering; none of the above was not an option. Like a typical teenager, he didn't know what he wanted, which was alright as Zor Singh made the choice for him. He never forgave his father for pushing him into a field in which he had little interest. Zor Singh was proud that his son had become a doctor; there were no other doctors in their family. He had a dream of his son becoming a successful doctor in Canada and rubbing it to the relatives, but things didn't pan out and it was the relatives who rubbed it to Zor Singh. There were misgivings on both sides; the father-son relationship remained as cold as Manitoba winters and thaw in their relationship remained as elusive as ever.

"Sadeep, what's going on?" Zor Singh said. "How come you

got involved with politicians?"

"Nothing is going on. I went to an event and asked a question to the Minister. Anyone could have done that. She gave a weird answer, that's all."

"And you didn't even tell us. I saw your video on WhatsApp. I couldn't believe it."

"It's not a big deal."

"It has become such a scandal. Be careful. Don't mess with politicians."

"Come on Dad, it's Canada. There is no need to fear politicians."

"You listen to me. I have seen more life than you. You lie low and live your life peacefully. Life hasn't given much to you but whatever it has, hold on to it."

"Thanks, Dad."

He threw away the phone on the bed. He couldn't afford a new phone, so throwing it on the floor was not feasible. He had to show anger but within limits.

"Why do parents think that they know better?"

"This affliction is not confined only to parents," Qubit Preet said.

"I know but when your own parents don't appreciate you, it hurts like hell. You wouldn't know."

"That's harsh, even by human standards."

"I am sorry, I am angry and disappointed. I wish I were you."

"Your wish is your destiny. Sooner or later, you would end up in the dark matter."

"I am not afraid of dying. Not anymore."

"Then you're lying."

"Okay, maybe a little afraid. I want to make my life meaningful. What's my next consignment?"

"You talk like an assassin."

"I have come a long way from an anxious existence. Thanks to a ghost, I am no longer afraid."

"That was not the intention."

"Intentional or not, here I am."

"We are climbing up the ladder. We can't directly go after the Prime Minister. We have to take one step at a time. We need to go after one of the richest persons in Canada. He is close to the Prime Minister. We are getting a 2-in-1 deal."

"I never pass on a good deal."

CHAPTER THIRTEEN

Crème de la Crème

R obert Own owned many things: a house in Bridle Park, Toronto; a condo in Knightsbridge, London; a mansion in Beverly Hills; a penthouse in Manhattan; and a beachfront property in Nice, France. He owned Ferraris, Lamborghinis, private jets, and a chain of exotic islands in the Pacific. He owned hundreds of pairs of shoes, thousands of clothes, millions in cash, and billions in debt. He was not only rich, but he was filthy rich, ultra-rich, crazy rich, super-rich. Rich people called him rich; accountants called him a billionaire; poor called him greedy; institutions called him a benefactor; politicians called him a lobbyist, and he called himself an unapologetic capitalist. He inherited wealth and added some. Own family had been rich for generations. They knew which way the wind would blow. They built railroads across Canada when it was lucrative. They made auto parts when automobiles became accessible. They built cellular networks when the internet revolution was starting, and they were ready with windmills and solar panels when a climate emergency was declared.

The family business had tentacles in all parts of the Canadian economy. The business was designed to be too big to fail, which had several perks attached to it. Credit rating agencies considered it investment grade and Robert Own considered it his fiduciary duty to take on more and more debt. The strategy paid rich dividends, which were distributed among shareholders. It was free money. Interest rates were kept low by central banks to boost growth and the risk of default was minimized by the government, which was ready to provide generous loans. Robert Own gave the government enough reasons to justify bailing him out. He kept a large workforce which was supported by paying minimum wages. He made his headquarters in Montreal. He aligned his fortune with the prosperity of Quebec and the national unity of Canada.

It was a cunning move and politicians had no choice but to play along. A Quebec-based firm that employed thousands of employees could not be allowed to go bankrupt. The Quebec government considered saving it only fair, but to the federal government, it was a dare. Quebec's relationship with Canada was fragile and any further tension could snap the bond forever. A referendum was a one-way street, and it was always around the corner, thanks to sovereigntists, who dreamed of Quebec's sovereignty day and night. It was an in- law-like relationship; when in-laws ask for something, saying no is not an option. Robert Own did his part in wooing Quebec, which primarily involved learning French and requiring all his employees to be bilingual. He kept language standards flexible though; Bonjour and Au Revoir were good enough for an employee to be qualified as bilingual.

He felt emboldened to take risks as downsides were limited. The biggest risk he took was to start a new bank at the height of the 2008 financial crisis. He was wise enough not to buy struggling banks, who were available dirt cheap, but came with liability that knew no bounds. He had no interest in buying struggling American financial institutions and to get under the preview of the Federal Reserve, which was beyond reproach. Canadian banks shined in the crisis and got away with much less stringent regulations. It was a golden opportunity for Canadian banks to expand, but they were scared to take risks.

Robert Own added risk to his middle name and starting

a bank certainly amounted to that. He had high interest in running his own bank and offered even higher interest on saving accounts to his customers, who by the way had to pay high fees in return. The bank had high interest in getting deposits and provided above-market interest rates, only to be negated by fees that were hidden in the fine print. The bank offered mutual funds, real estate investment trusts, exotic investments, which were once available only to wealthy clients. The bank marketed itself as a cheap alternative to hedge funds and promised great returns on investment. The definition of great returns was deliberately left vague. The running costs were kept low. It was a branchless bank. It was entirely digital, and its app was simple and effective. The bank was a roaring success. It cemented the reputation of Robert Own as a financial genius.

The bond between the wealthy and the powerful is as strong as a covalent bond. They may not share electrons, but they share many other things that make their bond long-lasting. They share the same space, whether it's corporate boards or donation dinners. Ministers are one vote away from becoming ex-ministers and one nomination away from becoming corporate board members. The flow can reverse of course, and corporate leaders can become politicians. It is admittingly difficult but not impossible. You may think that's not fair, but fairness is a marketable commodity; it goes to the highest bidder.

Politicians are expected to keep their mouths shut on corporate boards, which is a tall order for them as they are inclined to engage in shouting matches. They are handsomely rewarded for their silence and for showing up at the meeting to listen to boring and incomprehensible financial statements of the company. It's a symbiotic relationship and like any relationship, it requires give and take; the wealthy give the money, and the politicians take the credit. Dinner is a good meeting place for both parties, where besides pleasantries, a lot of other things are exchanged. Limits have been put on corporate and individual donations, but money is like water, it finds a way. Quid pro quo becomes inevitable though it is not advertised as such for legal and ethical reasons. It's understood by both parties that favors granted way out in the future don't come under the preview of quid pro quo. It's a barter system that has stood the test of time. No amount of bitcoin can replace the convenience and flexibility of this barter system.

Robert Own was a charitable man. He granted many favors, starting with himself. He did it with a smile, which was expensive to maintain and painful to endure. He had a team of orthodontists to take care of that. He charmed ladies with his looks, politicians with his generosity, Wall Street with his greed, and creditors with his promises. It did not take too long for him to charm the Prime Minister. John and Robert had known each other since childhood but they were not childhood friends. Families had known each other and had several get-togethers. That was the extent of their relationship. In fact, they started on the wrong note.

It was Christmas time and there were gifts to be given. They were children and only two years apart, which meant they competed for gifts. John wanted a train and so did Robert, and when Robert was the one who got it in a lucky draw, John objected; in other words, there was pushing and pulling and shoving and cries. Parents intervened, and guess who had to give in? Robert was older and being the host, he had to part ways with his gift. John stole his Christmas. Robert eventually got his train, a real one many years later, as part of a railway contract in lieu of his generosity, but what he really got was a lesson in realpolitik. Patience is a virtue that gives exponential returns over time. Robert had to give up the toy train but when the time came, it was John who handed him the contract for a real train and not just one but hundreds of them. It was followed by another contract for building railroads and bridges, which further cemented their ties. Robert reciprocated by building a factory in the Prime Minister's constituency. Relationship and nation-building went hand in hand. Childhood fights were long forgotten and were replaced by a friendship that was endearing and enduring.

Rich people have a lot of things in abundance, except time.

It makes them restless. They want things others don't have or can't have, and that too as fast as possible. They could be demanding, and some do behave like irritable pricks. Companies know it and churn out special and limited editions to calm their volcanic rage. A limited-edition tourbillon watch, or a one-off hyper car would do just fine, only if they could get it in time before the others. They don't mind being in line if they are the first in line. Who cares about the second or third one in line, whether it's to the throne or to be the winner of a lucky draw? People only remember the first person on the moon or the fastest man on earth. When a lot of rich people get together, they form a rich country. Its behavior is not too different than its constitutents. But the selfishness is excused in the name of national interest. Survival of the wealthiest is considered synonymous with survival of the fittest.

Robert Own was also obsessed with being first in line for everything he ever wanted. He was the first to arrive and the last to depart at auctions. He was a collector par excellence. He was a connoisseur of arts and culture and collected paintings, historic relics, and classic cars. He rationalized his self-indulgence as a safe investment. He was a hoarder of collectibles. He never sold any. He considered it a part of his legacy. He had secret vaults to store the ever-increasing size of his collection. There was one painting that got away. He had an eye on Leonardo da Vinci's Salvador Mundi, but the price tag of over 400 million dollars was pushing it even for him. If he was pushed a little further, he would have splurged the necessary amount for it.

Rich people often have regrets. They regret getting into the wrong relationships. It's worse than a tax audit as the penalty could be half the wealth plus spousal support. Rich people regret passing on investments: I wish I had invested in stocks when they were dirt cheap; I wish I had bought real estate in 2009. These are the regrets of omission. I wish I had sold tech stocks in 1999; I wish I had foreseen the 2008 financial collapse; I wish I had not sent that tweet, are the regrets of commission. This wishful thinking only causes misery to an otherwise privileged life. Robert Own had his share of regrets but they were not what you would normally consider regrets. He was married thrice. The first two marriages obviously failed but he had no regrets. He married into wealthy families. He had invested little emotionally and after the divorce, his wealth had increased substantially. There was no question of regret. It boosted his confidence. If he can come out of two failed marriages, stronger and richer, he could handle anything. He only regretted missed opportunities. He had his plate full, yet he had an eye on others half-full plates.

As they say, success is its own enemy. It's easier to become successful than to stay successful. Success creates admirers and breeds enemies and competitors. Successful people have to watch their backs while keeping their eyes on the goal. Robert Own had his reasons to worry. He built his empire on the corpses of several defunct businesses. He was ruthless like a warlord. He offered to buy his competitors and those who resisted were decimated. He explained to the antitrust division that bigger was better and they trusted him. He carried a security detail that only a head of state could afford. He had permission to carry firearms and could land his private jet in any airport in Canada. His private life was off-limits to the public, and he was successful in fending off the paparazzi. His public persona was meticulously managed. He had an entire PR firm dedicated to managing his social media accounts. His every tweet was vetted by a team of experts in mass media marketing. He was an epitome of the doctrine of "No-Drama Obama."

Robert Own was a perfectionist. He had an opinion on everything, and he was adamant that it was the right one. He was known for giving unsolicited advice. It was not easy to live with him. It needed a special set of characteristics to tolerate him. He was third time lucky and found the right person in Nina. She was unsure of herself and needed constant direction and validation. She knew how to take advice even though she had been a scientific advisor to Health Canada. He was mesmerized by her ability to respect other opinions. Her questions were as sweet as candy.

"Honey, may I ask you a question?"

"What should I do?"

And finally, was this seductive phrase,

"Honey, you are absolutely right?"

It was too much to ask, and Robert was a reasonable man; he settled for a milder affirmation.

"Honey, you may be right."

She wasn't a stunner, but she had decent looks. She was in her mid-thirties when they first met. He spotted grey hair, but he also spotted her kind and generous heart. He wasn't prince charming either. His face was dominated by a long sharp nose, which he loved to dig into other people's affairs. He knew they were made for each other. He made allowances for her careless-ness and casual attitude to life. They got married in a hurry, but they built slow and long-lasting bondage.

Rich people are often busy and Robert Own was no differ-ent. He was hardly ever home, and they spent little time to-gether, which was another reason for their successful marriage. Familiarity breeds contempt but their marriage remained like a freshly squeezed lemonade, which either of them could enjoy.

Nina was ready to go to a charity event to promote envir-onmental causes. She was dressed in a green suit, which was not the only green credential she was carrying.

"Honey, how do I look?" Nina asked.

It was a rhetorical question, which nevertheless required a firm answer.

"You look dapper my dear," Robert said.

"You know this suit is entirely made of recycled material. It's all natural fiber."

"Good, but the designer bag you are carrying has no such pretensions."

"Darn it, glad you reminded me. I don't want to be embar-rassed in front of a large audience by carrying a glittery leather handbag."

"Don't worry, money does the talking for you."

"I hate getting criticized when I am doing noble work. Why can't people be nice?"

"Do you expect some kind of sainthood?"

"I expect validation."

"I can pull some levers and get you nominated to the Order of Canada."

"Please don't," Nina said. "There was a lot of criticism when you got appointed to the Order of Canada. Can you imagine the raucous it would create if I got appointed as well? The critics would say we have bought it, which is not true. We have earned it."

"Either way, I am proud of you," Robert said.

"Thank you."

"Don't forget to take the electric car."

"I shall."

"Is it charged?" Robert asked.

"Don't know," Nina said.

"Is your phone charged?"

"Don't know."

"Who would know?" Robert said.

"I was hoping you would. But seriously, we hire people to do household chores. Why should I be bothered?"

"Fair enough. I would text Andy to get the car ready. He can drop you off at the event."

Andy was the driver. They had three housekeepers and two cooks and one gardener. There were hired contractors to plow snow on the driveway, which was bigger than Highway 401. There were two dogs and a cat and a parrot and an army of attendants and vets to take care of the spoiled brats.

Nina was not yet ready to go; she had an agenda, and it was time to reveal her real intentions.

"Why don't you ask the Prime Minister to help our charity?" Nina asked.

"It's not that simple," Robert said.

"Why not? We have helped him so many times. He owes us."

"He is already in trouble. Did you see the news? It's not the right time to ask for favors."

"It's for charity. We are not asking for a personal favor."

"There is intense competition for charity contracts. He can't just hand over grants to your charity. Why don't you ask the CEO of your charity to contact me? I will hook him up with the Prime Minister's Office. They would coach him how to bid for charity contracts."

"Thanks. You are such a sweetheart."

She was not done yet; she had saved the most contentious agenda for the last. They had arguments bordering on fights many times over the future of their children. Robert was an overprotective father and Nina was a cool mother. He wanted to homeschool, and she was ready to ship off her children to boarding school. They settled for a local private school. He helped with the homework, and she was involved in extracurricular activities. Division of labor worked well for them.

Once upon a time, humans roamed naked and then they made clothes and became civilized. Some people were trying to reverse that process by shedding their clothes. He didn't care for the uncultured or the latest fashion trends coming from social media, but he expected his children to see the virtue of dressing up properly. Nina was more relaxed and took fashion cues from gossip magazines. She liked high heels and put her foot down on fashion choices. They agreed on one thing: they would never come in the way of their children's careers; they would only push them hard from behind.

"I need you to do one more thing," Nina said.

"What?"

"Can you ask your PR firm to manage social media accounts for Rachel? She is going to university, and they don't teach that stuff over there."

"Why are you inviting trouble? She can't handle the pressure of social media."

"Don't underestimate her. She is our daughter."

"You don't know the trolls. They are vicious. She had so far been posting only for her friends; going public is a whole new ball game."

"We can't live in fear. She has dreams, and so do I. Don't you want her to be a celebrity?"

"Not really."

"Celebrities make tons of money. She could start her own clothing line, perfumes; the sky's the limit."

"I don't want that kind of money," Robert said.

"That's surprising, coming from you," Nina said.

"Canadians don't like vulgar displays of wealth."

"You don't have a frugal existence either and besides she doesn't need your permission to do what she wants. If you want to have some control then join us, otherwise, we'll do it without you."

Their tempers were flared, their voices were getting louder and sharper. Someone had to back off and lay down the arms; that honor went to Robert. He didn't give up, but he had to make a tactical retreat.

"Let me think about it. I'll get back to you."

You would think rich people would love to shop at one-stop shops, but they don't. Whether it's a convenient store or a general practitioner or the main road or an index fund, rich people try to avoid them if they can; it's because anything that's considered average is not good enough. Of course, there are exceptions but let's not quibble over details, it's much more fun to stick to crude generalizations. Rich people would rather go to a shop that sells spoons, visit a plastic surgeon that repairs only eyebrows, and pay hefty fees to a hedge fund investing in exotic strategies, all in search of an above-average experience. They would love it if these services could be delivered in the comfort of their home; I mean making a short trip in their limousine is an inconvenience. What is not inconvenient is to visit far-flung exotic places for exclusive travel experiences; virtual visits are not worth the visit.

This poses a particular problem in matters of the divine. God is the ultimate one-stop for all things; rich and poor alike must bow and pray and wait for His blessings. It's not an attractive proposition for the rich but nevertheless, they play along, and they have nothing to complain about. His blessings are galore for the rich; they are the chosen ones, to lead a luxurious and privileged life, which means they must be doing something right. Robert Own would have wholeheartedly agreed with this statement. He did not solely rely on God. He took his health seriously and did executive physicals once a year, where any test that could be done, did get done. The incidental findings that were found had to be explored and he explored every eventuality. His life was precious, and it was worth the hassle to find even the remotest possibility that could affect his health and wellbeing. It made him anxious and fearful. He wanted to do everything possible to delay the inevitable; he was not keen on dying.

He developed several fears: getting stuck in an elevator, falling into a crevice, swimming in a rip current, and a bird strike on both the jet engines. He reacted by running away from danger: taking stairs where he could, looking down than up, swimming only in a pool, and flying in quad engine planes. It was not easy but if anyone could pull it off, it was him. He was rich and could control his life much better than others. He could choose his holidays, his surgeon, his flight, and the pilot to some extent. What he could not choose was his diseases, his feelings, and his fate. He also chose virtual meetings before they were popular. Human touch was not his thing; he preferred buffering over suffering. The situation was the opposite for his staff, who were expected to be available 24/7 for virtual meetings and feared getting caught without trousers.

The staff were handsomely rewarded for their availability and pursuit of perfection. They were awarded generous stock options, which were tax-efficient and came loaded with conditions. It aligned their careers, wealth, and fate with the corporation. They were part owners and full-time well-wishers of the company stock. The bill of issuing stock options was paid by ordinary shareholders, who saw their shares get diluted by the deluge of employee stock options. Robert Own was no ordinary shareholder. He was the founder and had special provisions in the share structure to protect his dominance. The corporation had different classes of shares. Class A shares were held by Robert, class B shares were held by his family, and class C shares were held by everyone else. The value of class A shares was 100 times more than class B shares, which were in turn 1000 times more than the value of class C shares. He had a firm grip on the corporation, which even the fascist dictators would envy. The activist investors circled the corporation like hungry sharks but all they could chew were the unappetizing class C shares.

The Annual General Meeting (AGM) of the corporation was a nominal but festive affair. It was all about Robert Own and his accomplishments. His admirers in the form of shareholders gathered to pay homage to a financial genius. There was voting for directors and corporate resolutions. All shareholders got ballots to vote in the AGM to influence corporate policy; it was a farce. They had no say whatsoever, but it was made to look democratic. Shareholders didn't mind as they were no crusaders for social change; they were in it for the money, and they made tons of it. They came to celebrate their success and spared no expenses. The meeting was held in a convention hall in downtown Montreal. There were special discounts for the attendees in hotels and they brought goodwill and big valets to help the local economy. There were investing pitches, food stalls, and media at the event. It was at this event that Sadeep and the ghost decided to ambush their illustrious victim.

It was Sunday but Robert Own was working, so were his staff. They had to give the finishing touches to the AGM. Every little detail had to be checked and rechecked. Those with obsessive zeal were chosen to ensure nothing was left to chance. Dress rehearsals were done to avoid any last-minute glitches. The level of preparation was on par with a space shuttle launch and the level of precision was on par with an atomic clock. The meeting started with the Chief Financial Officer presenting financial statements for the year; analysts took notes, creditors took notice, and the audience took yawns. Voting for the directors and the resolutions was held in secrecy but it was a mere formality. What was not a formality was the lineup of speakers heaping praises at Robert Own. It was followed by a documentary on the vision and the future of the company. It put many to tears. Those were the tears of regret. Why didn't we buy the company stock before? Why did we come late to the party? It was better late than never, and they felt privileged in the company of a financial genius and being part of a world-class organization. Thank you address from the host was the highlight of the occasion. Robert Own was given a standing ovation, too many times to count. It was like a State of the Union address, but on steroids, where both sides of the aisle were up on their feet. The noise of clapping was so loud that Robert Own wore earplugs disguised as microphones to prevent hearing loss, but that didn't prevent him from being tone-deaf.

The event was to conclude with a press conference. The media and the analysts asked technical questions about debt-to-equity ratio, future acquisitions, and non-GAAP earnings but there remained a wide gap in what he answered and what others understood. He also took questions from shareholders. They were chosen from an online draw; only two lucky ones were allowed to ask questions. This is where the power of quantum computing came in handy. It was easy for Qubit Preet to hack into the online system and ensure Sadeep's name was chosen to ask the question. The net was drawn, and the prey was slowly but surely coming their way to be caught.

The first shareholder danced his way to the microphone. He was young and in awe of the man.

He asked a perceptive question, which was the only type of question that was allowed. Yes or no type questions were not entertained.

"How do you keep going? Doesn't winning become boring

after a while?"

"Good question. Let me answer it by asking a question: Have you had a failure in life?"

"Not yet, touch wood."

"Trust me, it sucks. The ladder of failure only takes you down. Success is more often than not, a recurring process."

There was clapping, cheering, and another standing ovation for a well-crafted zinger. Sadeep was next. He walked slowly, like a tiger taking a position to pounce on its prey, even though he was hunting a much more powerful enemy than him. He pretended to appear confident but inside his heart was pounding and his mind was racing. It was still less than the anxiety he had about finding a parking spot in downtown Montreal and not scraping the underneath of his low-lying sports car. He took a train to Montreal which had more stops on the way than stop signs in downtown Montreal. He took nothing to chance. He had prepared and rehearsed for it more often than the organizers of the event. He was no method actor, but he believed his method was the right one. He memorized his lines and enacted it in front of a mirror. There were no retakes allowed; he had to give his best in the first and only try. He had done it before but this time stakes were high. He thought of taking a drink or lorazepam or beta-blocker to calm his nerves, but he only took advice from Qubit Preet, who did motivational counseling. He needed moral support as he was entering the lion's den and was about to kick it in its groin. No one recognized him; it worked to his advantage.

"Sir, even a powerful corporation like yours needs help from the government. How do you ensure the help would be there when you need it?"

"Excellent question. You see, access leads to success. I am friends with the Prime Minister. I could call him anytime and he listens, and he acts. He has been kind enough to award us contracts and loans, which frankly we didn't deserve in many cases. We have reciprocated by adjusting his loyalists in our organization, donating to his charities, and taking his entourage on wild rides. It's a well-balanced relationship, and it works for both of us."

It was a long-winded answer, which was what Sadeep was looking for. He had hit the jackpot. It's the beauty of an open-ended question. It allows others to have free reign over their own destruction. There was no applause, only silence. Robert didn't realize what he had said. He had a confident smile which his subordinates did not dare to interrupt. He was like an emperor without clothes. The restlessness in the room led to a commotion. His staff ended the event abruptly and whisked him away from the barrage of media questions. Sadeep headed for the exit. He kept walking straight, avoiding eye contact, and made no impression as he sneaked out of the room. He feared for his safety. He was like a lone Indian cricket fan in a packed Pakistani cricket stadium. He had planned his exit; he ran to the nearest subway station and was out of the danger zone before others could lay hands on him.

Meanwhile, in the conference hall, clean-up was on. The audience slowly dissipated. The reporters were excited; they had got their scoop and it would keep them busy for weeks. Robert Own was informed of his transgression. He did not panic. He was no novice to mistakes. He could handle any situation. He knew from experience that the truth which tasted bitter could be sweetened with humor. He was informed that the guy who trapped him into answering the question was the same one who had started the political scandal with the Prime Minister. He used that to his advantage and recorded a statement:

"I know some people will take my answer to the man who was pretending to be a shareholder at face value. They need to loosen up. I recognized the imposter and decided to play along for fun. I apologize if my attempt at humor has caused any misunderstanding. I have never taken unfair advantage of my friendship with the Prime Minister and nor has he ever pressured me to do anything unethical. I have always acted responsibly in my dealings with any and all of the governments."

He personally rang up the Prime Minister and gave him

the same excuse. He advised the Prime Minister to laugh it off. Laughter was the only way to prevent a disaster. It was not easy for the Prime Minister to laugh when he was not happy, but he was a true politician; his emotions played no part in his public persona. They agreed to coordinate their responses. It was in their best interest to stay united and keep the opposition divided. They knew the focus had to shift from them to the one who was responsible for the scandal. They would ensure questions were asked about the true motive and modus operandi of the man who was wreaking havoc at the highest echelons of power.

CHAPTER FOURTEEN

No Questions Asked

Coincidences don't happen repeatedly. Sadeep was no longer an innocent party. He was at the crime scene more than once. The circumstantial evidence was pointing straight at him. He may have asked innocent appearing questions, but their answers were beyond the realm of what was considered normal behavior. He could no longer hide under the pretense of an innocent questioner. The sharks were after him and he was neck-deep in the water. The media asked the questions first: Who is this guy? What does he want? Is he a spy? Is he a fraud? Who's behind him? The questions were asked nonstop by the networks friendly to the aggrieved parties. The answers were so valuable that there were bidding wars to get them. It was worse than the bidding wars for detached homes in downtown Toronto.

Sadeep was the most sought-after man in Canada. The bidding price had reached seven figures for a thirty-minute interview. The media was desperate to find him, but it was not easy. He was a reclusive person. He had more credit cards than friends in his life. His friends were fellow immigrants whose accents made it difficult for the mainstream media to interpret what they were saying. He did have a social media account, which was flooded with messages, offers, thank you notes, and death threats. He had become a celebrity. His self-esteem had shot off to a geostationary orbit with a focus on him. His disdain for socializing was beginning to ease. He wanted people to recognize him and praise him; a cardinal sign of a newbie celebrity.

Sadeep was back at home safe and sound. He was a general who had come home victorious. He was a one-man army; a guerrilla army. He had done a hit and run job, which didn't involve any alcohol. He watched television and he was proud to see his name on every news channel. It was a dream come true, but what was also true was the messy situation at home. Trash cans were overflowing like Red River in the spring; organics bin was smellier than his armpit; there were more hair on the carpet and the floor than on his head; public toilets were cleaner than his washrooms, and bucket loads of laundry detergent were not enough to remove stains from his clothes. Things on the outside were not any better; people could get lost in his front lawn; there were more cracks in the asphalt driveway than in the Greenland ice sheet; shingles were flying off his roof like toilet paper on supermarket shelves during a pandemic, and his fence was one rodent away from collapsing.

"Can you help me clean up the house?" Sadeep asked.

"I already told you; you are barking up the wrong tree," Qubit Preet said.

"You have power, use some of it."

"I also have dignity and besides, my powers don't extend to the housekeeping domain. It's like asking a pathologist to do brain surgery."

"There's no job that's demeaning."

"That's what winners say to losers."

"Ok then, I would hire housekeepers. Have you seen the offers I am getting?"

"I haven't had the chance to hack into your email."

"You don't have to, I'll tell you. You would be glad to know that truth is not only scary but highly lucrative as well."

"How so?"

"A hedge fund manager is offering me ten million dollars

to interview his prospective wife, in lieu of a prenup."

"Smart guy."

"Media outlets are offering five million dollars for thirty minutes of my time."

"Tricksters."

"Mafia and foreign governments are offering blank cheques for my services."

"I see."

"What do you see?" Sadeep asked.

"You are a marked man," Qubit Preet said.

"I am not afraid anymore."

Sadeep went outside to cut the grass and root out the weeds, which were growing faster than his fame. He was in the grass-cutting attire: a pajama, t-shirt, slippers. He had un-combed hair and an untrimmed beard; he was going to do manual labor and there was no point in looking handsome. He readied the manual lawn mower, which was cheap and easy to use. As soon as he got out of the garage, he was photographed, and a bunch of microphones came right up to his face. He got poked in the eye by the microphones but no sorry was said by the aggressive reporters; however, he kept saying sorry and thank you to get out of their clutches. It was his first brush with fame, and it was not what he expected. His privacy was invaded, and his excitement was jaded. He had a red eye, which he caressed with water.

"I am going to sue the hell out of them," Sadeep kept mumbling to himself. There were curses and less charitable words which are best left to the imagination.

As a celebrity, he could not just walk out of his home. He had to plan his outings. He had to get dressed every time. He had to put his best foot forward, which meant no more shabby shoes. He had to hide his emotions, which was easy with black goggles. His attire had to be appropriate every time; no more offensive t-shirts; no more skinny jeans, which made his legs look like drumsticks. It was like going on a date every single day. The pressure was on him and so were the layers of makeup.

The media didn't give up; they were a tough bunch. They nudged the neighbors, who smelled of jealousy. The answers remained elusive as the guy in question was found to be reclusive. He was like an enigma machine whose code only he knew. His family was also hounded but they were in the dark as well. His sister told the media that Sadeep was a boring man who couldn't excite even a squirrel and as for special powers, his only power was to suck the air out of a party. It was harsh but she was telling the truth and defending her brother. Her parents answered in a simple but effective way, "No English."

Curiosity is a kind of animal that grows when left hungry. In the age of information overload, lack of information on Sadeep was making the media go berserk. The situation was ripe for conspiracy theories. They are like wildfire; no one knows who starts them, but they spread fast and are hard to tame. The most outlandish theories attract the most fervent followers, who cannot be reasoned with. The alien theory was conceived on forums and blogs. It took a life of its own. The proponents pointed to the circumstantial evidence, which proved their case beyond any doubt. His robot-like behavior corroborated their hypothesis. He was either an alien in human form or a human with an alien transmitter. They proposed that confirmatory evidence could be obtained by opening up Sadeep's brain. However, there was a problem: the law. But that didn't stop the alien aficionados to come up with a plan to dissect his brain and search for alien interference. It was a long shot, but they took themselves seriously when others did not.

Ultra-nationalists down south got worried about national security. They always were but it was code red for them. The United States and Canada shared the largest undefended border in the world and if it was not for practicality and money and common sense, they would have built a border wall all along the border. Since the border was porous, they had to pay attention to what was happening in Canada. What if the guy had asked questions to a US politician? It could have destroyed a political career. Another foreign actor, another election interference, another impeachment; no one was ready for a political nightmare.

It was not just elections; no secret would be secure. The American national security establishment had not seen a threat like that since the advent of e-mail servers. National security hawks considered Canada as the 51st state of the United States, notwithstanding the war of 1812. Canadian politicians pushed back, reminded the US politicians politely to mind their own business. Politeness was a sign of weakness; that's what the US security hawks saw, and they carried on with their plans. A draft proposal was made to liquidate the dangerous asset and it was awaiting the President's signature. It was a contingency plan that could be activated if required. The plan was code-named operation "Wisdom Tooth"; an appropriate name for a painful but necessary removal.

There was a problem in the implementation of the operation Wisdom Tooth. If far-right was bent on making the US government a hitman for its interests, the left was lobbying for Sadeep to be conferred awards, from Nobel prize to the Presidential Medal of Freedom. It was quite a range for the President to work through, who decided to play it safe and did nothing. He was asked at every press conference to comment, and he had a standard answer which he repeated verbatim, "We are carefully watching the situation. There are more questions than answers and we are seeking those answers from our closest ally, Canada. I want to assure all Americans that they are safe and secure and everything possible will be done to keep it that way."

The politicians in Washington were not satisfied with the diplomatic answer from the President. They knew it was wordplay and meant nothing. They wanted action and in Washington, it meant convening committees, hearings, witnesses, drama, and the like. The House and the Senate intelligence committees scheduled hearings and summoned the CIA director and the Director of National Intelligence. The members were briefed in secret by them, but a public spectacle was necessary to show something was being done. There was a suggestion to summon Sadeep but a wise and experienced Senator cautioned against it.

What if he started asking questions? Tables could turn and if an inadvertent truth came out, their political careers could end in front of live cameras. The risks were too high, and it was decided to forgo summoning him. There was a bipartisan consensus on that. A bipartisan bill was working its way through Congress. It called for a ban on any revelation of truth through "unnatural means." The bill was as clear as a nursery rhyme, but it was as hard to implement as prohibition.

It was not just the land of the free and the home of the brave, which was worried about unsolicited truth, all countries had reservations. They made it clear to the Prime Minister of Canada, who was receiving phone calls from world leaders, big and small. Canada was host to G7 and G20 meetings that year and the clouds of truth were hanging over the meetings. What if Sadeep showed up at the meetings and started asking questions left and right? World leaders expressed their sympathy with the Prime Minister, who himself had been burned by the truth. They sought reassurance from him that he would shed light on the matter. He listened to them patiently and advised them to be patient as well. He gave a statement that every politician understood, "We'll get at the bottom of this."

The world was not waiting. Politicians and governments work at warp speed when their interests are at stake. Dictators, despots, and royals were at an advantage; they didn't have to put up with questions from reporters or anyone else for that matter. They only asked questions even in the normal state of affairs, but these were unprecedented times and so they issued decrees that no one would ask them any questions. The moratorium created question-free zones around them, where asking a question amounted to asking for trouble. They decided to self-isolate themselves in their question free bubbles. The contagion spread to democracies and quasi-democracies alike. National security was used as an excuse to explain their actions and the President of the United States had the biggest excuse of them all. It was not only the secrets that were unsafe, but the jury was also still out if mind control could be exercised by an individual like Sadeep. No one was taking any chances. The White House press conferences were reduced to a mere formality where the press secretary jotted down questions and had a ready-made answer, "I would get back to you on that."

There was an outcry. Journalists took to the streets. News anchors pounded their desks. They were joined by a plethora of prominent lawyers but for a different reason. How could they defend a client by speaking the truth and only the truth? There would be no need for trials. The accused would incriminate themselves. They had as much right to lie as everyone else. The critics lambasted those lawyers that they were more concerned about their fees than for the fairness of the accused. Who would pay insane legal fees when the truth no longer needed to be twisted? It was not only lawyers who were facing extinction, the manufacturers of lie detectors were in deep trouble. They would be put out of business. It was not fair; liars put food on their table and were essential to their existence. Marketing professionals were in a panic. How could marketing be done without flexing the truth? Marketing without exaggeration would be like Indian curry without spices. The most worried lot were religious leaders and priests. Who would come to them for a confession? There would be no need to put a hand on a religious book to speak the truth. Taking God out of the business of truth would be a sin.

Not everyone was upset, of course, truth suited those who were asking questions from the position of authority. Police were gleeful. No need to torture to get a confession unless it was fabricated. "Were you going over the speed limit?" would take care of many municipal budget shortfalls. Immigration and customs would see people declare their goods and those with illegal articles would either refrain or surrender themselves. "What's the purpose of your visit?" would make visa issuance easier. Judges and jury would only need to look in the eye of the accused and ask, "Are you guilty?" Justice would not be delayed but it could still be denied, at least in certain jurisdictions. Innocents would still be hanged. An innocent person speaking the truth would not work if the verdict was preordained. Sham trials would still go on.

Truth is not a swiss knife that cuts through everything, but it does cut through the crap. It can help untangle the bond between love and lust. That's what the rich were hoping for. "Honey, are you in it for the money?" would save a lot of money and misery for the rich. It required some degree of courage to ask this question, which was not a problem for the rich. It only became a problem if courage was needed for let's say a military draft. Rich and famous would have additional benefits. They would get a straight answer to the question they most often asked their money manager, "Where is my money?" There had to be some amount of give and take, that's what paparazzi were hoping for. If celebrities could speak the truth about their affairs and their real feelings about working with their directors and co-stars, it would be a bonanza for the gossip magazines, which worked day and night to entertain people and reminded them that there were more miserable souls than them.

There were winners, there were losers, and there were those who didn't give a hoot. It was all speculation as nothing of consequence had happened to anyone save the people who were questioned by Sadeep. Nevertheless, it was worth fighting for and the fighting was taking place on social media. Trolls were ready with spam messages and ensured every user saw them repeatedly. Moderators were exhausted and AI was confused; viral videos were being generated and lies were being spread. Social media companies saw record engagement and revenues; their shareholders saw record profits. Traditional media was not far behind; there was extensive coverage and there was special programming on the nature, value, and revelation of truth. TV ratings went through the roof and so were the shouting and screaming by the hosts and the guests alike. There were passionate debates and indifferent attitudes and unceremonious exits.

TV channels called hypnotists and psychologists and neuroscientists and astrologers and those who were considered experts at giving opinions on anything and everything. Each had their own theory and version of events, which differed vehemently from the other. Physicists were notably absent from the expert panel who filled the airways. Physicists dismissed the entire exercise as mass hysteria and took pains to explain that the standard model and the quantum field theory couldn't allow for such ludicrous versions of events. Physicists didn't have the answers, but they begged the public to at least ask the right questions. Public and the tv networks had no interest in hearing their sermon, and so they were tuned out.

Truth dominated the conversation and became the most searched word on the internet. The literary world took notice and there was a race to publish books on anything related to truth and its implications. Streaming sites went full steam ahead to make web series focusing on truth and mind control. Late-night shows and stand-up comedians made spoofs of politicians caught speaking the truth. It was not all, the public was still hungry for more. Con artists smelled an opportunity to fool people and they were ready with their game plan. Advertisements claiming to extract the truth from one's enemies or friends through proprietary gadgets spammed e-mail and e-commerce sites.

A truth transmitter for $ 9.99; an affordable starter kit. It had to be placed on the subject to be compelled to speak the truth. It came in the form of a sticker, which could be placed on a lump of fat, preferably on a tummy or buttocks for optimal results. It presented a whole different set of problems. The truth spray was convenient to use but cost $ 29.99; a relative bargain. Options were many from tasty truth cookies to sparkling truth wine costing $99.99. There were lots of reviews that swore to their effectiveness, which lured customers and enticed con artists to go come up with more ways to dupe people. It presented a problem to authorities. They couldn't stop the sales, so they required a warning label on the products, "Claims of this product remain scientifically unproven." Sellers were fine with this requirement as they buried it in the fine print.

The fear of truth was creating fissures in societies. They

were being filled with paranoia and censorship. Any answer given to a question under duress, which was defined as interference in free will, was made a crime deserving strict punishment. The rules were first adopted in countries where the free fill was an afterthought. It had a chilling effect, which was felt even in the tropics. People stopped asking questions. They stopped receiving information unless it had a disclaimer: no question was asked to obtain this information. The right to information was replaced by the duty to be ignorant. It was too embarrassing to be enshrined into the constitution, but it was implemented with religious zeal. Informal guidelines were issued to ensure compliance.

Truth squads roamed the streets and did random checks on people. They were given permission to ask only one question to people, "Have you asked any question to anyone today?" An affirmative response meant a court date and if the question was posed to a stranger, an immediate arrest was made. "Can I ask you a question?" was still considered a question and thus prohibited. It posed practical problems. People stopped asking for directions. There were maps to take care of that but finding the location of washrooms became a rushed and frustrating affair. It led to changes in restaurants and offices where directions to washrooms were written in bold and capital letters at every nook and corner. Social norms had to change to accommodate the culture of not asking questions. "What's your name?" and "Where did you get this jacket?" were no longer available to start small talk. Information had to be voluntary and spontaneous. People learned; facial expressions and body language replaced the need for asking questions.

The problems didn't end there. Teachers were livid. How were they supposed to test their pupils without asking questions? They didn't get any support from parents, who were scared about teachers asking questions about what went on at home. Teachers reminded them that information was shared both ways; parent-teacher meetings became a slugfest. Students demanded exams to be postponed and they were. The situation was untenable. People were asking for special passes to ask questions. Some governments listened and the Ministry of Exemptions was set up, which was responsible for drawing out a list of allowable questions. It also drafted the eligibility criterion for asking those questions.

It was not only the human beings that were affected; love birds had a terrible time. "Will you marry me?" was left out of the allowable questions, instead a marriage proposal had to be sent to the government and if and only if no objection was stamped, the question could be posed. The questions that were explicit in nature were banned altogether. Lovers were daring and nothing, not even warnings from ex-lovers could stop them. They were joined by those who had no interest in love but every interest in lust. There were one on one meetings and small and large gatherings.

It posed a health risk. People were reluctant to go to doctors, who had their own issues about asking questions. Medical questions were allowed but social questions were censored. Abuse history was omitted and so was addiction history. "Where did you get these drugs?" could not be asked. It took longer for doctors to go through the medical history as they had to navigate the minefield of questions. It made getting consent easy. "Do you have any questions about the procedure?" was made redundant and so was the question, "Doctor, do you think this is serious?"

When would this nightmare end? This question was still allowed, and it was asked by almost everyone. The answer remained elusive. The guy who could shed some light on the matter was holed up like a rat in his house. The patience of people was wearing thin. Leaders were tired of calling the Prime Minister of Canada, who kept advising them to wait and watch. It was like watching a movie that was stuck at pause. If it was stuck at a pretty face, it would have been different, but it had stopped just before the climax. There was a heated debate at the United Nations Security Council and a resolution was put forward to compel Canada to allow international experts to investigate the phenomenon of truth revelation against free will; failing which sanctions would be imposed against Canada. All major powers were for the resolution but for the United States, which vetoed the resolution.

The United States considered North America as part of its exclusive domain and allowing international observers would have been a major embarrassment. It didn't mean America was letting Canada off the hook. The United States Congress authorized the President to take all necessary steps to ensure the safety of the American people and to engage with Canada to ensure free will which had helped mankind to come this far, remained alive and well. The President appointed a special envoy to Canada, who arrived in Ottawa to gauge the situation. He didn't come empty-handed. He had a bouquet of promises in one hand and a garland of threats in the other. The stakes were high; stick and carrot were inadequate for the occasion. Canada wanted access to markets for its products and the United States wanted access to classified information.

The special envoy Mr. Green Oilfield was an experienced negotiator. He was familiar with the Canadian psyche. He had spent time in Canada as a CEO of an energy company. He had to navigate the Canadian bureaucracy, which was as slow as an oil tanker, and environmental activists, who were as tenacious as tar sands. He was embraced by Alberta politicians like a long-lost sibling. The warmth was not reciprocated in Quebec where he got booed by local politicians, who disliked his love for fossil fuel. He understood the East-West divide in Canada. It was as ugly as the Red-Blue divide in the United States. Alberta desperately needed its oil to be transported to oil refineries down south, but it was not easy; it was a political and legal quagmire. The oil pipeline was stuck in legal limbo. It resulted in Canada's crude being sold at below-market prices and it also meant huge losses for the oil sector.

Mr. Oilfield had a plan; it involved setting up a brand-new state-of-the-art oil refinery in Alberta. The United States would grant generous loans to set up the refinery. He had letters of support from the leaders of both political parties in the United States Congress, who had promised to pass legislation to that effect. That was not all; the tariffs on Canadian softwood lumber would be rescinded. It was too good to be true and it probably was, but the plan was presented with the authenticity of a street vendor. It was not all lovey-dovey between the two sides. Mr. Oilfield enumerated the consequences of non-cooperation. Visa-free travel would end; snowbirds would have to find their nest somewhere else. The free trade agreement would be suspended, and the United States would establish a permanent naval base in the Arctic and monitor traffic across the Northwest Passage; it was outrageous but that was the whole point. The Prime Minister pleaded for more time and explained to him that his own survival was at stake. Once he ensured his survival, meeting American demands would be his first and only priority. Mr. Oilfield gave him the benefit of doubt but reminded him that the clock was ticking.

The Director of the Canadian Security Intelligence Service (CSIS) was summoned by the Prime Minister. CSIS was not a glamorous organization like CIA or MI5 but that worked in its favor; discretion was its strength and secrecy at low cost was its unofficial motto. The director had seen it all, from UFO sightings to alien abduction to fake moon landings. Politicians wanted CSIS to investigate stuff like that and waste limited resources on a goose chase. He had a similar feeling about this truth revelation nonsense. He was dressed like a bureaucrat, he behaved like a bureaucrat and in all probability, he was a bureaucrat. He needed to be a bureaucrat as he had to push pencils to get his agenda across to politicians. Nothing was interesting about his looks except his eyeglasses, which were thick as a wall and made his eyes look smaller. It was hard to fathom if he could see clearly with those thick glasses but that was a deception; his perception of sight and situational awareness was at least two standard deviations higher than the average.

The director was shown into the Prime Minister's office. It was a large office, embellished with hand-crafted wooden furniture made in Canada. There were large paintings depicting Canadian history and political events, but the portraits of John Envy's parents loomed large over the others. It was ensured that everything in the room was made in Canada except the computer, the router, the telephone, the fax machine, wiring, the table lamp, pens, pencils, and security cams. The Canadian flag was made in Canada; not all of it but after carefully applying complex rules of origin, it was certified to be a Canadian-made flag. The Prime Minister was busy typing on the computer; he was using only one finger to do the typing. These were the sort of things that were noted by the director.

"Good morning, sir."

"Good morning. Sit down, Sam."

"I got briefed by your staff. I have brought everything we have on the man."

"So, what do you think is going on?"

"We have checked his phone records, his internet records, financial dealings, and his movements."

"And."

"Nothing suspicious so far."

"How's that possible?"

"Sir, I don't know but it's clear that there is no conspiracy or foreign power or organization behind him."

"The world has gone upside down. I am getting calls from foreign leaders every day. Americans are on my back. I need answers. How would you explain this hoopla?" The Prime Minister was about to break a pencil in his hand.

"Mass hysteria?"

"Do you want me to tell this to Americans? That's not good enough," the Prime Minister said, shaking his head.

"Sir, what do you want me to do?" Sam kept a poker face.

"Why don't you interrogate him? Use whatever degrees you have to use."

"Excuse me."

"Don't act innocent. It's not the first time."

"Sir, he is surrounded by the media everywhere. We have no probable cause to arrest him."

"What about a covert operation?"

"Again, it's impossible to arrest him without drawing attention. We could bug his home, which may give us some clues about his motives. But I need authorization."

"National Security Act has sufficient leeway to allow you to do these sorts of things. You have my permission."

"Thank you, sir."

The Prime Minister got busy typing with his finger again. It was time for Sam to go but he couldn't help but notice that the Prime Minister was doing online shopping on websites with dubious repute. He wanted to say something, but it was not the right time. He would indirectly pass on the message to his staff to clear the cookies and rinse the computer with a thorough antivirus scan. A ransomware attack would be costly and embarrassing to the government. He was however more worried about his own future. He was being asked to bend the rules to spy on a Canadian citizen; it was fraught with risk. He had to carry all the risk; if something went wrong, he alone would be blamed, but if it succeeded, the Prime Minister would take the credit.

He had seen this movie play out before; politicians did that to bureaucrats, but he was an experienced fellow. He made meticulous notes and kept all official correspondence and directions from the Prime Minister in case things went wrong. No verbal orders from the Prime Minister would be entertained. He however gave verbal orders to his agents, who would carry the risk for him. Odds were against him, but he was trying to spread those odds; if the ship of state was to sink, he would ensure he had a lifeboat, and the role of the captain of the Titanic would be assumed by the Prime Minister.

CHAPTER FIFTEEN

Paying the Price

Sadeep was having the time of his life despite being confined to his home. He was relaxed and felt confident. The same could not be said of the reporters who were camped outside his home or the spies waiting in the parked cars on the streets with parking tickets sticking out of their windshields. There were dozens of spy satellites zooming in on his house. Neighbors were not thrilled either; parking on the street became nonexistent, noise from the moving cars was a nuisance and they had to drive within the speed limit as cop cars were always lingering around.

He enjoyed this attention, but he got bored of it after a while. He stopped watching news. Watching movies was becoming stale and he had grown out of playing video games. He liked reading books, but he had to cut them short due to recurring headaches. He was under a self-imposed house arrest. He had to get out to get some fresh air. He didn't want to go too far. The local shopping mall was his camping ground and he found it cathartic to do some shopping and contribute to the economic growth of the country. He wore a baseball cap, put on the sunglasses, fired up the V8, and whisked away in front of the onlookers.

He was recognized but not acknowledged by people in the

mall. They knew who he was, but they were too scared to confront him. They glanced at him from a distance and moved on quickly. Sadeep could sense that; it was not normal behavior; it was the sort of behavior typically seen on the roads when cars slowed down on seeing a cop car. His home was empty, but he had set the alarm, which was not a problem for the spies to enter; the real problem was the media and the live streaming that went on 24/7. It was too risky to go in and hence the plan was abandoned.

The spies also followed Sadeep into the mall but kept their distance. Sadeep entered a departmental store. He needed new trousers and shirts. Sitting at home and munching on snacks had increased his Body Mass Index; he had to pull up his trousers and tuck in his shirt frequently, which was not a pleasant sight. He went to the change room, selected a pair of trousers and shirts, paid for it, and checked out without any incident. The spies had to trace his footsteps. They made a note of people he interacted with and who would be later interrogated for any anomalous behavior. The spies went into the change room with a Geiger counter to check for any radiation, which could explain his powers. There was none but they collected the data anyways. They were perplexed with the science stuff they had to do; they had never done it before, and it was beyond their comfort zone but those were the orders. Sadeep had his coffee and donuts and sat in the food court for a while, contemplating what had become of him. He was watching people but soon realized that people were watching him as well. He felt uneasy, got up, and threw the remainder of the coffee and the donut in the open garbage bin.

"I need his cup and donut," the senior spy said.

"Yes, Sir," the junior spy said with a grimace as he wore gloves and put the items in a black bag.

They had to be quick; they couldn't afford to lose sight of Sadeep, who was heading to the washroom. The junior spy sighed, "Oh no!" He knew what was coming. He too entered the washroom and came back with a disgusting look on his face.

Sadeep's hands were full of shopping bags, and it was time to head home. His car as usual was parked way back in the parking lot. He rushed to get there as his hands were barely holding on to the shopping bags. He was halfway through when two SUVs blocked his way: one at the front and the other at the back. Both SUVs had tinted glasses. Two men got out of the front SUV: they were tall, muscular, menacing, and stone-faced. Jim was in a t-shirt and shorts and his arms were filled with tattoos. Garry was in a t-shirt and jeans and had a big scar on his cheek.

"You need to come with us," Jim said.

"Why should I?" Sadeep said.

"Because I am the one with a gun." Jim pulled out a handgun and pointed at him. Spies were watching at a distance, but they didn't have a clear view of what was going on.

"I have my rights," Sadeep said.

"I don't give a damn," Jim answered with an attitude.

It dawned on Sadeep that these guys were not working for law enforcement. He was alarmed but did not panic. If these guys had guns, he had a ghost, and no bullet could ever harm a ghost.

"Who are you?" Sadeep asked with a shaky voice.

"We deliver people, alive, sometimes dead, for money of course," Jim said.

"Why me?"

Both guys looked at each other and smiled.

"Now that's a dumb question," Garry said.

"Are you guys friends?" Sadeep asked.

"Yes, we are," Jim said, pointing at Garry. "We always have a good time together."

"Like what?"

"I enjoy my time with him and his wife," Jim winked. "You know what I mean."

"What the....," Gary said as he pulled out his handgun.

Sadeep saw an opportunity to use truth as a weapon and interjected, "Have you slept with his wife?"

"Yes, I have," Jim answered.

Shots were fired; two shots stuck Jim. He was down on the ground. One bullet hit Garry's arm; he was bleeding profusely. Other guys came out of the SUVs and pulled both men inside and fled as fast as they could. In the commotion, Sadeep was left behind. He had a shot to the left side of his chest and was bleeding profusely as well. He was lying on the ground badly wounded but awake.

"Am I going to die?" Sadeep mumbled.

"I am not a doctor," Qubit Preet said.

"I thought you would save me."

"I have no such powers. You would be saved by professionals, not a freaking ghost. Now zip it, people are coming."

Spies rushed to help. They were more nervous than Sadeep; if he died, they could be held liable and lose their jobs or worse. They called an ambulance and tried to stop the bleeding with hand pressure. They did put some blood in a test tube. The ambulance came within five minutes, and he was rushed to a local hospital. The ER doctor realized his injuries were serious and arranged an airlift to a tertiary care hospital in Toronto. He was taken straight away into the operating room. The trauma surgeon was concerned; the wound was too close to the heart. Sadeep's blood pressure was low and falling; his heart rate was high and rising. He was given IV fluids to stabilize his vitals, but he needed blood, which was in short supply. His blood group came back as AB positive. "Lucky guy," the trauma surgeon remarked. His vitals stabilized once blood transfusion was started.

The trauma surgeon was ready with his scalpel, but he had one last thing to do. He looked at the chest x-ray to find out where the bullet was lodged.

"Oh, my word," the trauma surgeon said. "He's the luckiest guy alive. Erica, what do you see on the x-ray?"

"He's got dextrocardia," the surgical resident answered.

"His heart points to the right side," the trauma surgeon remarked. "He has his heart in the right place."

It was a quirky joke, and no one laughed except him. It was the norm in his operating room. He removed the bullet from the chest and inserted a chest tube. Sadeep was transferred to the ICU overnight but was moved to the surgical ward in the morning as his condition improved. The surgeon gave him the good news and prophesied he would be out of the hospital in a week. He was kept in an isolation room, not because of the contagion risk but for the security risk. A cop guarded the room around the clock. Visitors were kept to a minimum and only the immediate family was allowed. His parents and sister came to visit him and brought their fear and disappointment with them. Visiting hours were limited and he was thankful for that.

The spies gave their briefing to the Director of CSIS along with an analysis of the test reports. They revealed nothing. He was disappointed and reprimanded them for their lapse in judgment and allowing a deadly attack on Sadeep. He was himself reprimanded by the Prime Minister for the intelligence failure. The director defended himself and the agency; negative results also meant something. There was nothing special about Sadeep. A thorough analysis of his blood and DNA was completely normal except for borderline glucose, which could be explained by his dietary habits and sedentary lifestyle. As far as the attack was concerned, the director was more direct. He pointed out that the crime was revealing, and it revealed the vulnerability of Sadeep. He was a mere mortal and there was no need to fear such a man. The Prime Minister was not fully satisfied but he had something to tell the Americans and the other world leaders who were harassing him daily. The director saved his job and so did the spies but the same could not be said of the Prime Minister as a political storm was brewing in Ottawa.

Sadeep was happy to be alive but was disappointed in the ghost. If he had known that the ghost was a one-trick pony, he would have taken precautions for his safety. The fault was entirely his; at no time did the ghost promise him safety from goons or bullets. He assumed to his detriment that having a ghost friend confers some kind of immortality. He learned the hard way not to speculate either on money or on ghosts.

"Can we talk in here?" Sadeep asked.

"Don't worry old boy," Qubit Preet said. "There are no bugs in this room, neither artificial nor microbial. When we go back home, we would have to debug the whole place."

"What if I had died?"

"You would have become a martyr."

"I like the sound of that."

"Do you know who's better than a martyr?"

"I don't know."

"A hero."

"I like that even better."

"As far as I can see, you have no reason to be disappointed," Qubit Preet said.

"You are probably right," Sadeep said. "I shouldn't dwell upon it. What should we do with the Prime Minister?"

"We can't do anything. You are sick and you wouldn't be allowed anywhere near the Prime Minister. I must say I am astounded by the response we have got from our exposes. I am proud of what we have achieved so far. Seeing all those scared faces makes this endeavor worthwhile."

"What happens now?"

"Events have taken a life of their own. Our job is mostly done; enjoy the show."

Siyasat was in India when she heard the news of the attack on Sadeep. Her initial response was one of validation, "He deserved it for ruining my career." It was his karma that had brought him closer to the doors of death, but she didn't want him to die; that would be overkill. On reflection, she felt bad for thinking that way. She was superstitious by nature; insecure people usually are. She had to repent for her sins. It was easy; being in India, opportunities were plenty. She went on a religious tour and sought forgiveness, strength, happiness, and success. She didn't hold back in asking from God. People of Punjab didn't hold back either; they embraced her with open arms. She was a celebrity and was floored by their hospitality. She didn't expect such a warm reception considering she was no longer a minister. She thought a politician without power was like a fused bulb, good for nothing. She was happy to be wrong on that account. She realized that Punjabis, apart from eating good food and giving a good fight, adored those who spoke truth to power. She was coerced into speaking the truth but never mind that; she was a shrewd politician and was willing to accept any credit even if it was not due.

It was her first visit to India. She had always asked her parents to take her to India, but they were busy running the business and had no time for an extended vacation. She found Punjab to be colorful: predominantly green in color, which was the color of paddy fields. She got teary-eyed looking at the paddy fields; it was not due to overwhelming emotions, but due to the smoke that was coming from burning stubble in the fields. She imagined India to be like what was portrayed in Hollywood movies. She was expecting snake charmers and elephants on roads, but all she saw was rickshaw pullers texting while pulling. There were stray dogs and cows alright, but not in the numbers she expected. She could not find any muddy huts but there were plenty of palatial houses.

She found capitalism alive and kicking; if there were lots of beggars, there were also plenty of wealthy who in their high-end cars gave the unfortunate ones plenty of opportunities to pitch their pleas. The stifling traffic and chaos on the streets were no problems for her. She was given a police escort vehicle and its siren was loud enough to scare away the commuters and they knew who had the right of way. She became aware of the VIP culture in India. She had nothing to complain about; she had the VIP pass; doors opened quickly and widely for her wherever she went. She was a politician and was eager to meet local politicians to reinforce her credentials as a VIP. It made for a pleasant visit.

The villages were a world apart from her life in Canada. People were open and so were their doors. They locked it only at night. She got their unadulterated love along with unadulterated milk and butter. She was inundated with requests for facilitating visas to Canada. She had been a minister and was still a member of Parliament. Her recommendation carried weight. She explained her delicate position, but they were in no mood to listen. Their relationship with Siyasat was about to get sour. Siyasat had become a seasoned politician; she made vague promises, which were sufficient to keep her hosts happy. She had made plans to go on a pan-India pilgrimage, but her plans were cut short by happenings back in Canada. Ottawa was under a storm watch; and it was the type of storm where the affected ran into it, not away from it.

She said goodbye to Punjab but not quite; there were many so-called mini or little Punjabs and one of them was in Southall, UK. She had a layover in the UK; she visited her uncle there, but the real reason for her visit was to meet an MP. It was not a member of parliament, but a man of possibilities who she was desperate to meet. He was highly recommended by his uncle. He made things happen; he called them possibilities powered by the power of probabilities. He was a statistician who couldn't get a job in the UK after he immigrated. He spent his time pondering over the probability of his success, but he soon had an epiphany: it was much more lucrative to opine on other's future than his.

He catered to the elites, who were already successful, and the probability of their success was higher anyways; he added his two cents in return for thousands of dollars. They were looking for reassurance which he provided in the form of customized probability, that was wrapped in a veneer of science. His fees were high, but a discount was given to those who wrote rave reviews. Siyasat's dad rolled his eyes when she insisted on seeing this man and advised Siyasat to stay away from this hocus pocus. She had a simple response, "Advice noted." She visited his office in Soho; she had to fill a questionnaire and complete an aptitude test. The results came in the form of an envelope. She was excited to open the envelope like a fortune cookie and hoped that it would be sweet; the word "PM" was written inside. She understood the meaning and was elated. She paid the fee, wrote a five-star review, got her discount, and felt ready to climb Parliament Hill.

CHAPTER SIXTEEN

An Echo Chamber

It was fall, leaves were falling and so were temperatures. That was not the case on Parliament Hill, where acrimony and friction kept the temperature high. Many political careers were about to fall; they were hanging on till the next election. Fall is the election season in Canada, more or less. Canadians don't engage with politicians when they could go fishing at the cottage. That's what happens during the summer. Summers are short in Canada and voters have no patience in listening to long and boring speeches from politicians. Any politician who dares to call an election in the middle of summer and wants Canadians to cut short their well-deserved summer vacation is asking for trouble. An angry voter at the ballot box is not a good prospect for any incumbent. Winter on the other hand is brutal and not conducive to electioneering. Standing in line in -10c to vote is not fun. Spring is unpredictable and may or may not deliver on its premise, like a politician. There are always outliers as opportunity trumps conventional wisdom. A politician who doesn't avail an opportunity when it presents itself is left only with regret.

Politics is a zero-sum game, where participants are looking to checkmate others. If someone gets into trouble, others lend their hand, not to help but to snatch the valuables. Expressing gratitude for a retiring colleague is a code name for good riddance. There was no dearth of people who wanted to express their gratitude to the Prime Minister for his services, only if he could go away for good. John Envy had been Prime Minister for too long. It was not fair that he was stuck in the prime minister's chair like a tick. He had to be removed one way or the other; one way was if he resigned on his own, which was as likely as a Canadian team winning the Stanley cup. The only other way was to remove him through a no-confidence motion. It required the co-operation of all the members of Her Majesty's opposition.

Mr. Wright offered an olive branch to Dr. Green, and she readily accepted it. They deliberated various options, whether to go for the jugular or go the thousand cut route. It meant choosing between a no-confidence motion and a public inquiry. The public enquiry option was enticing; it would ensure drip, drip, drip of bad news for the government. It was a risky move and there was no guarantee that the outcome would favor them. If the government appointed a person of their choice to head the inquiry, which was highly likely, all bets were off. The other danger was that the news cycle could change, and people would tune out the non-answers given by politicians and bureaucrats at the public inquiry. The no-confidence motion was a better bet, though they were not confident if it would pass. It was decided to go the non-confidence way; the battle lines were drawn.

The fate of the minority government was dependent on the four independent members of Parliament. One was a former conservative member and he had declared that he would support the no-confidence motion. The other three had supported the government in the past and were likely to support the government this time as well. But their support like the Canadian weather was not guaranteed. Each asked for a favor: government investment in an electric car plant; a subway extension line; and funding for a local hospital. The price tag of their demands was in billions of dollars. The Prime Minister was willing to do the deal as he was offering promises and nothing more; promises didn't cost anything. He was used to making promises all the time and then breaking them from time to time. The independent members of Parliament were aware of this predicament, but they had no choice; it was an uphill task for them to win again on an independent ticket and it was wise to take whatever was offered.

Siyasat was in a bind. She was still in the party and was obligated by the whip of the party. Voting against the no-confidence motion would be an about-face for her. It would dent her credibility. Defying the whip would throw her out of the party and a politician without a party was like a writer without a publisher. Her ambition to run for the party leadership would be dealt a death blow. She did not have sufficient information to make a decision. If the government was to survive, she would vote for the motion as she saw no future in a party with John Envy at the helm. On the other hand, if the government was to fall, she would jump on the sinking ship to be a savior of the party. It was her plan, and she kept her cards close to her chest. The whip's office did call her as they were tallying their votes, but she gave an unequivocal maybe as the answer. She would decide after the debate; it was frustrating for the Prime Minister but with the support of the three independents, he was comfortable in letting her go.

Tempers were running high inside and outside the Parliament. There were plenty of protesters outside; they were outnumbered by the police by 2 to 1 and by the reporters by 3 to 1. The world media took an interest; Halloween scary nights were replaced by Parliamentary proceedings in run-up to the debate on the no-confidence motion. The focus on Canada cleared certain misconceptions about the country. Many outsiders were unaware that Ottawa, not Toronto, was the capital of Canada; not all RCMP officers patrolled on horses; it didn't snow all year round in Canada, at least not in Southern Canada; speaking French was essential in Quebec; Canada was not all wilderness; and Canadians though polite, were touchy about being pushed around.

The no-confidence debate started with the backbenchers

and moved up to the leadership level. The speeches were blatantly partisan, which was business as usual. There was a hint
that something was wrong: each speech ended with an admission, "We aren't any better." It was mumbled at the end of
the speech, which was not picked up by the microphones ini-
tially but with each subsequent speaker, it kept getting louder
and louder. It was not the only thing that was odd: claps were
noticeably absent, so were the smiles and so were the standing
ovations. There was a somber atmosphere in the House as if they
were attending a funeral. The speakers were reluctant to begin
and eager to end. No one asked for extra time; speeches were
short and kept getting shorter. It was up to the party leaders to
wrap up the debate.

Dr. Green started the debate with a passionate appeal
for environmental causes and her disdain for big business. She
linked the two together. The bigger the business, the bigger
would be its carbon footprint. She chastised the government for
cutting taxes while ignoring the cutting of trees. She kept repeating, "It's not fair."

"No one should be allowed to get rich; it's not fair. No one
should be allowed to keep getting elected; it's not fair. This government has lost trust. It has lost credibility, and I am confident
it will lose the next election as well. That's why we introduced
the no-confidence motion. I don't really care if he or his chief of
staff are bullies; to some extent we all are; that's how party discipline is maintained. But what I am troubled by is his closeness
to big business. I admit our party is close to labor unions, but
that's like comparing apples and oranges. Special interest groups
are ubiquitous in politics and it's only fair that we share closeness to labor groups, who only ask for fair working conditions.
The wealthy on the other hand want everything for themselves,
just like the Prime Minister. We need to destroy the big business
by raising taxes sky-high. We want to shrink the oil industry, the
lumber industry, and the auto industry. If the economy suffers,
so be it; that's the price of a fair society. I know we won't form the
next government, but I am hoping we would be big enough to

play spoilsport. Thank you, Madam Speaker, for allowing me the opportunity to share my views."

She sat down and was expecting her caucus to give her a raucous standing ovation. No one stood up or uttered a word; however, she mumbled, "It's not fair."

Mr. Dion was next. He neither had the motivation nor the energy to make a long speech. He kept it short, "Au Revoir Monsieur le Premier Ministre." It was the shortest speech of his political career but the most consequential one. He spoke so few words that it did not allow the unvarnished truth to come out and thus saved himself the embarrassment. He sat down and did not expect any reaction from his fellow Parliamentarians, and he was right. He was on his way out of politics and wanted to expedite it. He was offered the post of Director of Inconsequential Research at a sovereignty think tank in Quebec, which he gladly accepted.

It was Mr. Wright's turn. He was taking notes when others were speaking; not sure what was the point of that, but it made him look interested, which perhaps was the only point. He stood up slowly, adjusted his reading glasses, sipped from a glass of water. He was building anticipation for his speech. He had the demeanor of a Professor Emeritus, who had been ticked off by someone asking what his title meant.

"Madam Speaker, do you know how painful it is to lose election after election? I'll tell you: it hurts more than an ingrown toenail, which, trust me really hurts. What hurts, even more, is that the Prime Minister gets to dine with the President at the White House and the Queen at the Buckingham Palace; and I have to dine with my caucus who have nothing good to say to me. The Prime Minister gets to host celebrities, and I get to host a bladder infection, which at my age, makes going to the washroom a messy affair. The Prime Minister has the big business in his pocket, while my pocket has unpaid bills from the last election. He needs to go, for the sake of the country and for the good of my party. It's my last chance to become prime minister and I can't let it go. I want it so bad. I won't dwell on the accusations about bullying and favoritism; we are all guilty here, but the Prime Minister is on a different level. Thank you, Madam Speaker, that would be all."

The Prime Minister made no attempt to make eye contact or even acknowledge Mr. Wright. He considered Mr. Wright, a spent force and not worthy of his disdain. Dr. Green's policies were hopelessly impractical. Mr. Dion was an irritant and nothing more. He was more worried about an internal coup. His job was made easy; others had already admitted that they were no different than him, so what was the whole fuss about. He rose with confidence and arrogance that was worthy of his post, "Madam Speaker, I would like to thank the members who have expressed their opinion on this matter, not that I care. It's the sort of thanks which is reserved for special members of the family, namely in-laws. I won't take along; I am sure you are dying to get out of here as well. I have been accused of using colorful language with my staff and colleagues. Who here hasn't? Have I got rich and powerful friends? Yes, I have. Is it my fault? Yes, it is. Am I privileged? Yes, I am. We all are. Aren't we? Do I deserve it? I certainly do. Would you dare ask the same question to Her Majesty?"

"We are lucky that voters have given us the honor to represent them, and privilege comes with it. I have tried to help minorities get their due representation in politics; it's the right thing to do and it helps my party's electoral calculations. What's wrong with that? Siyasat knows that. She would never have made it to the Cabinet if I had not put my foot down, but she betrayed my trust. If you were in my shoes, you would have done the same thing. People say I don't practice what I preach. So do the others. Who drives under the speed limit? Who here hasn't sworn in public? Who here hasn't had the urge to punch others? Who here is perfect? We aren't even perfect hypocrites. Hypocrisy is part of democracy. Get over it. With that, I yield, Madam Speaker."

It was time for the Honorable Speaker to introduce the no-confidence motion and bring the proceedings to a close. The

Speaker stood up and asked the question, "Is the House ready for the question?"

Yeas affirmed the House was ready. She popped in the ultimate question, "Is it the pleasure of the House to adopt the motion?"

There was no dissenting voice. The Speaker was befuddled. She repeated the question again but there was no response.

She reluctantly declared, "The motion is carried."

The government had lost the trust vote. The Prime Minister would have to resign and order an election. The business of the House was done. The members huddled to get out of the premises. The reporters charged on them like hungry lions, eager to get a sound bite. Politicians would have none of it. They made a sprint towards their vehicles and gave no response to their conduct inside the House. The reporters made the best of what they could. It was an extraordinary story; unprecedented and scary. How can all members of Parliament agree to a no-confidence motion? Even the Prime Minister kept quiet, that was most intriguing.

The world took notice. Stock markets took a dive. Uncertainty freaked out the investors and they sold first and asked questions later. Stock indices fell precipitously; circuit breakers kicked in and trading was halted for the day. There were monstrous moves in currencies; the Canadian dollar fell below fifty cents to the US dollar. Gold was a winner; scared investors took solace in gold. Legislatures around the world were adjourned sine die. Protestors gathered around them to demand fresh elections. It was a crisis of epic proportions. Politicians usually don't let a crisis go to waste, but this crisis was radioactive even for them. They had to steer clear of it until they knew what was happening. The hypocrisy in politics was on full display and so was the scary nature of truth.

The public had no sympathy for the privileged few, but they were concerned about their own future. No one was ready to only speak the truth. No one was ready to share their dirty secrets with others. The consensus was limited to that only.

The fault lines in society were opening up. Anarchists had their dream come true; chaos was what they wanted. Like everything else, the level of fear was not equally distributed in society. The losers had less to lose, and they were the winners in this situation. Everyone was busy gauging their situation in the new world order.

Sadeep was engaged in meditation to reduce his stress. He was mindful that the present was gone before you could spell it. He did his mediation in front of a rotating globe. He felt better, not that he was somehow special, but he relished the triviality and futility of it all. He imagined the globe rotating backward, reversing the flow of time, which took him from his current worries about job, debt, bills, taxes, politics, heartbreak, health problems to a world where there were no winners or losers, no countries, no religion, no tyrants, no abuse, no life, and no worries. It was the sort of mental gymnastics that made him feel fresh. His mediation was interrupted by push notifications on his phone. It dragged him to the present and he was tempted to check what was happening in the Canadian Parliament. He saw the proceedings with much interest, and he was the only person in the world who had some clue as to what was going on. He had questions, lots of them; there was only one way to find out.

"If we over here, how come they are telling the truth?"

There was no response.

"Hello, are you there?"

Again, no response. He was concerned; Qubit Preet had always been prompt in responding. It was not normal. He began to shiver.

"How could you abandon me at this moment?"

"How could you?"

He felt betrayed, a sense of grief overcame him. No goodbye, no thanks, no parting words, it was the worst kind of break up. He was longing for the ghost. He dreaded return to a mundane life. He was pacing in the room. He grabbed his hair with both hands and shook his head. He made no effort to stop his tears. He had found a reason to live, thanks to the ghost. He had found a friend and a guide. He had found his path. He had hoped for a better finish. He felt abandoned. He was neither here, nor there. He was alone in the middle of nowhere. He had to acknowledge and appreciate the bright side of life. A Monty Python song did the trick. He came back from the melancholic thinking. His life had changed for the better. No one could take away that from him. He had learned a lot and a lot still needed to be learned. A motivation for him perhaps. His mind was a battlefield: a battle of glasses was going on, between glass half-full and glass half-empty. His mind was running fast, faster than a bullet train and it was throwing out all kinds of questions:

"Did I do something wrong?"

"Was he responsible for the Parliament fiasco?"

"Did he get help from his fellow ghosts?"

"Was it a one-off event or a sign of things to come?"

"How would society react to the unrelenting onslaught of truth?"

"Would truth lead to lasting change or only create apathy?"

"What would happen to me?"

The truth was folded into many layers. He needed his friend Qubit Preet to unfold the truth for him. It was not meant to be. He was left with the questions he had asked and the ones he could ask. The answers were unknown. It was not known when or if they would ever be known. What was known was that humans had always lived in fear: fear of others, fear of themselves, fear of God, among other things. Fear had taken countless lives and saved countless more. What would the fear of truth do? Would people continue to fall on the slippery slope of truth? It was not clear, and the end was nowhere near.

ABOUT THE AUTHOR

Preetinder Rahil

Preetinder Rahil writes fiction, non-fiction, and poems that rhyme. He tries to keep things simple, fun, and worth your time. If you have any feedback, please let him know. Listening to his audience will only let him grow.

Twitter: @preetpoet

BOOKS BY THIS AUTHOR

The Investing Geodesic

Quantum Mechanics: Basic & Advanced Concepts For Beginners

Special & General Relativity : A Beginner's Introduction To Basic & Advanced Concepts

Poems On Physics: A Collection Of Rhymes & Light Verse

For The Love Of Rhymes: A Collection Of Poems & Cartoons

Made in the USA
Columbia, SC
12 August 2021